Someone
to Love

JUDE DEVERAUX

Someone to Love

ATRIA BOOKS
New York London Toronto Sydney

ATRIA BOOKS

A Division of Simon & Schuster, Inc.
1230 Avenue of the Americas
New York, NY 10020

First Atria Books export edition July 2007

ATRIA BOOKS and colophon are trademarks of Simon & Schuster, Inc.

For information about special discounts for bulk purchases, please contact Simon & Schuster Special Sales at 1-800-456-6798 or business@simonandschuster.com.

Designed by Davina Mock

Manufactured in the United States of America

10   9   8   7   6   5   4   3   2

ISBN-13: 978-0-4165-5028-0
ISBN-10:   0-4165-5028-3

Someone to Love

1

Margate, England

The house was enormous, frighteningly ugly, and Jace Montgomery had just paid four and a half million dollars for it.

As he drove his car slowly through the wrought-iron gates that were set inside square brick pillars topped by stone lions, he dreaded seeing the house. Priory House was his now, but he could remember little from his one-time viewing with the realtor. The graveled road meandered through parkland that was quite pretty. He'd been told that the gardens had been laid out in 1910 by some famous landscape architect. The trees were now mature, the flowering shrubs were well established, and the grass perfect. If Jace were a horseman, which he wasn't, the parkland would have been a dream come true.

As he neared a big oak tree, he pulled over, stopped the car, and got out. In a moment the house would come into view, and he needed to prepare himself for it. To keep himself solvent, he'd borrowed the purchase price from his billionaire uncle. Since the house had been on the market for over three years, Jace knew that when the time came to sell the house, it would be a pain to unload.

He'd tried to rent the house, but the owner wouldn't consider it. The man wanted to get rid of the monstrosity free and clear.

"All right," Jace said to the realtor, or estate agent as they were called in England, "what's wrong with the house? Other than being ugly, that is." He imagined plumbing that was perpetually clogged, low-flying jets, murderous neighbors. At the very least, dry rot.

"It seems that there's a ghost," Nigel Smith-Thompson said with the air of a man who doesn't believe in such things.

"Don't all old houses in England have a ghost?" Jace asked.

"We were told that this ghost is particularly persistent. She appears rather often and it annoys the owners."

Scares the hell out of them is what you mean, Jace thought. "Is that why the house has changed hands so often?" When Jace asked to borrow the money from his uncle to buy the house, Uncle Frank had had it thoroughly researched. Since the late nineteenth century, the house had never been owned by anyone for more than three years. Uncle Frank's conclusion was that the house was a bad investment and Jace shouldn't buy it. Jace hadn't said a word, just handed his uncle the envelope he'd found inside a book that had belonged to Stacy. Frank took the photo of the house out of the envelope, looked at it in distaste, then turned the picture over. On the back someone had written "Ours again. Together forever. See you there on 11 May 2002."

It took Frank a moment to put it all together. "Stacy died on . . . ?"

"The next day." Jace took a breath. "On the twelfth of May, Stacy Evans, my fiancée, committed suicide in a room over a pub in Margate, England."

Frank picked up the envelope and read the postmark. "This was sent from Margate and the postmark is the eighth of April."

Jace nodded. "Someone sent that to her before we left for England." He thought back to the trip that had changed his life. Jace had worked in the family business of buying and selling companies since the day he graduated from college. Less than a week before he was to marry Stacy, his uncle Mike, Frank's brother, had called and said that the owner of an English tool manufacturing plant was pulling out of the sale. If that happened, three export deals would fall through and about a hundred people would be out of work. Since it had been Jace who'd negotiated the deal, he'd been the only one who could put it back together. He told Stacy he was sorry but he was going to have to fly to England. He promised that he'd work night and day and be back as soon as possible.

But Stacy had surprised him by asking to go with him. "I told her I didn't think it was a good idea for her to go," Jace said. "The truth was, I didn't want to have to deal with her stepmother. Stace had enough stress on her without a foreign trip thrown into it all."

"Yeah, I remember," Frank said. "If Stacy said no to purple daisies then Mrs. Evans went on a campaign for masses of purple daisies. Anything to cause problems—and to put the attention on herself."

Jace looked away for a moment. There had been no love between the young, beautiful Mrs. Evans and her stepdaughter, who was just a bit younger than she was but a great deal more beautiful—and a great deal more elegant. Stacy was the kind of woman who could wear a sweatsuit and people would know she came from money and breeding. Her father was a self-made man, but Stacy's mother had come from an old family: penniless, but with ancient bloodlines.

It was only after Stacy's death that her stepmother had professed great love for her stepdaughter, and she'd made Jace's life miserable. At the funeral Mrs. Evans had screamed that Stacy's suicide was Jace's fault. "You killed her!" she screamed in front of everyone. "Did you find somebody you liked better so you took Stacy out of the country, away from her family, so you could drive her to death in secret?"

It had all been absurd, of course, but it hurt just the same. Jace had loved Stacy with all his heart, and he had no idea why she'd killed herself just days before their wedding.

"You think this house has something to do with Stacy's death, don't you?" Frank asked.

"I have nothing else to go on." Jace got up and began to pace the room. "It's been three years, yet it's all I can think of. That moment when Stacy's sister threw the suicide note in my face and told me I had killed her sister haunts me every hour of every day."

"What did the psychiatrist say?" Frank asked softly.

Jace waved his hand. "I quit going to him. We spent six months talking about Stacy and me. What deeply buried, hideous things had I done to her in secret—secret even from myself—that made her take her own life? He got frustrated because I couldn't come up with anything, so he started on my family. When he concluded that I felt unworthy because I'd been born into a family that has money, I got out of there."

Frank looked at Jace hard. "So after you buy this white elephant of a house, then what?"

Jace sat back down. "I don't know. All I know is that I have to make this pain stop." When he looked at his uncle, his eyes were full of such anguish that Frank's breath stopped for a moment. "I haven't touched a woman in three years. Every time I take a woman out, I think about Stacy."

"No one truly believes it was your fault. I think Stacy must have been unbalanced. She—"

"That's what everyone tells me." Jace got up again, anger beginning to boil inside him. "But Stacy wasn't unbalanced. She was sweet and kind and funny. We used to laugh over the silliest things. She didn't care about my family name. She laughed when *Forbes* magazine declared us one of the richest—" He broke off and ran his hand over his face. "I've been over all this a thousand times, in my mind and with the doctor."

"And with your family."

"Yes," Jace said. "With everyone. I know I've been a bore and a pest, but I seem to be in the middle of a whirlpool. I can't go up, down, back, forth, nowhere. If I could put it behind me, I would. 'Get on with your life,' as everyone keeps telling me to do." Jace sank onto the chair. "If I could figure out what happened and *why,* maybe I could go on."

"And what if you find out something you don't like?"

"You mean that I might find out that I'm such a monster that she knew if she wanted to call off the wedding I'd refuse? Or maybe I'll find out that the only way she could get away from me was to kill herself."

"You don't believe that and neither does anyone who knows you. What's *really* eating at you?"

Jace looked away for a moment, then back at his uncle, his

face bleak. "I need to understand what happened. The horror of it is bad enough, but the mystery of it is driving me insane. Stacy and I were in a hotel in London and we had a fight." He took a breath. "Out of the blue, she told me she didn't want to have children. My mind was fully on getting that man to sell his company to us. He'd asked for verification of our family's good financial standing back seven years. The truth was, the man was a snob and I think he really wanted to know our family tree back seven generations. I was swamped with work and frantically trying to get back in time for the wedding. Stacy had to say it twice before I heard her, then I thought she was kidding. She said she had put off telling me, but she couldn't leave it any longer."

Jace took a breath, then let it out. "It was an argument that got out of hand. Everything I said seemed to make her angrier. When I said she might change her mind, she said I was accusing her of being a person who couldn't make a decision. Finally I told her it was okay, that I loved her enough that if we didn't have children it would be all right. That's when she started crying and ran out of the room. I thought she'd gone out for a walk to cool down. I didn't know it, but she'd taken the rental car."

Jace stopped talking, drained from yet again telling the same story. He'd agreed to be hypnotized in an attempt to remember more of that night, but even in a trance the events didn't change.

The next morning Jace awoke to find that Stacy hadn't returned to their room. At the time, he'd been more angry than worried, and he'd spent the day with the owner of the tool company. That night, after a long, hard day, he'd returned to their hotel room to find that Stacy hadn't been back. Jace called the police.

But by that time, Stacy's sister in the United States had been notified by the English police of the death by apparent suicide of her sister. Stacy had taken a full bottle of her own prescription sleeping pills. Her passport had been in her handbag and the person marked to notify was her sister.

Jace had not been allowed near Stacy's body and the police had looked at him as though he'd murdered her. In three days, Jace had gone from being a happy man who was looking forward to his marriage to a man who was reviled by his dead fiancée's family.

Since then, his life had not existed. He'd slept and eaten, and even worked some, but he wasn't really alive. The questions "Why had this happened?" and "What really happened?" haunted him incessantly. He'd tried everything he could to get rid of the doubts that now ruled him, but he was unable to. He'd gone on a few dates, but he couldn't be himself. He was polite to the point of coldness, and a first date never turned into a second.

Jace had thought that he and Stacy were a happy couple. He thought they'd had no secrets. Stacy was a legal secretary in an old, established New York law office, and even according to her bosses she nearly ran the office. She remembered where every brief was and every due date. And her classiness had fit their image of themselves. They always had her greet new clients. All of the young lawyers had tried to date her, but she'd have none of them. She used to smile graciously and say that when she met the man of her dreams, she'd know him.

And that's how it had happened. Jace had walked into the boardroom, a briefcase full of papers about a building in Greenwich Village that his company was buying, and he'd looked up and seen her. She'd been handing out documents to each lawyer, but with her eyes on Jace, she'd shoved them into the hands of a lawyer and left the room.

Jace hadn't been able to concentrate. For the first time in his life, he lost his train of thought and signed contracts that he didn't read. He was oblivious to the smirks and smiles of the lawyers around him. They had all tried with the beautiful, elegant Stacy, but she'd politely but firmly told them no. They could now see that her days of being the untouchable maiden were over.

After the meeting, Jace had stood outside the boardroom door and looked for her. Another secretary, smiling, had pointed the way to him and he'd walked to her desk. She was waiting for him, her coat on, and they'd left the office to go to lunch.

After that, they'd been inseparable. They'd talked and laughed and during the three years they knew each other, Jace had thought they'd told each other all about their lives.

But they hadn't. He had told her all about himself, but it seemed that Stacy had had secrets.

Jace looked back at his uncle Frank. "I can't go forward until I do all that I can to find out what happened and why."

"And you think this house has something to do with it?"

"Maybe not the house, but certainly whoever she was to meet that night. Stacy had some connection to that village and to someone in it. People there know things that they haven't told."

"Couldn't you hire—?"

"A private detective? I thought of that, but I think that if anyone walked into that small village and started asking questions, the people would clam up."

"So how does buying an expensive, ugly old house help you?"

Jace shrugged. "Maybe it won't, but I thought I'd say I was writing a book on local history. Some woman who robbed stagecoaches lived in the house and it's said that she now haunts it. Writing a book would give me an excuse to ask questions."

"Be careful. The lady highwayman may turn out to be an ancestor of ours."

"None of the women in our family would do that," Jace said and almost smiled.

"You did hear about our ancestor who was called 'the Raider,' didn't you?"

"Of course I did." Jace looked at his uncle pointedly. "Will you help me or not?"

"You couldn't rent the house?"

Jace gave his uncle a hard look. Jace had money of his own, quite a bit of it, but the bulk of it was tied up in long-term investments. He could have gone to a mortgage company, but his family liked to keep to themselves. Jace didn't like having to borrow money, but he also didn't like that his uncle was treating him like a kid.

"I'll give you the money," Frank said.

"Lend me the money."

Frank nodded, then looked at his watch. "I have a meeting. Tell me how much and where and the money will be wired."

True to his word, Frank had sent the money. Jace had already repaid part of it by selling the house he had bought for Stacy and himself. It had been vacant for years, partly furnished, ready to receive the bride and groom. Jace often remembered the day they'd closed on the house. He'd carried her across the threshold, both of them laughing and pretending the ordeal of the wedding was over. They'd drunk champagne while sitting on the new sofa they'd chosen together and talked about their future. Stacy had surprised him by saying she wanted to go back to school to get her law degree. Jace had agreed readily. He liked the idea of having a lawyer for a wife.

He brought himself back to the present and looked up at the

sky. The sun was shining brilliantly; a beautiful day. He had to get back in the car and go to that house. Already he missed his family, missed their concern and their efforts to cheer him up. In the years since Stacy's death, his family had never failed to listen to him and to try to understand. But he knew he was wearing on them. How many times could a person go over the same material? How long could he stand in one place and not move forward? Last month his uncle Mike told him that he had to either move forward or die. "Is that what you want to do?" Mike asked, his eyes angry. "Have you so glorified Stacy that you want to die with her?"

Jace couldn't meet his uncle's eyes, and that's when he realized he had to *do* something. Good or bad, he had to. A few days later, he was looking for a book when he'd pulled out a paperback that had fallen to the back of the shelves. He was still living in the small apartment that he and Stacy had shared. Her sister, in a rage after the funeral, had gone to the apartment and taken whatever she thought had belonged to Stacy. Jace had returned to an apartment that was cleaned out, almost as though Stacy had never lived there with him.

When the paperback fell on the floor, he saw that it was the one Stacy had been reading just before they left for England. For a moment, Jace forgot that she was gone and almost called out to her. When it hit him yet again that she was dead, he clutched the book and collapsed onto a chair.

He looked at the book with its gaudy cover and smiled. He used to tease Stacy that she had "low-class taste" when it came to novels. "I read legal papers most of the time," she'd said, "so at home I need fun reading. You should try them. They're great."

He got up, meaning to put the book by his bedside, but something fell onto the floor. When he picked up the envelope, his heart nearly stopped. It was postmarked "Margate," the English village where Stacy had died.

Inside was the photo of an ugly house and on the back someone had written that he/she would meet Stacy the night before she died. "This is why she wanted to go to England," he'd said aloud. It wasn't that she wanted to be with him but that she was meeting another person. Who? Jace wondered. Why? Was it a man?

For days he thought of nothing but the photo. He memorized the words. "Ours again." What did that mean? That Stacy had owned the house before? Jace spent sleepless nights going over everything Stacy had told him about her life. Her parents had divorced when she was three. Her mother had moved them to California while her father stayed in New York with his business. When Stacy was sixteen, her mother had died of cancer. One day she had a headache that wouldn't go away, so she went to a doctor. Six weeks later she was dead. Stacy was sent to live with her father, a man she'd seen only a few times in her life. Stacy used to laugh when she said that at first they "didn't get along." She'd meant it as an understatement. She was a teenager and angry that her mother had been taken from her, and angrier still that she was sent to live with her father, who was always working and never had time for her. Stacy said that she managed to be so bad that after a year her father sent her back to California to live with her mother's sister.

After Stacy graduated from Berkeley, she and her father finally became friends. But the friendship nearly died a year later when her father married a woman who was deeply jealous of Stacy.

Jace tried to remember all the places Stacy said she'd been. In the summers while she was in college, she used to go with a group of kids to Europe to "see the sights." "My hippie days," Stacy would say, laughing. Was that when she saw the house? Jace wondered. Is that when it was "theirs"?

He wanted to ask her father questions, but Mr. Evans had said that . . . Actually, Jace didn't want to remember what Stacy's father had said to him on the day of the funeral.

On impulse, Jace had gone to the Internet and brought up the name of the premier real estate agency in England, then typed in "Margate" for the location. The house was for sale. He recognized the photo as the one in the envelope and was sure that the picture of the house had been cut out of a sales brochure.

Jace downloaded the brochure for the house and read every word carefully. It was a very old house, part of it built on the remains of a monastery established in the early 1100s. When the Dissolution of the Monasteries was ordered in 1536, the brochure said it had been converted into a "stately manor house."

The second Jace saw the house he knew what he had to do. He knew in his heart that the secret to why Stacy had killed herself was inside that house. She had been there before. She had met someone who was so important to her that when he/she had written just a few words, Stacy had figured out a way to go there to meet . . . him. Jace felt sure that she was meeting a man. Yes, he was jealous, but he was sane enough to know that there could have been reasons other than love to explain her actions.

When Jace knew he was going to buy the house, he said nothing to his family because he knew that whomever he told would come up with a sensible reason for why he shouldn't. In the end, the only person he mentioned it to was his uncle Frank because he had the money that Jace needed to borrow to buy the big house.

When Jace got to the real estate office in London, the agent was cool and polite, but he got the feeling that the man and his office mates would be toasting with champagne if someone at last sold the odious old house. Maybe the realtor had an attack of conscience because he handed Jace a thick stack of brochures on other houses in England that were for sale. Jace had smiled politely, thanked him, then tossed them into the back of his brand-new Range Rover and left them there.

He saw the house only once before he bought it. It was a Sunday afternoon, raining hard outside, and the electricity had gone off. The darkness made the gloomy house even more dismal. But it didn't matter as Jace hardly looked at the place. At least not at what the realtor was pointing out. Had Stacy sat on that window seat and looked out? he wondered. Had she climbed those stairs?

Since it was Sunday, he hadn't met the housekeeper or the gardener. The realtor said that Jace was, of course, free to hire his own employees, but both of them had worked at the house for many years and—"Yes, I'll keep them," Jace had said. He didn't plan to stay long enough to go to the bother of hiring new employees.

So now he was ready to take possession of the house and the contents. For an extra hundred grand, the realtor had persuaded the previous owner to leave behind a great deal of furniture and housewares. Few antiques, no valuable ornaments, but some couches, chairs, beds, and china were left. During the price negotiation, the owner had taken more time discussing the furniture than he had the house. Frustrated, Jace said, "Tell him that the ghost might have attached herself to the furniture and might leave with it." He'd meant it as a joke and the realtor presented the statement as humorous, but the owner didn't laugh. Immediately, he stopped haggling and gave in to Jace's requests.

Now Jace got into his new car, turned on the engine, and continued to drive. When the house came into view, he sighed. Yes, it was as hideous as he remembered. From the outside, it looked to be an enormous square fortress, three stories high, with thick brick turrets pasted on top of each corner. The truth was that the house was hollow—or at least that's how he thought of it. Although it looked to be solid, when you drove through a gap between the buildings, you were inside a large, graveled courtyard. If the house were seen from the air, it would look like a rectangle with an empty interior.

Inside, it was almost as though there were two houses, one for the owners and one for the staff that it took to run such a large place. Two sides of the box formed a normal house, with large rooms, several of which had beautiful ceilings. The other two sides had smaller rooms that contained the service areas, including the laundry and a big kitchen. There were also two apartments for the live-in staff.

Above the owners' part of the house, there were two floors of bedrooms and baths. The master bedroom was huge, thirty by eighteen, and it had been connected to two smaller bedrooms that the previous owners used as giant closets. The third floor was a kids' paradise, with four bedrooms and two bathrooms, and a walk-in closet under the eaves that could be used for a "hideout."

Jace let the car roll through the wide opening between the buildings and into the courtyard. So far, he'd seen no one, not a gardener, nor the housekeeper, not even a kid on a lawn mower. He hadn't even seen any animals. Were there animals on the grounds? Dogs? Sheep? Cows, maybe? For a moment he sat in the car and reminded himself that he was now the owner of the estate and should know whether or not there was livestock on his land.

When there was a knock on his car window, he jumped so high his head hit the ceiling. Turning, he saw a little old woman standing outside. She was short and plump, with rosy cheeks and an apron full of green beans. He pushed the button to lower the window.

"Well, come on," she said in a thick accent that seemed to leave out half of each word. He had to wait a second before he understood her. "Are you gonna sit there all day or come inside and have some lunch? I'm servin' Jamie today."

With that, she bustled through a brick archway that was topped with a pointed roof. Jace hesitated for a second, then leaped out of the car and followed her. Life! he thought. She was the first sign of life he'd seen about the place. Besides, what with there being a north wing and a south wing and a main house, he feared she'd disappear and he'd never see her again. On the other hand, was *she* the ghost? She didn't look like a swashbuckling lady highwayman, but . . .

Inside the house, there was no sign of a human. It was dead silent. The thick brick and stone walls kept out all sound. He was in the main reception hall and in front of him was a beautifully polished oak staircase. Halfway up was a tall, leaded glass window with a little round insert of a couple of lions. Where could she have gone? he wondered as his stomach gave a growl. He hadn't eaten since early that morning and it was now after three.

He couldn't remember the floor plan from when the realtor showed him the house. He took a right and went down a hallway, peeping into rooms as he went. He saw a big living room with oak paneling three-quarters of the way up the walls. Next to it was a kitchen. Eureka! he thought, but there was no one there. The cabinets were beautiful, the floor slate, the windows stone-cased. He opened the refrigerator. It was empty. Maybe the woman cooked outside. On a grill, maybe.

Vaguely, Jace remembered the realtor telling him that there were two kitchens, one for the family and one for Mrs. Browne. The man never called her "the housekeeper" but always referred to her by name, as though she was someone of significance.

Jace turned right and went past another little sitting room, then into a second drawing room. Huge, floor-to-ceiling windows ran along one side, while the other wall had nothing on it. "I'd put bookcases there," he said aloud. "If I were staying here, that is." The ceiling was rounded and covered with delicate designs done in plaster. There was no door except the one he'd entered through.

Turning, he backtracked until he got to the entrance hall. This time he took the old oak door to the left. This led into a narrow passage that took a sharp left turn. He went past a laundry big enough to take care of the crew of a submarine, an office, a little room that contained another staircase, a walk-in closet, a powder room, and a door to the outside. He had his hand on the knob to the exterior door when his nose made him turn left. He walked into a big kitchen that looked like something out of a history magazine. It was as unlike the other kitchen he'd seen as it could be. For one thing, there wasn't one built-in cabinet. The walls were lined with a mixture of tall wardrobes and a Welsh dresser that displayed an amazing array of old dishes, none of which seemed to match. There was an old sink along one wall, one of the constantly on, beloved-by-the-English, multidoored Aga ranges on another wall, and a huge oak table in the middle of the room. The legs on the table were about a foot in diameter and turned into huge rounds.

Mrs. Browne was at the sink, her back to him. "Had trouble findin' the place, did you?" she asked.

"Totally lost," Jace said.

She turned around to look at him. "You're a big one, aren't you?" In her hand was a plate with a long sandwich on it. "And near as handsome as our Prince William. But not as handsome as my Jamie. Now sit down there and eat. You look starved. I imagine you been livin' on sausages and burgers in the States. Now, sit and have a good meal."

Like a child, Jace did as she told him to, pulling out an old oak chair and sitting down. The sandwich she put before him was divine: roast beef, cooked onions, and cheese on what he was willing to bet was homemade bread.

"Good," he said, his mouth full. "Excellent."

"It's from me Jamie."

"He your son?" Jace asked when he'd swallowed.

"Oh, heavens no! Wish he were, but then we all wish Jamie was our son." She nodded toward a framed photo on the wall. Since it was half-buried under hanging pots, dish towels, and strings of garlic, he could barely see it. The photo was of a handsome young man, blond, blue-eyed, and he looked vaguely familiar. "He's Jamie Oliver," she said and seemed to expect Jace to know who that was. When he didn't, she gave a look of disgust, her eyes wrinkling at the corners. Jace thought that whatever her age, it didn't match her little-old-lady looks. He thought she was either a lot older than she appeared, or a lot younger.

"Jamie Oliver!" she said louder, as though Jace was deaf as well as ignorant.

When he still looked blank, she grabbed a thick book off the countertop and put it on the table beside him. It was a cookbook and on the cover was the young man in the photo on the wall. "Ah," he said, "a cook."

"Julia Child was a cook," Mrs. Browne said, going to the cabinet beside the sink and opening a door. Inside was a refrigerator of a size that Americans would use to hold their drinks on the family boat. She withdrew a bottle of something dark and brown, poured a big glassful, and set it on the table in front of him.

She was looking at him as though he was supposed to say something.

"If this sandwich is an example of what Jamie Oliver can cook, then I say he's an artist."

She looked at Jace for a moment as though trying to figure out if he was lying, then she smiled, showing that her top left canine was missing. She seemed to be pleased and went back to the range to stir a pan.

Jace smiled, feeling that he'd passed Test Number One, and took a deep drink of what he assumed was beer. He didn't usually drink beer in the afternoon, but he didn't want to offend Mrs. Browne—again. The brown liquid was beer, but it was so strongly flavored and so strongly alcoholic that he thought he might choke. Mrs. Browne had her back to him, stirring her pot while she told him all about Jamie Oliver and what a magnificent chef he was and how she followed his advice to the letter. Behind her, Jace was quietly trying to rebound from the swig of beer. His eyes were watering and his head swimming. He thought he might have to lie down on the stone floor to recover.

Mrs. Browne turned around and looked at him, her eyes narrowed to slits. "That beer's too strong for your American stomach, isn't it? I told Hatch it wouldn't suit you. 'That's English beer,' I told him. 'Yanks drink things that say "light" on the bottle. They don't drink that homemade concoction of yours.' Here, I'll take it."

As she reached for the glass, Jace felt that he was representing all of American maledom and he held onto the glass. "No," he said, then cleared his throat since his voice had come out in a squeak. "No, it's fine. I love it. See?" he said, then picked up the glass and drained it.

When he finished, he thought he might pass out, but by strength of will, he stayed in his seat and looked at her. He hoped his eyes weren't going round and round as they felt like they were.

Mrs. Browne gave a little smile as though she knew exactly what was going on, then she turned back to her bubbling pot. "Well, maybe I was wrong about you Yanks. You go tell Hatch that you like his beer and he'll give you more."

"That'll be a treat," Jace said under his breath, then tried to pick up his sandwich, but missed. His hands went one way and the sandwich another. "Who is Hatch?"

She turned on him, hands on hips. "Didn't that uppity estate agency tell you anything? Hatch is the gardener. Of course he hasn't been here as long as I have, and I have no idea what his parents did before he came here, but he's been here a while. He'll be wantin' instructions from you as soon as you're finished here."

Jace again tried to get his hands onto his sandwich but again missed.

Frowning, Mrs. Browne moved the plate under his hands. When Jace got hold of the sandwich, he smiled at her in accomplishment.

"Instructions about what?" Jace asked, his mouth trying to hit the sandwich. He bit his hand twice, but it was numb so he felt nothing.

Mrs. Browne was watching him and shaking her head. "The gardens. Hatch will want to know what you want done to the gardens."

"I have no idea," Jace said as he sank his teeth into the sandwich. That the little finger on his left hand was in the bite didn't bother him. "I know nothing about gardens."

"Then why did you buy this great bloomin' place?"

"To see the ghost," Jace said, chewing and wondering how much of his little finger was left.

Mrs. Browne smiled warmly. "And she'll be glad for the company. The last two families were scared to death of her. Poor thing."

"Then you've seen her?"

"No," she said, turning back to her pot. "Never seen her or heard her. I'm not a 'sensitive,' as they're called. Some people can see her and some can't. She talked to a few of 'em, but they all got scared and run away. You gonna be calm when she comes clankin' down the stairs in the wee hours?"

"Maybe I'll give her some of Mr. Hatch's beer. That should loosen her chains."

Mrs. Browne laughed. It was a rusty sound, as though she didn't laugh often. "You go on now and have a look-see. Unless you need to lie down a bit on a count a the English beer."

Jace heaved himself up by his arms because he was dead from the waist down. "Tell me, Mrs. Browne, am I bleeding anywhere?"

Again came that rusty little sound. "You go on now. I'm spendin' the afternoon with me Jamie so you can have a good dinner. Hatch makes wine as well as beer."

"Lord save me," Jace muttered as Mrs. Browne put her strong hands on his lower back and gave him a push. When he opened his eyes he was standing outside and the door was being closed behind him. The sunlight threatened to crack his brain open.

"So you came to see *me,* did you, Mr. Montgomery?" said a soft voice behind him, a woman's voice.

Jace turned as fast as he could, but considering the state of his body, that wasn't very fast. No one was there, but he thought he smelled something. Flowers and wood smoke, he thought. It lasted only a second, then it was gone.

He turned back, put his hand over his eyes, and looked out across the gardens. Green trees, green grass, flowers. He saw it all, but there was no person in sight. Had he just been spoken to by a ghost? He smiled. Maybe he should have been frightened, but he had an odd thought. He could say anything to a woman who was already dead and he wouldn't have to worry about the consequences. "You can't hurt someone who's already dead," he said aloud.

"That proves that you didn't meet the nasty little boy who lived here in 1912," came the woman's voice, so soft the wind in the trees almost drowned it.

Jace gave the first semblance of a laugh that had passed his lips in years. He put his hands in his pockets and tried to lift his neck, which was nearly as numb as his feet, and went in search of the gardener.

2

When Jace awoke the next morning the inside of his mouth felt like it had been used as a lint filter for a dryer. Worse, for a long moment, he couldn't remember where he was. Enough light was seeping in between the heavy curtains that he knew it was morning, but he couldn't remember how he got wherever he was.

He lay still on the bed, blinking into the gloom. He remembered Mrs. Browne's lunch, then being pushed outside and meeting Mr. Hatch, the gardener. He was a little gnome of a man, so short he made Jace, at six two, feel like a giant. But for all Mr. Hatch's small stature, he was certainly strong. When Jace first saw him, he was using a big handsaw to cut up a huge limb that had broken off a tree and fallen across a path.

"You wanta grab that end?" the man said in an accent that made Mrs. Browne's sound as though it was from an English drawing room. "My helper is out sick today. If you ask me, what's made him sick is that girlfriend of his. Too pushy, that one. Makin' the boy think he's somethin' he's not. Mark my words, she'll be the downfall of him. All uppity, but she cleans the toilets over at the school. What's the matter with you, boy? Can't you pick up that thing? What they teachin' you at that school?"

Jace stood up and looked at his hands. He could see them but he couldn't feel them, so he couldn't pick up his end of the heavy log. "I don't know what school you're talking about and I have no strength because Mrs. Browne fed me a bottle of the beer you made."

The little man stood up straight and under his weathered skin Jace thought he saw a glow of pink. "You're the new owner."

" 'The Yank,' as Mrs. Browne calls me. Jace Montgomery." He held out his hand to shake, but the little man didn't take it.

"Beggin' your pardon, sir, I thought you was the lad the vicar said he was sendin' to help me. What with you bein' a big, strappin' fellow, I thought you . . ." He trailed off, not seeming to know how to get himself out of the jam.

"I'll take that as a compliment," Jace said, trying to put the man at ease. "Shall we try again with this log?"

"No, sir, the lad'll be along soon now. He's one of the vicar's charity cases and the vicar is savin' the boy whether he wants to be saved or not."

"Maybe he'll run off with your other lad's girlfriend and you'll get rid of both of them at once."

Mr. Hatch gave a smile and Jace again tried to lift his end of the log. This time, with great concentration, he was able to help move it to the far side of the path.

"Where does this lead?" Jace asked, looking down the graveled path.

"Yonder," Mr. Hatch said. "All the paths lead nowhere, then they connect up and lead back to the house. They were made for a lady of the house that didn't ride. Ain't no stables anywhere on the property, so if you're wantin' a horse you'll have to build somethin' to put it in. But then, you won't be stayin' long enough to build anythin' so no need to worry about that."

"And why won't I be staying?"

"On account of the ghost." He looked at Jace with his wrinkled, weathered face twisted into something that Jace assumed was meant to be frightening. "A real fright, she is."

"How so?" Jace asked.

Mr. Hatch looked around to see if the young man the vicar was sending over was coming, but they were alone. "Come with me and we'll share a glass of my wine and I'll tell you everything. I've been here thirty years and I know all there is to know."

Jace couldn't resist the temptation to say, "Do you know more than Mrs. Browne?"

"Hmph! That one? She spends her days droolin' over some boy on the telly. That cook. Now, mind you, I'm as open-minded as anybody, but is cookin' a fit job for a man? And callin' himself 'the naked chef.' Is that a proper thing for a man to do?"

Jace thought about asking Mr. Hatch if planting daffodils was a manly occupation but thought better of it.

When they reached a brick shed, Mr. Hatch stepped into the dark interior and returned with a blue glass bottle and two stained ceramic mugs. "Over here, under her tree," he said. "We'll have a bit of rest and I'll tell you all that you want to hear."

I'm going to regret this, Jace thought as he took the cup of wine. It was made from raspberries and was delicious, but it was even more lethal than the beer. Mr. Hatch downed two cups full for every half a cup that Jace drank, but even so, after forty-five minutes, Jace wanted to curl up under the tree and go to sleep.

But for all Jace's questions, Mr. Hatch didn't tell him anything about the ghost. He talked at length about putting in a bed of dahlias, but he didn't mention the ghost—and he evaded Jace when he tried to ask. Jace got the impression that Mr. Hatch was so sure that Jace, an American, would stay at Priory House for so short a time that he wanted to do as much to the garden as possible before the house was put up for sale again. And he didn't want to hasten the end by talking about the ghost that had scared so many other people away.

Maybe it was a feeling that two could play at this game, but Jace didn't mention that the ghost had spoken to him, and that she didn't sound like anyone's idea of a lady highwayman.

"Ah, here he is now," Mr. Hatch said, emptying his glass for the fourth time. "I'll get him to help you up to your room."

"I'm fine," Jace said as he put his hand on the tree and tried to stand up. Legs that were once numb but functioning had now turned to rubber. "I'll be fine. I want to hear about the ghost and about—"

That's the last thing Jace remembered before he awoke in a strange room with his tongue feeling like it had turned into a caterpillar. Surprisingly, his head didn't hurt, but his mind was fuzzy. Eventually, he remembered the two soft comments by an unknown voice.

"Are you here?" he whispered, but there was no sound. He lay still, listening and thinking about what he'd heard. Yesterday, in between two drunken sessions, he thought he'd heard a woman's voice. She'd even made a joke to him. Could that have happened, or was it just the byproduct of some outrageously potent booze that he'd been given?

"Please answer me," he said. "If you're here, please talk to me. I want to contact someone." Until he said the words out loud, he hadn't realized he'd thought them. He'd told his uncle Frank that a ghost in the house didn't bother him, but now he was seeing that he liked the idea of a ghost. Maybe she could contact Stacy for him. He wanted to ask her what had been so terrible in her life that she couldn't bear to go on living.

When there was no answer to his questions, Jace began to feel silly. He had no idea where he was in the house. He remembered that the master bedroom had an enormous four-poster bed in it. The man who had remodeled the house back in the 1850s had bought the bed from an auction of the furnishings of a bankrupt duke. The bed was made of heavily carved, age-blackened oak, and the mattress was eight feet square. To make sure the bed stayed in the house, the remodeler had had the room built around it. The only way to get the bed out was to cut it into pieces. Over the years, the bed had come to be included in the sale, like the windows and the sinks.

But now Jace was in another room. It was half the size of the master bedroom and much prettier. There were windows on two sides, one set forming a pretty alcove where a deep window seat had been built. He could imagine Stacy curled up there with a book while the rain lashed against the windows. She'd always loved the rain.

For the first time since Stacy's death, Jace felt at peace. He closed his eyes, wanting to go back to sleep, but he knew he couldn't. How long had he been asleep? Since he passed out under what Mr. Hatch called "her" tree? The man said he was going to tell Jace about the ghost, but he hadn't. He'd spent their short time together enumerating all that needed to be done to the outside. There were ditches that needed to be cleaned, plants that needed replacing, things like manure that needed to be bought. "You need some animals around here," Mr. Hatch said, draining his cup of the potent wine. "We need the manure. That a place this size should have to buy cow dung goes against what's right." Thirty minutes later, Jace found out that there were a lot of things that Mr. Hatch thought went "against what's right."

Now, lying in the bed, he thought, Someone is doing this. Someone is making me feel calm. Part of him thought that was absurd, but another part knew that he hadn't felt this calm since Stacy died. "If you're here, please talk to me," he said.

There was a rustle of fabric near the window and he turned, fully expecting to see a transparent white shape, but there was nothing. However, there was no wind in the room to make the curtain move.

Sighing, Jace swung his bare feet off the bed. He was fully dressed, but his shoes and socks had been removed. Wonder who took them off? he thought.

He went in search of the nearest bathroom. One thing he'd learned about English houses was that no matter how much they cost, a bathroom that wasn't "down the hall" was a rare thing. On the Internet, he'd seen twelve-million-dollar houses with a third floor that had seven bedrooms and only a powder room to share. To bathe, people had to go downstairs.

He found a bathroom en suite, as the English say, meaning that a door opened into the bedroom. As his head began to clear, he realized that the room he had slept in was one of the bedrooms that the previous owners had used for storage. When Jace had seen the room, it had been full of big packing boxes and racks full of garments in zippered bags. His visit had been cursory and his mind hadn't been on the house itself, so he'd not realized the room was as beautiful as it was.

When he saw that his toiletries were on the sink, he realized he was in the master bathroom. He was glad to see that there was a shower as well as a huge tub. He stripped off his clothes, took a long shower, brushed his teeth eleven times, then put a towel around his waist and went in search of his clothes. While he slept, someone had taken his suitcases out of his car and unpacked them.

Suddenly, his calmness was gone, replaced by panic. Where was his suitcase? With a growing sense of foreboding, he searched for his large case. It took him a while, but he found it in the back of a built-in cupboard in one of the closet-bedrooms. He pulled the suitcase out and opened it, then searched the lining. When he felt the leather case of the photo, he breathed a sigh of relief. He had brought only one photo of Stacy and he'd hidden it under the lining of his suitcase. He'd decided that it would be better if he kept what he was doing and why a secret. He would tell people he was interested in their lady swashbuckler ghost rather than in a woman who'd committed suicide just a few years ago. Jace feared that if he showed the photo and asked questions, someone would warn the person Stacy had met to get out of town. He wasn't sure how he was going to do it, but he knew that his questions had to be subtle and he had to work around what he actually wanted to know.

"So you found me!" Mrs. Browne said when Jace at last found her kitchen.

"No problem," he said, lying. Once again, he'd taken a wrong turn. Frustrated, he'd gone outside and tried to find another way in. For such a big house, it had extraordinarily few exterior doors. In the end, he had to circle the entire house before he found the door that Mrs. Browne had pushed him out of the day before. Seeing that the long walk had made his heart beat faster, he knew he'd made the right choice when he put on a sweatsuit. A run around his seventy-two acres would be good for him.

"It's late, but I think I can still make you a breakfast," Mrs. Browne said.

He looked at the clock on the wall. It was 8:05 in the morning. "That would be kind of you." He took a seat at the big table in the center of the room. "Where do you live?" He knew there were two apartments in that wing of the house. He was told that the housekeeper lived in one but the other one was vacant. He wanted to be sure he didn't accidentally wander into Mrs. Browne's private territory.

She had her back to him at the Aga and when he saw her stiffen, he knew she'd taken his question the wrong way. "Do you mean to evict me?"

"Throw out Jamie's girl? How could I do that?"

She rewarded his jest with a bit of a smile and a platter of food: three sausages, three fried eggs, broiled mushrooms and tomatoes, and two thick slices of fried bread. It was accompanied by a pot of tea strong enough to float fishing weights.

Jace looked up at her in astonishment. "This is from Jamie?"

"No, that's a good English breakfast. But if it's too much for the likes of you . . ." She reached out to take the plate away.

Jace stopped her. Living alone, he tended to eat a boring bowl of cereal for breakfast, but since he'd slept through dinner last night, he was ravenous. "I'll manage," he said, picking up his fork.

"See that you do. You're a mite thin to be livin' in England."

Jace looked at her back and thought that no matter what he accomplished in his life, to Mrs. Browne he'd always fall short because of where he was born. The food was delicious. It was high calorie, cholesterol laden, and bad for him, but wonderful tasting. "So where *do* you live?"

"Across the way," she said, waving her hand in the general direction of "outside."

Jace wanted to ask more, but just then Mrs. Browne saw a girl walking through the courtyard.

"There that dratted girl is again! Mark my word, she's stealin' raspberries. That old man Hatch says the birds get 'em, but I think they're in it together. She's sellin' 'em is what I think. If I ever catch her, I'll sack her." With that, she bustled out of the kitchen, running for the outside door. Minutes later, Jace saw her running across the courtyard after the poor girl, who seemed to be guilty only of shaking the dust out of a rug.

Jace took the opportunity of Mrs. Browne's absence to look about the kitchen. There were three doors in it; one was the entrance, so he looked at the other two. One door led to a room full of cabinets and a sink. A quick glance showed him the cabinets were full of dishes. None of it seemed to be the "good" china. No names like Herend or Spode or even Wedgwood were on the bottoms, but there was enough that he could give a dinner party for a dozen or more. If I knew anybody, he thought.

He stepped back into the kitchen, saw that Mrs. Browne was still bawling out the poor cleaning girl, then he went to the other door. It was a pantry with three skinny windows on one wall and slate shelves on the other. Cans, bags, and boxes filled the shelves, as well as jars of homemade jams and pickles. There was a big jar labeled "peaches in rum" that looked interesting.

"I'm turning into an alcoholic," he said, then at a sound, he looked out the narrow windows. The view was almost obscured by strings of herbs and sausages, but he was looking at the entryway into the courtyard. Interesting, he thought. No one could enter or leave that Mrs. Browne, enthroned in her kitchen, wouldn't know about. He saw her hurry through the opening, but she turned left into a narrow door. "Her apartment," Jace said, smiling and feeling that he'd solved a mystery.

When she returned to the kitchen, Jace was back at the table, finishing his platter of breakfast. He looked at her for praise, but she just said "hmph" in a way that was becoming familiar to him.

After Jace finished his meal, he found the outside door and went into the garden. From what he'd seen so far, the grounds were beautiful and Mr. Hatch did a splendid job of keeping them up. The breakfast sat heavy in his stomach and he was still feeling the effects of the beer and wine from the day before, but all in all, he felt better than he had in, well, in three years. Again, he thought there was something being done or said to him that was making him feel good.

As he wandered about the acres near the house, he marveled at them. There were several flowerbeds, lush and full, with not a weed in sight. There was a pretty pond full of big goldfish and surrounded on three sides by tall evergreen hedges. His favorite thing was a row of topiaries in the shape of animals. There were four of them: a swan, a bear, a big fish, and something that could be a dragon if you looked at it at the right angle.

He walked under a long pergola with square brick pillars and wooden beams overhead. Lacy-leaved vines nearly covered the beams. There was a rose garden, and everywhere benches seemed to be tucked in some cool, beautiful spot.

At the end of the rose garden was a young man digging a hole, but there was something about the way he was digging that made Jace think the boy had almost been caught doing something else. His clue was that the young man was using a rake to dig with.

"Good morning," Jace said.

"Morning, sir. You the new master?"

Jace smiled at the old-fashioned term, then followed the boy's glance toward the trees. A small foot moved. "Are you the one with the girlfriend who's going to be the downfall of him? Lead him into wicked ways?" Behind them, a girl giggled.

"Yes, sir, I am," the boy said. "I'm Mick, the first garden assistant."

The young man was tall, strong, and looked intelligent. "Planning to take over after Mr. Hatch leaves?"

Mick laughed as though that weren't possible, but the girl came out of the trees, clutched Mick's arm possessively, and said, "Yes, he is."

Jace thought that if young Mick had any ambition it was because of her. There was something about them that made him like them. "So when's the wedding?"

Mick looked at his feet, but the girl smiled. "In the autumn. I'm finishing a secretarial course, but my dad won't pay for it if I'm married."

Jace remembered that Mr. Hatch had said the girl was "cleaning toilets" so he guessed she was paying for most of her tuition herself. She had ambition and spunk; he admired that. "Wise decision. So where do you meet in the meantime?" When Jace saw Mick turn away nervously, he knew they'd been meeting in his house. And why not? It had been empty for years.

"Mick," Jace said, "and . . . ?"

"Gladys."

"Isn't there an empty apartment, a flat, over Mrs. Browne's kitchen? Would you two like to live there after you're married?"

Mick's eyes widened in disbelief, but Gladys's face turned pink with delight. "Oh, yes, sir," she said. "And you wouldn't be needing a secretary, would you?"

"Gladys!" Mick said. "That's askin' too much."

"Actually," Jace said, "I do need a secretary. Maybe you two could look at that office by—"

"The laundry," Gladys said. "Yes, sir, I know it well."

When they looked at each other, Jace knew that had been her plan all along. Yes, with her around, Mick would do well for himself. "Perhaps you could make a list of what I'd need to set up an office—computer, printer, all that—and give me a price list. And let me know your salary requirements. We'll have everything in place for you to start by the time you graduate."

"Oh!" Mick said. "She can start before she graduates. She can work evenin's, if that's all right with you, sir."

"Perfectly all right. Now, Mick, you better stop digging a hole there or Mr. Hatch will have your hide, and, by the way, even I know you dig with a shovel, not a rake."

Gladys laughed but Mick turned red.

He left them to continue his tour of the garden. He felt that he'd just made a couple of friends and had gained a secretary to take care of the bill paying and the . . . He wasn't sure what else he needed a secretary for, but he knew he wanted people in the house. Not that their apartment was anywhere near the main house, even though it was connected by a long passageway, but he liked that they'd be nearby. Talk and laughter might keep him from missing his family so much.

Standing at the end of the formal garden, just before the woodland park began, Jace looked back at the house. Yes, it was hideous, but now that he was really seeing the place, there were things to recommend it. To his American mind, it was odd having two kitchens, but his mother always said that there was no kitchen on earth big enough for two women. If a family lived in the house, Jace thought, it might be nice to have a place that was just for the husband and wife and the kids.

Stacy would like this house, he thought. When she wasn't working she could make pancakes for the kids on Sundays and—

He stopped that thought. It seemed that Stacy had known the house, but she'd never mentioned it to him. And as for having children, that argument had started everything.

He walked along a path in the woodland, which was acres of beautifully manicured trails shaded by fabulous old trees. He saw copper beech, sycamore, horse chestnut, as well as oak and elm. Most of the trees he didn't recognize and figured they were exotics, specimens that didn't usually grow in England.

Someone has loved this place very much, he thought.

He took a left at an intersection of pathways and came to a tall brick wall with an oak door. Opening it, he saw a beautiful vegetable garden. Neat rows of vegetables were surrounded by foot-high boxwood hedges. A long greenhouse stood at one end, and there seemed to be half an acre of cages that kept birds away from the berries planted inside.

As Jace looked about, he saw the pretty girl Mrs. Browne had been chastising scurry from behind one tall bean tower to another. She was followed by another girl. They didn't see him, so Jace stepped behind the end of the greenhouse and watched.

One young girl was plump and pretty, the other skinny and plain, and they were sneaking toward the raspberry cage. They opened the door slowly so the hinges wouldn't creak, then tiptoed inside. Since the garden was huge and enclosed by a tall brick wall, he wondered who they thought might hear them.

Jace stayed hidden and watched them fill little tin buckets with ripe raspberries. There were row upon row of bushes, each one dripping fruit. He remembered Mrs. Browne's complaints about the theft of the berries, but he or his employees couldn't eat all of them, so why not let the girls have them?

He opened the cage door, noting the oil glistening on the hinges, popped a raspberry in his mouth, and said, "They're good, aren't they?"

The girls jumped at his voice, then the pretty one looked as though she was going to cry. The thin one put on an air of defiance. "We can pay for them," she said, glaring at him.

"Will you call the police on us?" the other girl asked.

"You are . . . ?"

"Daisy, sir," the pretty one said. "I helped put you to bed last night. I took off your shoes and socks even though Mr. Hatch said to leave you the way you were."

"Thank you." He turned to the other girl. "And you are . . . ?"

"Erin."

"Do you both work for me?"

"Yes, sir," Daisy said. "We clean your house."

"And do whatever vile task Mrs. Browne can come up with for us to do," Erin added, watching Jace to see his reaction to that statement.

His instincts didn't allow him to trust these girls as he had Mick and Gladys. He was afraid that they would tell Mrs. Browne whatever he said. "So what do you do with the raspberries?"

The girls exchanged looks and seemed to decide to tell the truth. Daisy said, "Our mothers make raspberry tarts, then they sell them at the local shop."

"May I assume that you do the same with . . ." He looked around the garden at the other bushes and had no idea what they were.

"Strawberries, blackberries, gooseberries," Erin said.

"And apples, quince, medlars, apricots, peaches, pears, and cherries," Daisy said.

"And mulberries," Erin added. "My mum makes mulberry jam and they sell it at Harrods."

"That's impressive."

Erin took a step forward. "But the only way we can turn a profit is if the fruit is free. No one's lived here for years, so the fruit was going to waste." She glanced at the cage. "Not even the birds could get to it."

"What does Mr. Hatch know of this?"

"Everything. We couldn't do it without him."

"And Mrs. Browne?"

The girls again exchanged looks, but said nothing.

"If she knew for sure, she'd fire you, right?"

"Yes," Erin said. "If she caught us here we'd be sacked in a moment."

"What if I told her she couldn't fire you? I do own the place, you know."

The girls smiled. "Beggin' your pardon, sir, but do you? Owners come and go, but Mr. Hatch and Mrs. Browne stay. They make the rules."

"I can see how that would happen." He didn't say so, but he knew that he, too, would be leaving soon. "Perhaps if I tell Mrs. Browne that you two have my permission to pick all the fruit you want—"

"Oh, no, sir!" Daisy said. "She'd make our lives a living hell, and we can't quit because our mums need the fruit, and we all need the money. There are six women, all with children, who work in the business. And no men. My father is ill and Erin's ran away with the postman's wife, so—"

Erin gave her a look that cut her off. "She means, sir, that we have families to feed and while it's kind of you to offer to help . . ."

"It would be better if I kept my nose out of it."

"Exactly, sir," Daisy said, dimpling prettily.

Looking at her, Jace felt sure she'd be married and pregnant in another year. "All right," he said, smiling. "I won't—"

"Crickey!" Erin grabbed Daisy's arm and they crouched down in the bushes.

Jace, not knowing what was going on, remained standing, then he saw that Mrs. Browne had just entered the garden, a trug over her arm.

"Will you give us away?" Daisy whispered, looking up at Jace with big blue eyes.

He shook his head and took a step forward, but Erin grabbed his pant leg.

"She'll come in here and see us. Could you distract her so we can get out of here?"

"Maybe take your shirt off," Daisy said, then put her hand over her mouth to stifle her giggle.

In spite of himself, Jace felt his face turning red. The girls were no more than eighteen and at his thirty-two, they made him feel like a lecher.

"He's blushing," Erin whispered, then nudged Daisy and had to cover her own laugh.

Mrs. Browne had picked some beans and was now heading straight for the raspberry cage. Jace had to distract her, but how?

As he was thinking what to do, he saw an extraordinary sight. To the left, the nearly transparent form of a woman stepped through the brick wall. Mrs. Browne had just stooped to cut something from a plant and was bending over, so she didn't see the figure.

The woman stopped inches from Mrs. Browne, then reached out to take something from the wall. He couldn't see what it was, but she cupped it in her hands. When Mrs. Browne stood up, the woman—the spirit—opened her hands in front of Mrs. Browne's face and blew on them. For a split second, Jace saw what looked to be a spider go from the woman's hands to Mrs. Browne's face.

The next moment Mrs. Browne was slapping at her face. She dropped her basket of vegetables and ran for the door, swatting at herself as she ran. Beside him, Daisy and Erin stood up and watched the show, laughing.

But Jace's eyes were on the woman who was standing by the wall and smiling. He could see through her. She had on a high-necked, long-sleeved white blouse; her slim waist was encircled by a wide belt above an ankle-length skirt and soft, lace-up boots. Her long, dark hair was tied back at the nape of her neck, forming a thick tail that hung down her back almost to her waist. Her face was in profile and he saw delicate features, a perfect nose, and long-lashed eyes. Through her, he could see the bricks of the wall.

Daisy and Erin were laughing and doing a little jig, but Jace stayed frozen in place, not even blinking as he stared at the woman.

Smiling, the spirit woman turned to look at Daisy and Erin, who didn't seem to see her. When she saw Jace staring at her, her eyes opened wide in surprise, and for a moment their eyes locked. She was pretty in a quiet way, like someone in an old ad for shampoo or soap. Her eyes were dark blue and her mouth was small and perfectly shaped.

When she realized that Jace could see her, she registered surprise, then for about three seconds, her body had more substance. She wasn't solid by any means, but he could see more of her and less of the bricks. In the next second, she was gone. No poof of vanishing, just there, then not there.

Jace stood still for a moment, not moving, before he realized that Daisy and Erin were staring at him.

"You look like you saw the ghost, sir."

Reluctantly, he pulled his eyes away from the wall. "No, just recovering from ten pounds of breakfast. You better get your berries and get out of here before Mrs. Browne returns."

"Yes, sir, thank you, sir," they said as they ran out of the fruit cage. At the door in the brick wall, Daisy stopped, smiled prettily, and said, "If you're needin' anything, let me know. Anything at all. A foot massage, maybe. Or a—" Erin grabbed her arm and pulled her through the door.

"Make that six months before she's pregnant," Jace muttered.

For a while, he stood inside the fruit cage and stared at the spot where the spirit of the woman had been. She had protected the two giggling girls who were raiding the raspberry patch, he thought. She had picked a spider off the wall and blown it into Mrs. Browne's face so she would run away and not see the girls snitching raspberries.

What amazed Jace was that neither the girls nor Mrs. Browne had seen something that had been so clear to him.

"It's you," he heard to his right and turned to see Mrs. Browne opening the cage door. "I thought I saw someone in here."

"Yes, I confess. I was eating raspberries." He looked again at the place the woman had appeared. "Did I see you dancing a moment ago?"

"You might call it that. A spider fell off the wall and onto my face. I told Hatch what I thought of his gardening. He lets those boys of his slack off. They do no work."

"Not like your girls."

"I make them work, if that's what you mean." She was trying to get to the raspberries behind him, but Jace was firmly rooted to the spot. "You have that look on your face."

"And what look is that?"

"The ghost look. Did you see her? Will you be puttin' the house up for sale?"

Jace made himself look at her. "Sell? And miss out on your breakfasts? How could I do that?"

She gave her rusty little laugh. "You're a smooth one, aren't you, Mr. Montgomery? Why don't you have a wife and children? Fill this house with young 'uns. That's what it needs."

"Are you proposing?" he asked and she smiled.

"Go on now, go find somethin' to do and leave me to my work."

Jace went to the cage door, but turned back. "Mrs. Browne," he said seriously, "about this ghost. Do people see her inside the house or out?"

"Inside. I never heard anybody say they'd seen her outside. Ol' Hatch would be scared to death of her if she showed herself out here."

"But didn't you tell me that some people can see her and some can't? Maybe she appears outside but no one has seen her— or can see her in the daylight."

Mrs. Browne squinted up at him. "Are you tryin' to tell me that you saw Lady Grace outside the house? Maybe here in this garden?"

Jace grinned. "I'm trying to use you as a research tool. If I'm going to be writing a book about Lady Grace, I need to find out all I can about her, don't I?"

"Write a book about a woman that won't leave the earth? Well . . ." she said, "if that's what you want to do, but I have better things to do with my time."

"So no one has seen her outside?"

"Not to my knowledge and I know—"

"All there is to know," Jace said with a sigh. She might know things, but it was difficult to get information out of her. He dreaded trying to find out about Stacy from her. If Stacy had met someone here and Mrs. Browne knew of it, he was more likely to get a morals lecture than information.

"I think I'll take a run," he said. "Work off some breakfast in preparation for lunch."

"It's Jamie's roast chicken," she said. "With rosemary."

Smiling, Jace started jogging backward. When he reached the spot in the wall where the ghost had stepped through, he pretended to have a pain in his ankle. Mrs. Browne was watching him intently. As he rubbed his ankle, then stood up, he felt the wall. It was solid and old. There was no doorway there and he didn't think there ever had been.

3

Jace jogged around the parkland for over an hour. He often stopped to look at places. When a piece of land had been occupied for nearly nine hundred years, the people left their marks behind. He came across four sheds, all of them locked, and the ruins of two more. He found a pretty stone shelter with a dome top and a marble floor that was beginning to crumble. To get to it he'd had to fight through rampant vines and run out a family of small, furry creatures that moved too fast for him to see what they were. There were stone half circles next to what he'd been told was a dry riverbed. The monks had kept fish in the stone-lined ponds.

When he got back to the house, he just had time to shower before lunch. He ate in Mrs. Browne's kitchen and was subjected to a long complaint about the raspberry bushes having been denuded. She questioned Jace closely about who he'd seen. He lied smoothly. Of course to tell her the truth would have been worse than lying. Tell her that the ghost blew a spider on her? Not quite.

After lunch, which was delicious, he went upstairs and called Nigel Smith-Thompson, the estate agent, and asked questions. What Jace wanted to know was whether or not the previous owner had lent the house to anyone in the three years it was last for sale. Who had stayed there? The agent said no one had been there. The owner and his family walked out of the house in the middle of the night and returned to their native country, never to visit the house again.

"Are you *sure* he didn't lend the house to *any*one?" Jace persisted.

"I can call him and ask," the agent said, but he obviously didn't want to.

"Please do," Jace said, then gave the agent his cell number. "I want to know who had permission to stay here."

"I can answer that one. Only the housekeeper was allowed to stay. The gardener lives in the small house at the south end of the property."

"But perhaps the owner had a friend who *used* the house."

"The previous owner left the care of the house to us and I can assure you that we allowed *no one* to use it." His voice was becoming strained, as though Jace were accusing him of something bad. "I think, Mr. Montgomery, that you should talk to Mrs. Browne. If anyone who wasn't supposed to stay there did, then Mrs. Browne knows about it."

"I'll talk to her," Jace said, sighing because he knew he'd get no information out of the woman. "But you will call the owner right away and ask?"

"Yes," the agent said tiredly. "I'll call."

Jace thanked him, then hung up and dressed to go out. On his way out he stopped by the kitchen and asked Mrs. Browne if anyone had stayed in the house while it was empty. As he knew she would, she took offense and told him that *no one* had stayed there. He left in the middle of her lecture and went in search of his car. Outside, hidden behind a turn of the house, was a three-car garage, which he'd somehow missed seeing before.

It took him a while to find his keys in a little box hung on the wall. When he opened his car he saw that dirt had been vacuumed off the floormat and on the passenger seat was a file folder. Inside was a neatly typed piece of paper listing supplies and computer and other equipment needed to set up an office. Jace smiled when he saw that the items came from four different sources. "I tried to get the best prices," Gladys had written at the bottom. "I could buy it all on Monday and start work on Tuesday at two. I have classes until one."

Jace had to walk around to the other side of the car to get into the driver's side. It was going to take him a while to adjust to the steering wheel being on the opposite side of what he was used to.

He backed out of the garage, looked for the device to close the door but couldn't find it. Out of nowhere, Mick appeared and pulled the door down. Jace put the window down, stuck his head out, and said, "Tell Gladys yes. Tuesday will be fine." Mick smiled and waved thanks.

On the road into Margate village, Jace's cell phone—or mobile as it was called in England—rang. Nigel said that the owner had said emphatically that he'd never lent the house to anyone. "Thank you," Jace said and hung up.

Either someone was lying or Stacy and whomever she'd met had broken into the house. Or had they? Jace had no proof she'd kept her meeting. Maybe she'd gone to the house, waited for the person, but he didn't show up. Maybe in despair she'd taken her own life.

"But if she loved *him* so much, why was she marrying *me?*" he said out loud, then swerved to miss an oncoming car. Out of habit, he'd moved to the right side of the road.

Jace pulled his Range Rover to the side, stopped, and put his head on the steering wheel. Short of taking Stacy's photo into the village and asking questions, he wasn't sure how to proceed. He'd read the reports on her death. No one had visited her at the pub that night. She'd arrived late, the owner's wife said she'd given Stacy a key, and that she'd nearly fallen on her way up the stairs. The woman also said Stacy looked as though she'd been crying. The owner had asked if she could help. "No, I'm fine," Stacy said. "I just need a good, long sleep."

When Jace had driven to the house before, he'd turned into Priory House before reaching the village, so he'd not seen it. Now he saw that it was quaint and cute, but then most English villages were. All the grocery shops were divided, so there was a butcher shop, a bakery, a fruitier, a greengrocer, and a wine shop. At one end of the main street, named High Street as it was in most villages, was a pub and another one stood at the other end of the street.

Which pub was it? Jace wondered. His copy of the police report was hidden in the back of his photo of Stacy and he hadn't thought to bring it. Maybe he could visit the place where Stacy had . . . died—he could hardly even think the word—and find out . . . Find out what, he didn't know.

When he passed a small brick building that said Margate Historical Library, Jace had an idea.

He parked his car on the street and walked toward the library.

Everyone he passed stared at him, then nodded. He had no doubt that they knew he was the latest owner of Priory House. He could almost hear their wanting to ask if he'd seen the ghost yet. He thought he'd answer, "Yes, but she got scared of me and vanished."

When he got to the library door, he realized he hadn't so much as a pen with him. He couldn't pretend to be an author doing research if he didn't have pen and paper.

Turning, he looked about the village, and across the street was a stationer's shop. He crossed the street and went inside. As with most shops in English villages, it had two of each item rather than twenty-five of each as American stores carried, and there wasn't a piece of Plexiglas in sight.

"Here you are," said a tall, thin, gray-haired woman from behind the counter as she shoved a box toward him.

"I beg your pardon."

"It's all there," she said. "Take a look."

"I think there's been a mistake. I haven't purchased anything."

"Alice Browne called and said you'd seen the ghost outside in the garden. No one's done that before, so we knew your next stop would be the library to find out about her, and of course you'd be wanting something to take notes on, so here's everything you need."

When Jace didn't move, she pushed the box until it was about to fall off the counter.

"Go on," she said. "It's been put on your account and I'll send young Gladys Arnold a statement at the end of the month. Mind you, though, I don't take kindly to her buying some of her supplies in Aylesbury. You can tell her from me that it doesn't pay to antagonize the local vendors."

When Jace still didn't move, she looked impatient. "Is there something else you want?"

"No," Jace said slowly, then took the box and headed for his car. Shoving the box onto the passenger seat, he got behind the steering wheel. He needed some time to calm himself. Even though he'd told Mrs. Browne that he had *not* seen the ghost in the garden, she hadn't believed him. She'd called the local stationer's shop and told the clerk that Jace would stop in there on the way to the library.

His impulse was to call Mrs. Browne and tell her off, even to fire her. How dare she blab to the whole village what he was doing?

After a few minutes of anger, it occurred to him that this was good. He wouldn't have to work to make people believe he was interested in the ghost and thereby cover his real interest. No, it was assumed that Jace was just like everyone else.

"Good," Jace said. "This is good. A premade cover."

Relaxing his tight muscles, he looked at the box on the seat beside him and began to go through it, shaking his head in wonder. It was filled with all that a researcher could want: six black pens, four colored pens, two notebooks, one with lines, one without. On and on. There was even a little battery-powered booklight in the bottom.

Jace took out a large paper wallet with a string tie, and stuck in the unlined notebook and two black pens, then headed toward the library.

The librarian, a woman about the same age as the stationer clerk and Mrs. Browne, greeted him with, "I have everything you want right here." She pushed a box toward him. "We call it the Priory House box and we don't even put the books away anymore. I hope you have a video player. Alice said you don't have much in the way of furniture, just the leftovers of the last owner. If you need video equipment, we can rent some to you."

"Thank you," Jace said as sincerely as he could, but it was difficult not to make a smart retort. "I have video equipment on order."

"Oh? Alice didn't tell me—"

"Mrs. Browne doesn't know everything about my life," Jace said stiffly.

The woman blinked at Jace a couple of times. "I see. Perhaps you don't want these books," she said and started to take them off the counter.

In spite of his intentions, it seemed that Jace had offended yet another English person. "I very much want the books," he said, picking up the box before she could take it away. "And it was kind of you to assemble this for me."

She didn't soften. "I didn't do it for you. I put them together for Mrs. Grant."

"Oh?" Jace asked, smiling, trying to ingratiate himself. "I don't know her."

"Of course not! She was four owners ago." The woman was glaring at him as though he was taking up too much of her time. "Now, if you don't need anything else . . ."

"Actually, I'd like to look around. At other subjects. If I might be allowed to do so, that is."

She didn't answer, just turned away. Jace took the box and set it on a table. What he really wanted to see was a local newspaper for the day after Stacy died. He wanted to know what had been written about her and who had been involved.

He knew the librarian could answer many of his questions about where to start looking, but he also knew she'd probably call Mrs. Browne five minutes later. And ask her permission? Jace wondered. Would the librarian ask Mrs. Browne if it was all right for Jace to look at three-year-old newspapers?

He found what he wanted without asking and put the newspaper on the microfilm reader.

The day after Stacy's body was found, the headlines had been about the local garden contest, so her death was on the bottom of the second page. He felt some resentment that her death wasn't front-page news, but he was also glad that speculation about Stacy hadn't been made the center of attention. Her death had been dealt with quietly and with dignity, he thought.

The story was written by Ralph Barker. The paper was written, edited, and printed by him. He wrote the name and address down in his notebook.

He knew he was dawdling to postpone reading the story. Taking a deep breath, he began. It was a straight news story, just the facts given, no melodrama, no speculation.

At 3:00 p.m. on 12 May 2002, the body of Miss Stacy Evans, an American woman aged twenty-seven years, had been found above the Leaping Stag pub by the owner's wife, Mrs. Emma Carew. Mrs. Carew told constable Clive Sefton that Miss Evans had come into the pub about midnight and asked if she could rent a room for the night. Mrs. Carew said that Miss Evans looked the "worse for wear" as her blouse was torn at the shoulder and she had makeup under her eyes as though she'd been crying. Mrs. Carew asked her if she was all right. Miss Evans said she was, just that she was very tired and wanted a long sleep. She asked not to be disturbed the next morning and said that if she had to pay for two nights she would. Mrs. Carew said she could smell liquor on her breath, so she figured the woman had been drinking and didn't trust herself to drive. As Miss Evans went up the stairs, she tripped.

The next day, when Mrs. Carew heard nothing from Miss Evans, she began to worry. Her husband, pub owner George Carew, told her to leave Miss Evans alone, but Mrs. Carew wouldn't. She used her master key to open the door, but found it chained shut. She said she could see Miss Evans sprawled across the bed and her instinct told her the woman was dead. She called the police.

Constable Clive Sefton arrived on the scene at 3:06 p.m. and he and Mr. Carew broke into the room. Miss Evans was dead.

Constable Sefton found Miss Evans's handbag, removed her passport, then called the number listed to be used in case of an emergency.

The article said that, pending investigation, Miss Stacy Evans's death was apparently a suicide.

Jace fast-forwarded through two days of newspaper pages filled with articles and photos about the village garden contest. He noticed that there was no mention of his house or Mr. Hatch's beautiful garden at Priory House in the contest.

Three days after Stacy's death, he found a second article, this time on page six, again at the bottom. It briefly recounted the original story, then said that Miss Evans's married sister, Mrs. Regina Townsend, had flown to Margate to take the body home to the United States. When questioned, Mrs. Townsend told Constable Sefton that her sister had been despondent for quite some time, that she had committed to getting married, but was having second thoughts and didn't know how to get out of her promise of marriage.

Jace leaned back in his chair, feeling as though he'd been kicked. For a moment he couldn't get his breath. At Stacy's funeral, her family had vented their anger at him, but his family had protected him from the worst of it. Truthfully, Jace had been numb with shock, unable to comprehend what they were saying. Only later did he remember what they'd said, and then only partially.

But here it was in print. Stacy's sister, a woman he'd thought was his friend, had told the police that Stacy didn't know how to get out of her promise to marry. "A promise to marry *me,*" Jace whispered.

"Yes, Mr. Montgomery?" the librarian asked coldly. "Do you need something?"

"No, I just . . ." She was looking at him expectantly and when she took a step toward him, he turned off the microfilm machine. He didn't want her to see what he was reading.

"I was wondering why Hatch didn't enter anything from Priory House in the local garden contest," he said as he rewound the microfilm and put it in the basket.

"That's what everyone wonders," she said. "Whoever does win the competition is told that she, or he, would not have won if Mr. Hatch had entered *his* flowers. It is frustrating when one strives all year to be declared the best. Perhaps now that you own Priory House, you could speak to Mr. Hatch."

"I most certainly will, and I will say now that if the roses in the front of this building are any indication of your expertise, I'm not sure Hatch will win."

"I do my best," Mrs. Wheeler said, obviously pleased by his observation.

Smiling, Jace thanked her again, then went outside. For a moment he had to concentrate to be able to breathe. He put the box of books about the history of the house in the car. Now what? he thought, but even as he wondered, he headed down the street to the Leaping Stag pub. His uncle said that Jace might find out things he didn't want to know. Was he going to find out that Stacy wanted out of the marriage? That she despised him?

By the time Jace got to the pub, the last thing he wanted was more information. What he really wanted was a drink and to forget for a while.

The pub was full of old beams and shiny horse brasses, a tourists' vision of what an English pub should look like. There was a young couple at a table in a far corner, but otherwise, the place was empty except for the man behind the bar. He was tall, in his forties, and had an apron pulled tight across his big belly. He had an air about him that said he was the owner of the pub.

"You don't have any McTarvit single malt, do you?" Jace asked.

With a half grin, he poured Jace a shot of the dark gold whiskey.

"So," the man said, "you've met 'the three.' "

Jace looked up in question.

"Mrs. Browne, Mrs. Parsons at the stationer's, and Mrs. Wheeler at the library, and now it's time for a whiskey. Another one?"

"Make it a double."

A pretty woman, about Jace's age, with a good figure, came out of the back room. "Oh, my, you *are* a looker," she said. "I was told you were, but my goodness."

"Hands off, darlin'," the bartender said good-naturedly. "By the way, I'm George Carew, and this cheeky lass is my wife Emma." He nodded toward Jace. "He's just been through the trio."

Emma's face changed to sympathy. "Poor thing. I'd offer to feed you up, but I imagine Alice has done that already."

"How much weight can a person gain in twenty-four hours?" Jace asked.

"She'll have cobbler for tonight—if she can find any raspberries, that is." Her pretty eyes were twinkling in conspiracy.

"How can those girls keep a secret like that in a village like this?" Jace asked, his voice low. The whiskey was relaxing him, but he knew he couldn't have any more for fear he'd say something he shouldn't.

"Everything is done over at Luton," Emma said. "The only reason I know about the fruit is because my mother started it all."

"And how is Mr. Hatch involved?" Jace asked.

"His youngest sister is in it," Emma said.

" 'Young' is a relative term. She has to be eighty if she's a day," the pub owner said.

For a moment a look of love and such intimacy flashed between them that Jace wanted to grab the bottle of whiskey and drain it. He thought he'd had that with Stacy, but it seemed that he hadn't. "Yes, I've heard of your wife," Jace said before he thought, then realized he couldn't tell them where he'd heard of Emma Carew.

But the bartender just grinned proudly. "So you've already read the book."

"Yes, of course I did," Jace said, but Emma was watching him. He felt sure she knew he was lying. He wanted to open his notebook and write, "Find book. Read about Emma."

"Mr. Montgomery—" Emma began.

"Jace," he said quickly.

"Jace." She smiled at him in a way that made him feel good. "How about a beer and some of your American chicken wings?"

"Who made the beer?" Jace asked fearfully.

"Don't tell me you drank some of ol' Hatch's beer?" George asked.

"A pint of it."

"And you're still alive?"

"And I had two cups of his wine in the same day."

"It's a wonder you aren't blind."

"No wonder you slept through dinner last night," Emma said, then laughed at Jace's expression. "Daisy told her mother, she told my mum, who told me. You're the major topic of conversation around here. Big, gorgeous thing like you all alone in that giant house. It's the general opinion around here that you need a wife. In fact, there are quite a few unattached women who are dusting off their high heels right now."

"Who needs a wife? Other than me, that is?" came a voice from the doorway.

Jace turned to see a young man, late twenties, blond, blue-eyed, and strongly built. He was in a policeman's uniform and Jace intuitively knew he was the man who had opened the door and found Stacy.

He took a seat on a stool by Jace and ordered a lemonade. "On duty," he said. "Clive Sefton. So why did *you* buy the house?"

Jace didn't crack a smile. "Loved the beauty of it."

The three of them groaned.

"Mrs. Browne's cooking? The gardens?"

They groaned more.

Jace took a drink of his beer, a nice, light-colored American-style beer, ate one of Emma's fiery-hot chicken wings, and pushed the plate toward Clive to share. "Okay, so I made a little money from some good investments and I wanted a place to live so I bought a house."

"Why *that* house?" Clive persisted.

"To write a book about the ghost, of course."

"You and everyone else," George said.

"Sorry, dear," Emma said to Jace, "but you won't last there. Too bad."

"Tell me," Jace said, "exactly what does the ghost do?"

"It's all over town that you saw her in the garden this morning."

"What I saw were two girls stealing my raspberries. Mrs. Browne took it from there." It wasn't really a lie, but it also wasn't the truth.

Emma looked at Clive. "So tell him what you've been told."

Clive finished his fourth chicken wing. "The last owner told me he saw the outline of a woman sitting around his seven-year-old son. The boy was inside the ghost and they were playing Xbox together."

"Xbox?" Jace asked.

"Xbox. She reads over people's shoulders and when they go too slow, she turns the pages. The eldest son of two owners back said he heard her ride a horse up the stairs, but I think that kid smoked things he shouldn't."

"What about 'her' tree?" Jace asked.

"That's from long ago," Clive continued. "It's said that she hanged a man there. He betrayed her, so she ordered her men to hang him. Get Mr. Hatch to show you the place where the rope used to be. The rope was kept there until about ten years ago, when the owner before last cut it down.

"There's another story that she buried her loot under that tree. Mr. Hatch has spent more than one night sleeping under it with a shotgun across his lap. The lads around here are always saying they're going to chop the tree down and see what's under it, so Hatch protects the tree."

"Interesting," Jace said, looking at his beer, then blurted, "are there any unsolved murders in this village?"

Emma smiled. "I see. You want to write about murder in an English village, don't you?"

"It's the only kind of murder mystery that sells." Jace took a drink of his beer. "Has anyone ever done a study of the population of England versus the number of people supposedly killed in clever ways in remote English villages?"

"Can't say I've heard of it," George said, smiling. "But if somebody proposed it, I'm sure the government would pay for the study."

"My opinion," Emma said quickly, before her husband started on politics, "is that remote English villages are so boring that people think about murder just to liven up the place." She was looking at her husband pointedly.

"Emma wants George to take her to London for a night out," Clive explained.

"If he doesn't, you'll have a murder to investigate here in Margate."

"So nothing has happened here other than the ghost and the Xbox?"

"That's a good book title for you," George said. *"The Ghost and the Xbox."*

Clive was looking at Jace in speculation. "Any particular crime you're interested in?"

Jace looked away. He'd had too much to drink and there were too many ears listening. He was glad when half a dozen men, off from work, came into the pub. Music was turned on and everyone dispersed.

In the end, Jace stayed at the pub until 2:00 a.m. He laughed and talked with people and did his best to forget what he'd seen in the morning and read in the afternoon. Some man with red hair and freckles drove him home.

4

The next morning Jace decided to spend the day at home. He wasn't much of a drinker, but he'd had two days of falling into bed and that was enough. At breakfast, Mrs. Browne asked after his liver. Jace didn't reply, but in the next moment, Mrs. Browne was asking him what he'd researched other than the ghost. Jace knew he had to say something or the rumors would create their own explanation.

He looked down at the French toast—à la Jamie Oliver—and acted as though there was something he was trying not to say. She was cleaning the big Belfast sink and waiting.

Jace gave her some time, then said, "Why wasn't *my* garden in the local garden show?"

Mrs. Browne immediately launched into a diatribe against her favorite subject: Mr. Hatch. He never entered the village contest because he thought it wouldn't be fair to the other entrants.

After all, he was a professional. Mrs. Browne told Jace what she thought of Mr. Hatch's gardening skills.

Smiling, feeling as though he'd distracted the watchdogs, Jace went up to his bedroom, where someone had put the box of books the librarian had lent him. Might as well get started on them, he thought.

Last night he'd slept in the big oak bed in the master bedroom, but even asleep it had felt too big and too empty. A door had been cut into the wall so the previous owners could use the room on the west end as a closet, so Jace went to the east into what was becoming his favorite room, where he'd slept the first night. He smiled as soon as he entered it.

One wall contained a beautiful, carved marble fireplace; another wall had floor-to-ceiling windows that looked over the gardens. The wall before him had a deep bay with enormous windows all around it and a window seat below. The bed was against the fourth wall, as was the door into the bath.

He sat on the window seat and looked out at the parkland, across rolling fields of grass, dotted with . . . He really must ask Mr. Hatch if those sheep were his or not.

He turned back to the room. There was little furniture, just the bed, or rather a mattress and springs set on a frame, and a single chair by the fireplace. He knew that downstairs he had several huge rooms with sofas in them and if he had any sense he'd go down there with his books, but he wanted to stay in the bedroom. For one thing it was the only room that didn't feel empty. Even Mrs. Browne's kitchen, filled to the brim as it was, had a feeling of loneliness in it. But here, in this bedroom . . .

"Keep on, Montgomery," Jace said aloud, "and they'll lock you away." He told himself that the light in the room was good, there was the window seat, and that was all he needed.

He stretched out on the bed, the box on the floor beside him. The first thing he read was a small blue book published in 1947, about the wicked Barbara Caswell, Lady Grace. Born in 1660 to an impoverished family, she had been a beautiful woman who was bored and restless. When she was eighteen, she'd married the rich man who owned Priory House, and had assumed that her life would be one long round of parties. But her husband hated London, hated all social life. Bored to the point of insanity, the young wife sneaked out of the "chintz room," up a secret staircase to one of the four tower rooms, donned men's clothes, then went down the staircase to the ground. She whistled to her favorite horse, then set off to rob people, not for the money, but for the excitement of it.

After a few months of this, Lady Grace met another highwayman, Gentleman Jack, and had an affair with him. For years, they robbed people together. But eventually, the woman's boredom got the better of her and in her quest for more excitement, she began killing people. She shot a boy she'd seen grow up, and when an old servant found out about her, she poisoned him. When she found Gentleman Jack in bed with another woman, she gave his name to the sheriff. The highwayman was arrested, tried, and hanged. Barbara Caswell's only worry was that he might expose her when he was on the gallows. But he was true to his name and didn't give her away.

Two-thirds of the way through the book, Jace could hardly read any more. The story made no sense to him, yet it was supposed to be true. Barbara Caswell had gone out night after night for years. Didn't anyone notice that she was gone? Wasn't there even one thing that happened at night that caused people to have to get out of bed so they discovered she was missing?

Reluctantly, he continued reading. After years of murder

and betrayal, Mrs. Caswell fell in love with the fiancé of the only person who was suspicious of her, and she reformed. Ah! Jace thought. The power of love. Supposedly, overnight, Barbara Caswell went from being a cold-blooded killer to being content as a housewife—except that she was plotting to poison her husband to get rid of him so she could marry the man she loved.

By the time Jace got to the end of the book, he could hardly keep his eyes open. He knew he was supposed to believe the story was wildly romantic, but he didn't. When he read that Lady Grace went for one last raid and was shot by the man she loved, he was relieved.

"A well-deserved death," Jace said, tossing the book back into the box. He wanted to take a nap, but then he remembered Emma Carew and wondered what he was supposed to have read about her.

He picked up a huge paperback, *The History of Margate*. Since the book weighed several pounds, he didn't think he'd start from the beginning. He looked in the index, found "Carew," then turned to the page. There was a photo of Emma, taken about ten years ago, wearing a conservative swimsuit, a crown on her head and a scepter in her hand. "Miss Margate," it read under the picture. "Voted the prettiest girl in the village."

Smiling, Jace closed the book and looked at the other items in the box. There were four brochures from when the house was being sold. He glanced through them and saw that not much had changed except for the furniture. One owner had filled the house with chrome and glass and black leather. In the bottom of the box was a booklet about haunted houses in England and Priory House rated a long paragraph. He read how the ghost of Barbara

Caswell, the lady highwayman, had often been seen. Among other things, she lit candles in the tower window and rode her horse around the inside of the house.

"But her husband had no idea what was going on," Jace said as he tossed the booklet into the box.

He leaned back against the pillows on the bed and looked about the room. The ceiling was undecorated, but it was plaster. The walls had old oak paneling halfway up and the floor was oak parquet. "Wonder what the room used to look like?" he whispered just before he fell asleep.

Instantly, he began to dream. He dreamed he was in the bedroom, standing where the bed was, but he could see a narrow bed on the opposite wall. He looked down at his legs and realized his left leg was inside a big wardrobe. Startled, he stepped to the right, out of the cabinet. Curious, he put his hand through the wardrobe, then through a chair beside it. He knew he was dreaming, so he was enjoying the sensation. He walked toward the fireplace, stepping through a big green ottoman, and smiled as he went through an upholstered wing chair.

At the fireplace, Jace tried to pick up ornaments but his hand passed through them. What a wonderful dream, he thought, enjoying the magic sensation of seeing but not being there. And what a marvelous room his mind had created. Victorian wasn't what he would have thought he would have chosen though. If he'd guessed he would have said he'd choose Priory House when it was a monastery.

This room belonged to a woman, he thought as he kept walking, pausing to run his hands through the pretty bottles on a little dressing table, then looked at the titles of the books jammed into a tall, skinny bookcase. They were mostly children's books, but there were some nature books as well. "Birds," he said, but he couldn't hear his own voice. "She likes birds." When he heard no sound, he thought, Like a silent movie, this is a silent dream.

He wasn't up on his history of antiques, but he guessed the room was from about the time of the American Civil War.

When Jace had fully circled the room, he stopped by the wardrobe. To his left, the door into the hall opened. As Jace had thought, the other two doors, the ones into the master bedroom and the bath, weren't there. Those were later changes.

Even though he knew he was dreaming and knew that what he was seeing wasn't real, when he heard voices, his heart nearly stopped.

Two women came into the room. One was tall and slim and had her hair pulled back to the nape of her neck. Jace recognized her as the woman who'd blown the spider onto Mrs. Browne. His impulse was to say hello, but he so wanted to see what would happen that he inched his way into the wardrobe, disappearing into the side of it. His view was darker, as though he was wearing sunglasses indoors, but he could see them and wondered if they could see him.

The second woman was shorter and plumper. She had a beautiful face, even if her eyebrows were unplucked, and she wore little makeup. By twenty-first-century standards she was on the heavy side. However, Jace marveled at what she'd done to her body. For all that the top and bottom of her were rather large, her waist was small enough that he could have spanned it with his hands. In a way she looked great, but in another way, he thought that if you cut the straps to her corset, she might expand into a blimp.

He thought the taller woman would probably look great in a bikini.

"Ann, it's beautiful," the plump woman said. She was wearing what had to be fifty pounds of green silk and probably a hundred yards of fringe and braid.

The thinner woman, Ann, was holding up a pretty dress of pale yellow silk. It had half the yardage and half the trimming of the other woman's dress and Jace liked it better.

"Do you think so?" Ann asked. "But do you think Danny will like it when I wear it on our wedding day?"

"I think Danny Longstreet would like it better if it were red-and-black–striped taffeta and had purple fringe along the skirt."

Ann smiled. "Probably. Mr. Longstreet said that once I'm his daughter I can go to London to shop. Can you imagine, Catherine? London!"

"Something that father of yours would never allow," Catherine said, then her face brightened. "You will stay with me in London, won't you? The children are clamoring for the latest chapter in your story."

"Of course I'll stay with you, dear Catherine. And I'll be your alibi for the time you spend with your latest . . . What is his name?"

"He's my lover and you very well know his name. Sergei. Oh, Ann, you should see him. Gorgeous doesn't begin to describe him. And that Russian temper of his!"

"How does your husband like him?"

"I have no idea. Peregrine has an actress for a mistress."

Ann shook her head. "I thought you loved your husband."

"I do. Very much. In fact, I think our last child might be his."

Ann laughed. "You are incorrigible."

"Me? Here you are marrying a man who is one generation away from being the housekeeper's son, but *I* am incorrigible?"

"As you well know, my dear cousin, our family are but three

generations out of the factories. It was your face and your waist-line that caught you an earl for a husband, not your ancestry."

"Yes, but now that I've caught him, it reflects on you. You could have better than Hugh Longstreet's son. It's this old house the man wants and he's marrying his son to you just to get it. Your father has used *you* to get what he wants. Are you *sure* you won't change your mind about marrying him?"

"Absolutely certain." Ann put her wedding dress on the ottoman and started toward the wardrobe. "I didn't show you my going-away outfit. It has a cashmere jacket."

"I'd love to see it. I—Ann! What's wrong?"

Ann had opened the door to the wardrobe and there Jace was, standing inside. When he knew she was about to open the door, he'd tried to hide but he couldn't move back—which would have made him go through the wall—and for some reason his body wouldn't go sideways to hide behind the other door.

He felt bad about the terrified look on Ann's face, but he couldn't do anything about it. Unlike she did in the garden, he couldn't seem to disappear at will. He smiled at her and even gave a little wave, but that only frightened her more. Her skin was so pale he feared she'd pass out.

Raising her arm, Ann pointed at the wardrobe and Catherine went to it. She saw nothing unusual. She tossed the clothes out and picked up boxes and threw them out.

As Catherine bent down to look inside the deep wardrobe, Jace had the unsettling experience of her head going through his chest. When she tossed out a hatbox, it went through his legs. He couldn't take his eyes off what Catherine was doing, but after a while he began to see the humor in it all. He looked up at Ann to share it with her, but she was about to fall to the floor in fear.

Jace yelled at Catherine to see to Ann, but his voice made no sound. He pounded on the wardrobe wall, but that made no sound either.

When Ann's body hit the floor, Catherine looked back. Ann looked at Jace again, her eyes fluttered, then she went limp. The second she lost consciousness, Jace awoke to find himself on the bed.

For several minutes he lay there, blinking up at the ceiling, disoriented, not knowing where he was. Gradually, the barren room came into focus. It was the same room as in his dream, but nothing else was the same. Her—Ann's—wallpaper above the paneling had been cream with little sprigs of wildflowers tied with blue ribbons. The bed had been mahogany, narrow but tall. The carpet—

Jace ran his hand over his eyes, sat up, and looked at his watch. He'd been asleep only ten minutes.

As he came more fully awake, he began to remember what he'd heard. Names. Danny Longstreet. Ann, Catherine, Peregrine.

He grabbed the thick paperback, *The History of Margate,* and looked in the index. Hubert and Daniel Longstreet were under the chapter about Priory House.

Hubert "Hugh" Longstreet was the father of Daniel, who had been engaged to Ann Stuart, daughter of the owner of Priory House. But when the marriage didn't take place, Hugh and his son left Margate and were never heard from again.

"But what about Ann?" Jace asked aloud. "Why didn't she marry Danny Longstreet?"

As Jace flipped the pages, he thought of all the diseases Victorians had. What awful thing had happened to Ann so she didn't get to marry Danny Longstreet?

Two pages on, there was an essay written by N. A. Smythe titled "The Tragedy of the Priory House Stuarts."

Quickly, Jace read the story, then slowed down and read it again. Smythe wrote that Arthur Stuart, beloved son and owner of Priory House, had eschewed the rich young woman he could have married and had, instead, married for love. He married the sweet and lovely daughter of a vicar of a rural parish, and took her back to Priory House. Alas, she and his beloved father died the next year. But Arthur wasn't left alone as he had his beloved daughter, Ann, to comfort him.

"Beloved," Jace said. "Everyone is beloved of everyone else."

In 1877, it was found that the house needed massive repairs, but Arthur Stuart, a renowned scholar, didn't have the money to pay for them. Hubert Longstreet, a rich American, wanted to buy the house, but he also wanted his son to marry into what he considered the aristocracy, the Stuart family. Although there was no longer any title, it was believed that there had once been a connection to the royal Stuarts, and even a connection to the British throne. Longstreet wanted to elevate his status above his lowly American roots, and Arthur Stuart was desperate to preserve the home of his ancestors.

The two men struck a bargain. They agreed that their children would marry and they'd all live together in the big house. But it was a devil's bargain. Danny Longstreet was an uneducated lout who drank and gambled and frequented houses of ill repute. Ann Stuart was a lady of the highest reputation, quiet and scholarly, beloved by everyone.

"Ann tried to obey her father," N. A. Smythe wrote, "but when it came down to it, she couldn't go through with the marriage. Two hours before her wedding, she drank a bottle of poison. She killed herself rather than marry a good-for-nothing like Danny Longstreet.

"Ann was buried in her wedding dress, but unfortunately, she had to be buried outside the sanctity of the churchyard because of her suicide.

"A few weeks after the marriage was supposed to have taken place, a local Margate girl revealed that the father of her illegitimate child was Danny Longstreet.

"Poor Ann, may she rest in peace."

Jace closed the book. No, Ann Stuart didn't rest in peace. In fact, she didn't rest at all. She was doomed to wander about Priory House for . . . How long? he wondered. Until someone found out she had been murdered and hadn't commited suicide?

He sat up straighter. Murder. When Jace first heard that the woman he loved had committed suicide, he'd said she'd been murdered, but no one would listen to him. Stacy had been an insomniac, so she'd always had sleeping pills. But in the years they'd known each other, she'd gradually come to stop using the pills. He hadn't even known she still had a prescription. After her death, a doctor he'd never heard of had called to apologize for giving Stacy a new prescription. "I heard about her death," the doctor had said. "She was a new patient and I had no idea she was an addict or a manic-depressive." "She was no such thing!" Jace had said before his uncle Mike took the phone. Mike spoke quietly to the man for a few minutes, then hung up. Mike's face was red with anger. "I think he's worried we'll sue so he's trying to establish that Stacy was mentally unsound." All Jace heard of that sentence was the word "was." Stacy was gone.

During the weeks in hell that followed Stacy's death, all Jace seemed to hear was that Stacy was "unstable" and had had years of counseling. Her family seemed to agree that being engaged to someone like Jace, so busy with work, always traveling, had sent her over the edge. She'd wanted out of the marriage but didn't know how to say the words. Stacy's stepmother said that Stacy hadn't wanted to hurt Jace's feelings. "So she *killed* herself?" Jace said. At that, Stacy's stepmother had started crying, Stacy's father had led her away, and Uncle Mike had taken Jace away.

It hadn't taken much thought to see how much Stacy's stepmother had to gain with Stacy's death being a suicide. With Stacy gone, she had all her husband's attention. The man had never cared much for his other daughter, Regina, who had married young and produced four homely children. Stacy had been the one to laugh, the one to put a sparkle in her father's eye.

Jace closed his eyes and let himself remember something he'd tried to forget: Stacy's funeral. Mr. Evans's face had been bleak, his eyes dull and red with grief. Stacy had been his favorite. He used to say that she'd caused him problems, but she was worth it. At the funeral, Mr. Evans was slumped in a chair, numb from shock. Hovering over him were his young wife and his unloved second daughter, consoling him over the suicide.

What would have happened if Stacy's death had been declared a murder? Jace thought. Roger Evans wouldn't have needed the comfort of two women. He would have been a lion in a rage. He would have put his life on hold until he found out who had killed his precious daughter.

Jace's mother always said that if you wanted to know why someone did something, then you should look at the result. When Stacy's stepmother and her sister had blamed Jace and told the English police that Stacy was deeply unhappy, they'd achieved two things. They'd claimed Roger Evans's undivided attention, and they'd rid themselves of the Montgomerys. Jace was well aware of how pleased Roger had been that his daughter was marrying into the Montgomerys, a family of wealth and power. That must have hurt Regina, as her husband couldn't seem to hold a job.

Jace ran his hand over his eyes. Right now everything seemed clear. At least the motives of the people who were still living seemed clear.

But what about Stacy?

Jace looked about the room. He knew without a doubt that he'd been led to this house. It seemed that the letter he'd found had waited for him for three whole years. He'd needed time to get over his grief and shock about Stacy, and he'd needed time to realize that he *had* to find out the truth. He couldn't continue in his life afraid that each woman he met was going to . . . He couldn't bring himself to think of the possible consequences.

Murder, not suicide. It was an idea that had always been in his head, but who, why? *How?*

The one thing he was truly sure of was that it was no coincidence that he was seeing a ghost who was believed to have committed suicide.

Jace picked up *The History of Margate* and looked at the story about Ann again. From the little bit he'd heard in his dreams, it seemed that everything in the story was wrong. From Catherine's tone of voice, he didn't think Ann was Arthur Stuart's "beloved" daughter. And far from wanting to get out of marrying a rogue like Danny Longstreet, Ann was looking forward to it.

"What happened?" he asked aloud. "And what can I do about any of it?" He knew Ann had shown herself to other people—or been seen by them—but only he had seen her outside. That had to be significant.

Jace stood up. He knew he needed Ann Stuart. He needed what she'd seen happen in this house, and he felt that she needed him too. It was his guess that she'd been searching for . . . He calculated. Was it was possible that for a hundred and twenty-seven years she'd been searching for someone to help get her body into the sacred ground of the churchyard?

"You help me and I'll help you," he said, but felt no response. The room, even the house, felt empty. It made Jace smile when he thought that twice now he'd frightened Ann: once in the garden and once in her own time. For all he knew, right now she was hiding in Barbara Caswell's tower room and planning to never come out.

He needed to talk to her and tell her of his problems with Stacy. He had to get her to come to him.

A slow smile spread over his face. He was going to court her. Entice her. He was going to create a web, then draw her into it.

Still smiling, Jace went into the big bedroom to pack his overnight case. It wasn't going to be easy, but he knew he was going to have to trust some people.

5

Gladys put down her paintbrush. "I need a rest."

"Sure, as soon as—" Jace looked at Mick and Gladys and saw the way they were looking at him. They were young and in love and they wanted some of the weekend to be alone. It was three o'clock on Sunday afternoon and he'd had them working since two on Friday.

"Go on," he said, "I'll finish here. You two—" They were out of the room before he finished the sentence.

"It looks good," Gladys called back to him as she and Mick ran down the stairs.

Jace had to control his feelings of jealousy as their laughter rang through the house. "This house needs some laughter," he said, then stepped back to look at Ann's room. It did look good.

On Friday he'd told Mrs. Browne he was going to spend the weekend in London. He'd politely listened to her explain that in

England one spent the week in London and the week*end* in the country. "But I'm not English, am I?" Jace said, knowing that, to her mind, "not being English" was worse than any crime.

When he got to his car, as he hoped, Mick was nearby and Jace offered him a weekend job.

"In London? With my girl?"

"If you don't mind staying at Claridge's," Jace said and thought Mick was going to faint with happiness. Even country folk knew Claridge's was a world-renowned hotel.

Since Jace didn't want the village to know what he was doing, he met them in St. Albans, they left their car in a parking lot, and the three took Jace's Range Rover into London. Mick drove, Gladys sat beside him, and Jace sat in the back and made sketches and wrote notes on the big pad of grid paper that Mrs. Parsons at the stationers had included in her box of supplies.

Jace didn't give the reason behind what he wanted to do and the young couple didn't ask questions. He just said he planned to re-create the bedroom on the southwest corner of the house as it had been in 1878.

"The chintz room," Mick said, looking in the rearview mirror at Jace.

"*That* room is the chintz room?" Jace asked, remembering that it had been Barbara Caswell's room. "How do you know that?"

"My mother used to clean at Priory House when I was a boy. I used to hide when we heard Mrs. Browne because we knew she'd fire Mum if she found out I was with her. She did and my mum was."

Jace opened his mouth, but Mick spoke first. "No, sir, I didn't find the secret staircase. No one has found it."

No one alive, Jace thought as he looked back at his sketches.

He wasn't an artist but he'd sketched ornaments, china, furniture, fabrics, wallpaper, and the dresses of Catherine and Ann. "Mick?" Jace asked. "Does Mrs. Browne fire many people?"

Spontaneously, Mick and Gladys burst into loud, raucous laughter. He had his answer.

In London, they checked into two connecting rooms in the fabulously expensive Claridge's Hotel. Jace ignored the looks on Mick's and Gladys's faces. He could see that they'd like to do most anything other than search out antiques, but it wasn't five yet, so Jace gave them their assignments. Mick was to rent a trailer to haul what they bought back with them, then he was to go to a flea market and buy knickknacks from around 1878.

"I don't know about ornaments," Mick protested, glancing at Gladys.

"I know a bit," she said, moving closer to him.

"You can't go together," Jace said. "Gladys, I want you to do some research." He handed her a piece of paper. "That's all I know about a woman and her husband who lived in London in 1878. I want you to find out everything you can about her, and I want all the pictures you can get."

She looked intrigued by the assignment and stepped away from Mick. "Eighteen seventy-eight?"

"And after. What happened to the woman and her children? Mick, see that you get me lots of picture frames. Little ones." He gave them each a stack of cash.

In spite of Mick's complaints about his assignment, the three of them set out with enthusiasm. They met back at the hotel for an eight o'clock dinner in Jace's room and took turns telling about their day.

Mick had booked the trailer, then taken a cab to a flea market where he'd met a little old lady who delighted in helping him. "I told her I worked for the BBC and I was supposed to decorate a bedroom for a young lady of 1878. She asked me questions about the room and I told her about Priory House. All I had to do was listen to her tell me the history of every object." He unwrapped perfume bottles, a silver brush, a comb and hand mirror set, china ornaments, pretty hairpins, three brooches, and a pair of stockings. "If you want more, she'll be there tomorrow. It seems that all she does is haunt the markets. Her eldest daughter—" Smiling, Mick stopped talking and looked at Gladys. "What did *you* get?"

Jace smiled in memory of the rivalry between lovers. It was something else he missed.

"What about you, sir? What did you get?" Gladys asked.

Jace realized there hadn't been much time, so maybe Gladys hadn't found out anything. He didn't want to embarrass her. He'd visited four antique stores and found a bed very like Ann's and a big green ottoman. One store owner told him that what he'd chosen were the most common pieces of the Victorian era and that if he were a connoisseur—

Jace had cut him off, not wanting to waste time hearing a sales pitch. That the furniture in Ann's room was the "most common" reinforced his belief that she wasn't "the beloved daughter" of Arthur Stuart.

For a moment, Jace thought of upgrading the furniture. Maybe he should buy the four-poster rosewood bed that was a ringer for the Lincoln bed in the White House. But no, the idea was to re-create a familiar-looking environment for Ann, so he stuck with what he'd seen.

After Jace told of his purchases, he turned to Gladys. "Did you have time to find out Catherine's last name?"

Gladys excused herself from the table and returned a few

minutes later with a half-inch-tall stack of photocopies. "The aristocracy in England keeps track of its own."

Jace took the papers and began looking through them. Catherine Nightingale Stuart married Peregrine Willmot, the earl of Kingsclere, in 1872. They had nine children.

"I stopped by a tourist information shop and got this." With a little cat smile, she handed Jace a triple-fold brochure advertising a castle to see. It had acres of parkland, a maze, a playground for children, and—

Jace drew in his breath as he unfolded the last page. There was a photo of a portrait of Catherine. "Castle Veraine's most beautiful inhabitant, Catherine Nightingale Willmot," it read below the photo. "The mother of nine children, but she never lost her eighteen-inch waistline."

Jace looked at Gladys. "Tomorrow—"

"I've already checked the train schedules to go there tomorrow. I'll be back in time for dinner. I'll buy every book that has her name in it and every photo they have of her."

"Good girl!" Jace said, then saw Mick and Gladys glance at each other; they'd been talking. Gladys wanted more than praise; she wanted information.

"So why are you doing this?" she asked.

Jace didn't want to lie. "To attract a ghost."

Mick looked like he wanted to run away, but Gladys was interested. Mr. Hatch was right, Jace thought. Either Mick will come up to her level of ambition or she'll drop him.

"You're redecorating the chintz room. Lady Grace's room," Gladys said. "But aren't you a little concerned about her reputation of being a murderer?"

"What if I told you the house was haunted by a young Victorian lady who people believe committed suicide?"

"Ann Stuart," Gladys said and Jace smiled.

"Gladys knows all about the history of Margate," Mick said. "She wants to be on the village council someday."

"I could believe that Gladys might someday be prime minister," Jace said. Mick laughed, but she blushed prettily.

Jace had told them all he was going to, so he changed the subject.

On Saturday morning the three of them parted again. Mick didn't ask to go on the train journey with Gladys. After her triumph of the night before, Mick seemed determined to outdo her. He had a copy of Jace's sketches made and left before 9:00 a.m. "Gotta date," he said, teasing Gladys as he left the hotel.

Jace had the most trouble with the wallpaper. He could find a reasonable facsimile of Ann's wallpaper, but no one had enough in stock to do the room. When he was told someone had just ordered many rolls of that pattern, Jace asked the shop owner to call and offer double the amount for them. He could hear her thoughts of "Americans!"

Jace got the wallpaper, then bought a tea set that was like the dishes he'd seen on Ann's mantel. The salesman, who looked old enough to have known Ann, assured him that the pattern had been in production in 1878.

Jace made four trips around London to pick up his purchases and pack them into the trailer Mick had hired. At eight that night they all met in his hotel room. Jace was ready to return to Priory House right then and start wallpapering, but after one look at Mick and Gladys, he gave in. They wanted another night in the hotel.

But Jace roused them at five the next morning and they set off. Mrs. Browne was off on Sundays and she'd told him that she spent the day with her friends Mrs. Parsons and Mrs. Wheeler.

Jace wanted to redecorate the room while she wasn't there. If possible, he wanted to keep what he was doing a secret from the nosy village.

He dropped Mick and Gladys off at their car in St. Albans, then drove back to Priory House alone. He was glad he didn't have to go through the village with the trailer on the back.

It took them three hours to move everything into the house, then they started on the wallpaper. Jace had no idea what he was doing, but Mick and Gladys were old hands at it. They bossed him around and laughed at how inept he was.

At noon they raided Mrs. Browne's tiny refrigerator and the big pantry and covered the table with a Jamie feast. Jace had missed several dinners and most of them were still there. They had roast lamb, carrots, parsnips, and spinach that looked as though it had just been picked from Mr. Hatch's garden. Gladys dug around in the stone-shelved pantry and found a tart full of raspberries.

Jace didn't know if they knew about Daisy's and Erin's picking, so he didn't want to tell outright. "I'm glad Mrs. Browne could find enough raspberries," he said, and Mick and Gladys burst into laughter.

They were easy with each other now. In the last days the "sirs" had been dropped. They'd gone from being a boss and two employees to being competitors. Hands down, Gladys had won in the research competition and winning had given her confidence.

"Shall we get back to work?" Jace said after they'd eaten.

By three the wallpaper was up—thank heaven for prepasted—and all the many things they'd bought were in the room, but the small things were still wrapped. Jace wanted to be alone when he set up the ornaments, so he was glad they wanted to leave.

As soon as they were gone, he knew he wasn't alone in the room. He could feel Ann's presence. She was quiet, willing to sit without moving and watch, but he could feel her strength.

The furniture, even the wardrobe, was in place. The salesman had shown Jace how it disassembled so it could be carried upstairs in pieces, then quickly put back together.

Jace had bought a small stereo and some CDs, so he put on Mozart and began to unpack. Slowly, he unwrapped the wonderful things that Mick with his little old lady had found. "Hope it was all right that I gave her a hundred-pound note to say thanks," Mick said, wanting to please his new boss, but also loving being able to tip someone a hundred pounds.

First, Jace made the bed. Thick, rough sheets that no amount of bleaching could make white again went on. A wool blanket next, then a beautiful, hand-crocheted spread that had little tassels on its diamond-shaped edges. Big, linen-covered pillows went next, plus a pretty little blue and white round pillow embroidered with wildflowers that nearly matched the wallpaper. Jace felt sure the woman who had chosen these things for Mick had enjoyed herself.

Jace unwrapped a dozen fragile little glass bottles and set them on the dressing table he'd bought. Ceramic dogs went by the fireplace, and two ballerinas on the mantel.

He opened another box. Gladys had stayed up late last night cutting out the photos she'd collected at Catherine's husband's home. She'd bought postcards and books and pamphlets, gathering all the pictures of Catherine and her children she could find. One by one, Gladys had cut the pictures to fit into the twenty-three Victorian frames that Mick had bought, and stuck an identification label on the back of each one.

Carefully, with slow patience and some drama, Jace unwrapped each portrait. Twenty-three times he made a show of where to set the frame. And each time he unwrapped one, he said aloud who it was. "Catherine's next to youngest daughter, Isabella. She was born after you left, so you never saw her. She grew up to be almost as pretty as her mother."

He opened another package. "Ah, yes, Catherine's youngest daughter, Ann. She *was* as pretty as her mother." When the scent of flowers and wood smoke wafted around him, he smiled but he didn't turn.

He finished unloading the box. There was a photo of Catherine's latest descendants, Lord and Lady Kingsclere. There was a look of Catherine about the eyes of Lord Kingsclere. His mother was named Ann.

The scent grew stronger, and even when he heard the rustle of Ann's skirt, he didn't turn.

When the box was empty, he was careful not to look up abruptly. He cleared away the trash, tossed it into the big master bedroom, and closed the door.

There was one more package to unwrap. It was covered with newspaper and tied with string, and was propped against the fireplace. Last night Gladys had made a production of telling her story, then unveiling what she'd found. It was a two-foot-by-three-foot reproduction of the portrait of Catherine. One of the women who'd worked in the gift shop said that years before they'd sold them, but they were too big to carry on a plane so they'd quit stocking them.

With laughter, Gladys recounted how she'd told the woman her American boss had fallen in love with the ghost of a woman who was Lady Catherine's first cousin. She said the portrait was a gift to Ann Stuart's ghost from her boss. The woman, who'd worked there for thirty-odd years, said that Gladys's story was, of course, poppycock, but that few people knew Lady Catherine had a first cousin named Ann Stuart. She looked at Gladys with narrowed eyes. "How did Ann die?" "Suicide, poor dear," Gladys said. "Where did Ann live?" the woman asked. "Priory House in Margate, Bucks." Gladys said her love-besotted American boss had bought the house. The woman lifted an eyebrow and said, "Wait right here." Fifteen minutes later she'd returned with the big portrait printed on cardboard, and she'd charged Gladys the original price of two pounds. To say thanks, Gladys bought an expensive, huge, gilded, wooden frame she'd had trouble getting on the train back to London. With a flare for storytelling, Gladys told them that on the train she'd looked through the books and seen that the woman who had found the picture for her was Lord Kingsclere's mother, Lady Ann.

They all laughed hard at the story, even Jace, although he was embarrassed by Gladys's story of his love for a ghost. He made a mental note to be more careful of what he told her in the future. She saw too much.

After her story, Gladys presented the portrait with the fanfare worthy of a circus act.

After Jace saw it, he called room service and ordered champagne.

Now, as slowly as he could manage to do it, he cut the strings and unwrapped the package. Catherine stared back at him, slightly smiling, a woman of great beauty. She was sitting on a chair so her tiny waistline could be seen. The date of the portrait was 1879, the year after Ann died, and Jace thought he could see a hint of sadness behind Catherine's eyes. A nail was in the wall over the fireplace, so he lifted the portrait and hung it there.

Jace stepped back slowly and didn't stop until he was at the far side of the room, the bed on his right and the wardrobe on his left. As he knew she was, Ann was standing to the left of the fire-place and staring up at the portrait.

Jace stood still, afraid to even breathe, as he looked at her. She wasn't as transparent as she had been when he'd seen her in the garden. He could still see through her, but there was now more substance. She was looking up at the portrait, her face turned away from him, but he admired her figure, tall and shapely, with thick hair that he'd like to touch.

When she turned to him, he was smiling, pleased with himself at what he'd done. All the work and expense of making the room look like it once did had paid off. She was here, and now he would find out about Stacy.

He was pleased with himself to the point of smugness, so when she turned it took him a moment to register that she was angry. She looked as though she'd been crying, but now what he saw on her pretty face was old-fashioned rage.

When she took a step toward him, Jace would have backed up, but he was already against the wall and couldn't go any-where.

"Did you think I needed to be reminded of what was taken from me?" she said loudly and clearly as she came closer to him. "Do you think this existence isn't bad enough that you had to make it *worse*?"

He was pressed against the wall, a ghost was shouting at him, and every horror story Jace had ever heard was running through his head. In another second her ghostly body would reach his. In two seconds, would he be alive?

"Leave me alone," she said when her face was nose to nose with his. Since he was taller than she was, that meant her feet weren't touching the ground.

As Jace opened his mouth to defend himself, she ran through

him, then through the wall behind him. She took his breath with her.

He stood there gasping for air, but none would reach his lungs. A minute passed but no air. Clutching his throat, he could feel himself growing weak. Had she killed him? He fell against the bed and in the next second his breath came back to him. He lay there, panting, his vision blurred, his senses dizzy. When the room stopped spinning, he looked at the portrait of Catherine. "That went well, didn't it?"

After a few moments, he collapsed back onto the bed. Now what did he do? Yet again, he'd hit a brick wall. Literally. He looked at his watch. "I wonder if the pub's open. I need a drink."

6

Jace was sitting on the stool in the Leaping Stag pub, nursing a beer. Beside him sat the young policeman Clive Sefton. George and Emma were behind the bar, filling the orders of the few other people in the pub. Jace had just finished telling them how much he hated the story of Barbara Caswell, Lady Grace. "How could anyone think that woman was a character who should be romanticized?"

"You do know the truth, don't you?" Emma said. "The whole story is made up."

"But I thought it was a true story," Jace said.

She lowered her voice. "Don't tell the tourists. Lady Grace gets us in every haunted England book written."

"It all started with a book about ghosts," George said while filling a big glass full of stout.

Emma leaned toward Jace. "In the thirties someone wrote a

book about the ghosts of England and said that Priory House was haunted by the spirit of an aristocratic lady who used to slip out at night and rob people. That's all there was to it. In 1946, some writer made up the rest of the story and passed it off as true. Did you see the movie?"

"I didn't have time," Jace said.

"We heard you were in London," Emma said, glancing at her husband over her shoulder. "So what was London like?" she asked loudly, and George shook his head.

"Same as always," Jace said, then waited for Emma to ask him about making a room in his house look like a set for a Victorian play. When she said nothing, Jace hoped that he'd at last been able to keep one secret. "I don't want to write what someone else has. Are you sure there haven't been any other mysteries in this village?"

Clive looked down at his beer. "There was one."

Emma and George groaned.

"Not again," Emma said. "Don't get him started. It's Clive's favorite topic, and he's argued about it until we're all sick of it. It was suicide, pure and simple."

Jace took a breath and tried to keep himself calm. "Suicide?"

"Yes!" Emma said, looking pointedly at Clive. "Suicide."

"But you don't think it was?" Jace said, gripping his beer so the shaking of his hand wouldn't show.

"I think . . ." Clive began slowly.

Emma started washing glasses. "About three years ago, a young woman—"

"A real beauty," George interjected.

"Yes," Emma said, "a beautiful young woman committed suicide in a room upstairs. She'd been drinking and crying and she stopped in here and asked if we had a room for rent."

"*Still* had a room for rent," Clive said.

"I don't know if that's what she said. I know I said that right after we found her body, but later I wasn't sure. It was noisy in here and I may have misheard her."

"But you found her the next day," Jace said, his voice soft as he tried to keep it steady.

"Yes. Poor thing. She'd taken most of a bottle of sleeping pills. I called George and he looked at her through the chain lock on the door, then he called Clive—who, I might add, was brand new on the force and didn't know anything."

"Not that he does now," George said, but Clive didn't smile.

"But you think it was murder," Jace said to Clive, but the young policeman said nothing.

"Go on, tell him," Emma said, but Clive was silent.

George took Jace's empty glass and gave him another beer. "Her sister and her mother came from the States and—"

"Her mother?!" Jace asked, then had to cover himself. "That must have been hard for her to have seen." He took a deep drink of his beer.

"It was," Emma said. "The two women were beside themselves. They kept saying that they knew it was going to happen sooner or later."

"It seems she was a real nut case," George said. "Her mother showed us a stack of letters from psychiatrists about the girl. She'd tried to kill herself before."

"And her mother showed up with these papers?" Jace asked. "You'd think that she would have been too distraught by news of her daughter's death to think of getting papers out to prove that the girl was crazy."

Clive looked at Jace with his eyes wide. "That's just what I thought. It was as though those two women wanted to prove to us that she was insane. The mother asked that it not be put in the paper that she'd been there. If those women hadn't been in the States when it happened . . ."

"What?" Jace asked.

"I would have thought they did it."

Emma threw up her hands and George snorted.

"Tell him *why* you think she didn't commit suicide," Emma said. "Go on, tell him."

"She tripped on the stairs," Clive muttered.

"What?" Jace asked.

"She tripped on the stairs," Emma said loudly, then lowered her voice. "Clive, I've told you a thousand times. She was drunk. I smelled it on her breath. She was drunk and when she went up the stairs, she tripped. Simple."

Jace was looking at Clive. "What does tripping on the stairs have to do with murder?"

Clive lifted his head, turned on the bar stool, and faced Jace. When he spoke, there was energy in his voice. "You see—"

"He's off and running," George said.

Jace tried to keep the annoyance off his face and out of his voice. "Let's get a table," he said and they took their beers to a booth in a far corner. "I think this might be the case I'm looking for," Jace said, "so I want to know everything. You wouldn't want to start at the beginning, would you?"

"I'll bore you."

"I swear that you won't."

"Okay," Clive said, "but I warn you that all of this is based on a feeling I have and nothing else. The evidence was that a young American woman, named Stacy Evans, had a fight with her boyfriend, she stopped at a pub, asked if they had a room, then went upstairs and took a bottle of sleeping pills. Her family was called and her mother and sister flew in right away and presented papers as proof that the girl had been a problem since she was a kid. Her mother died when she was young and it very nearly sent her over the edge."

"Her mother died? So who showed up here?"

"Her stepmother, but she said she'd been Stacy's mother since she was a child so she loved her." Clive looked down at his beer.

"But you didn't believe her."

"No, I didn't. I told the superintendent that I didn't, but he said I'd been reading too many fairy tales about wicked step-mothers. There were no signs of foul play, but then there was only one door into the room and it was locked from the inside. She had a purse full of money, and she was wearing diamond ear-rings. Nothing was stolen, and there was no evidence of recent sexual activity."

Jace had to put his beer mug up to his face to hide his expres-sion. It didn't matter, of course, but he was glad that Stacy hadn't been unfaithful to him.

"It was an open and shut case," Clive said. "A nutcase offs herself. The end."

Jace winced at the young man's crudeness. "But she tripped on the stairs."

"Yes," Clive said. "You see, this pub used to be a real bad place. When I was a kid . . ." He smiled. "Better not tell you about what I was like when I was a kid. You've heard of the vicar and the way he helps kids like me?"

"Actually, I have," Jace said. "You were one of his triumphs?"

"I was one of his harder cases. I grew up with . . ." Clive waved his hand. "My life story doesn't matter except to say that I spent many a wasted hour here getting into trouble. You wouldn't think that a quiet little village like Margate could have such an evil place, but it did. Gambling in the back room, girls upstairs, drugs sold in the loo. If you wanted it, you could get it here."

Jace was beginning to understand. "The stairs were changed."

"Yeah. When the old man that owned this place died, the Carews bought it and tore it apart. They pulled out the back wall and drove a JCB in here."

"A backhoe?" Jace asked.

"Probably the same thing. They tore out all the old stuff." Clive gave a little smile. "They burned a lot of it and by then I was trying to reform, but I stood around with the other kids and breathed deeply of that smoke."

Jace made himself smile at the story, but he wanted Clive to continue about Stacy. "Everything was changed?"

"Everything. Due to my wasted youth—fun but wasted—I knew the place well, but after Emma and George redid it, I didn't recognize it. After I became a cop, I had to go up those stairs several times and I always tripped in the same place. The stairs are where they used to be, but now there's a funny little curve in them. Emma had it built that way so she could put in that fancy jar. See it?"

Jace gave a cursory glance at the big brass vase on the stair landing, then looked back at Clive. "What you're saying is that you think this young woman . . . what was her name?"

"Stacy Evans."

"You think that Miss Evans had been in this pub so many times that she was familiar enough with it that she tripped on the new stairs?"

"That's exactly what I think."

"But even if that was true, why would that make murder more likely than suicide? Maybe she met an old boyfriend here in Margate, had a fight with him, then took her own life because of it."

"That's what everyone said happened."

"Then why don't *you* believe it?"

"You'll laugh at me."

"No, I won't."

"She didn't look unhappy. Does that make any sense? I was in a school—at least that's what they called it, but it was really a prison for kids—so I saw some attempts at suicide. There was a point when I played with it myself. There's a look about people who want to off themselves that's like no other. It's around the eyes and . . ."

"Miss Evans didn't look like that?"

"Naw, if anything, I'd say she looked happy. She was lying there on the bed with a little smile on her face. Man! She was beautiful. I just couldn't believe that that woman had anything to be unhappy about. Her father was rich, she was . . . what's that you Yanks say about dropping dead?"

"Stacy Evans was drop-dead gorgeous," Jace said quietly, making Clive look at him.

"Yeah, she was."

"And she died with a smile on her face. Maybe she was smiling because she was at last going to get out of her problems. Didn't you say she was engaged to be married?"

"No," Clive said quietly, staring at Jace. "I didn't say that. Nobody did."

"I guess I assumed it. Was she supposed to be married?"

Clive was looking at Jace hard. "You're him, aren't you? Stacy had your picture in her wallet. I used to look at it and wonder why you didn't come over and see about her."

Jace took a moment to make a decision. Should he try to lie his way out of this? No. "I wasn't told of her death until her body was already back in the States," Jace said. "Will you—"

"Tell on you? No. I have so many secrets about the people in this town that you wouldn't believe it. See that little old man over there? When he was nineteen, he killed three men in a barroom fight. He spent most of his life in jail. Now he grows peonies. See that woman? Oh, well, you get the picture. So did you buy that huge place, Priory House, just to find out what happened to Stacy? I guess I should call her 'Miss Evans,' but I spent so much time on her case that I feel as though I know her. What was she like?"

Jace took a long drink of his beer. "She was funny and smart and loved marshmallows. She liked them toasted, plain, in chocolate, however she could figure out a way to use them. She had a photographic memory. She was very kind and I was mad about her. When she died I wanted to die with her. She wasn't crazy and I think she was murdered."

Clive looked at Jace for a while and thought about what he'd said. He lowered his voice. "Who else knows who you are and why you're here?"

"Only you know and I didn't mean for you to find out."

"I won't give you away. If someone did kill Stacy, then they might come after you."

"Do you have any suspicions of who did it?"

"None whatever. Not a clue." Clive was talking so low that Jace could hardly hear him. "I showed her photo around for a year, asking questions anywhere I went, but no one admitted seeing her. I had to ask questions in secret because if the superintendent found out about it, he would have tossed me out. He didn't want to have anything to do with me in the first place because of my past here in Margate, but—"

"Why didn't you go somewhere else? Is your family here?"

"Don't have one. Orphaned young, passed around. I did

some damage here when I was a kid and I wanted to repay it, so I came back here to work," Clive said.

"You wanted to show the people who'd said you'd never amount to much that you could achieve something."

"Exactly," Clive said, smiling. "Exactly."

"But you couldn't show anybody anything about Stacy if you were caught disobeying an order, could you?"

"No. So what have *you* found out?"

"Nothing," Jace said, then decided to take a chance. He really wanted someone to talk to about what had been going on in his life lately. "I've been trying to get Ann Stuart to tell me something, but she says she hates me, so I don't know where to go from here."

"Ann Stuart? I don't believe I know her. She an American?"

"Ann Stuart is the ghost in Priory House."

Clive's expression changed little, but then he'd had a lot of practice pretending to believe preposterous stories. "Rides about the hall on her horse, does she?"

"Sorry I said anything," Jace said, but he knew it was too late. "To answer your question, I haven't found out anything that isn't in the newspapers. I've had to deal with Mrs. Browne and her two snooping friends and—"

"So what's your ghost look like?" Clive asked, smirking. "Rotting clothes? Missing eyeballs, that sort of thing?"

Jace signaled George that he wanted his bill so he could leave. "I trust, Constable Sefton, that you'll keep what we discussed to yourself."

"Sure," Clive said, still smiling. "I'll keep everything—if you know what I mean—to myself."

"Yeah, I know what you mean," Jace said as he left the pub.

7

The next morning Jace awoke before daylight and lay there thinking about what he'd learned so far. He was elated that Clive also believed Stacy had been murdered, but Jace was no closer to finding out who or why than he had been. He wished he hadn't told Clive about Ann. She was Jace's secret and he shouldn't have said anything.

He got up, dressed, and tried to figure out where to go next.

Mrs. Browne was in her kitchen and she was in a snit. "I never saw such a mess," she was saying. "Dirty dishes everywhere when I came in and my larder emptied. You must've had a party with twenty people here."

It was obvious she was trying to get information out of him. "We had an orgy," he said seriously. "Naked Americans running everywhere."

"Humph!" she said, then put a platter of bacon, eggs, tomatoes, toast, and mushrooms before him. "If you were naked you'd've got wallpaper paste on you. What did you do to that lovely room upstairs?"

Another request for information. "You mean the room the last owners used to store boxes? *That* lovely room?"

"They had no taste. Horrible people. I was glad when she scared them away."

"She who?"

"The ghost, of course," she snapped. "The one you saw in the garden."

"Ah, that one. Big woman? Flaming red hair? I didn't want to tell you this, Mrs. B, but she was riding a huge black horse and coming right at you. She doesn't have any reason to be angry at you, does she?"

"No, of course not," she said, but her face went pale, then turned red as she realized he was teasing her. "Go on, get out of here. I have work to do."

Smiling, Jace went upstairs, got his laptop, and took it outside to sit in the shade of a rose-covered arbor. He pulled up his word processor, started an outline, and began to write down all that he knew about Stacy.

When he had two pages of facts, he saw that there were some things that puzzled him. Stacy's sister and stepmother had shown the English police a stack of papers from psychiatrists saying Stacy had serious "problems." The only problem he knew she'd had was an inability to sleep for more than three hours at a time. But as soon as Stacy had moved in with Jace and he'd begun blocking her family from getting to her, the sleep problems had stopped. Before Jace stepped in, her sister would call her at 3:00 a.m. She was up with her kids, so she called Stacy for "support."

"True sisters support each other," Regina would say. Of course, Stacy would never think of calling anyone at 3:00 a.m. Jace began unplugging the phone at night. His family had his cell number, but no one in Stacy's family had it.

Up until the day of Stacy's death he would have sworn that there were no secrets between them, but he'd found out that she had spent years in therapy. Considering that her mother had died when Stacy was young and that her father hadn't bothered to make time for her, therapy was understandable. But how had she been labeled as "troubled"?

He closed his eyes for a moment. He was being brainwashed by Regina's family's lies. He and Stacy had been in love. They'd told each other everything.

But they hadn't. She hadn't told him about knowing of Margate and when she'd been there before.

Yet again, it came to him that the ghost of Ann Stuart would know if Stacy had visited the house. She saw everything, but she wasn't speaking to him, and he hadn't felt her presence all day.

After lunch (Jamie Oliver's stuffed chicken breast), Jace wandered about the chintz room and idly pushed on every panel. The lady highwayman story had been a lie, but maybe it was based on some fact. Maybe the hidden staircase was real, and maybe if he found it, he'd find out something about Ann, which would lead him to—

A knock on the door interrupted his thoughts. Frowning, he opened the door to see pretty little Daisy standing there, her face flushed, as though she'd run up the stairs. She was looking over her shoulder like she expected Mrs. Browne to jump out from behind the cabinets. Not now and not this, Jace thought, and opened his mouth to begin a lecture on her age and his.

Daisy thrust a tightly rolled newspaper at him. "I think you should see this, sir."

"What is it?"

She looked over her shoulder again, then took a step closer to him. Jace held his stance in front of the door. He wasn't about to let her inside the room.

"It's the village paper," she whispered, holding it out to him. It was rolled into a tight little tube and seemed to have something clear and gelatinous on it. "Sorry about the egg," Daisy said, "but I pulled it from Mrs. B's rubbish bin. Don't let her see that you have it and you wouldn't tell her I gave it to you, would you?"

Jace frowned harder. This fear of the housekeeper had to stop! "No, I won't tell her," he said in a normal voice, not a whisper. "But not because I'm afraid to but because you asked me to. Truthfully, I think—" He broke off because Daisy heard a sound from downstairs and took off running down the hall.

Sighing at the absurdity of it all, Jace took the newspaper into the room and closed the door. His frown turned to disbelief when he saw the headline. Smack in the middle of the front page was a photo of him that had been taken many years before when he was in college. He'd been drinking with his fraternity brothers and singing every raunchy song they could come up with. One of the guys had been snapping pictures. Jace hadn't seen the photo in years, but there it was, taking up half of the upper section of the paper. His hair was standing on end, his shirt was undone, and he had his arms around two of his frat brothers while holding two bottles of beer. He looked like a poorly groomed alcoholic.

IS THIS WHAT WE WANT IN MARGATE? the headline read.

Jace stumbled back until his knees hit a chair. He sat down and began to read.

As everyone in Margate knows by now, Priory House has been purchased again. But this time the venerable old house hasn't been bought by a family that wants a home here. It's been bought by a rich American who, in just a few days, has earned himself quite a reputation around town. He's in the pubs every night and it's reported that he even drinks Mr. Hatch's brews. And he's already taken one mysterious trip to London. When asked about his trip, he refused to tell why he went, but we residents of Margate didn't have to wait long before we found out. It seems that he went to London to buy furniture and accessories so he could tart up the notorious chintz room of Priory House into a bad reproduction of a Victorian movie set. Is this the prelude to opening the house to the public as some House of Ghostly Horror?

What all of us in Margate want to know is what Mr. Montgomery is up to.

This reporter, through diligent searching, has found out that the Montgomery family's wealth goes back centuries. They have mansions all over the world. Mr. Jace Montgomery has purchased a house with the reputation as one of the most haunted in England. And he has bragged to anyone who will listen that he saw the ghost of Lady Grace in the daylight in the garden.

Does he plan to exploit the murdering ghost of Priory House? Will our village fête be replaced with re-creations that glorify Lady Grace and the innocent people she killed? Will quiet, beautiful Margate be changed into a town of horror? Will plastic ghouls be hanging from the lovely old stone windows of that magnificent house? Will Mr. Montgomery put fake movie blood on the stones? Is this what we want for our town?

Is this very rich American here to turn magnificent, history-laden Priory House into a tourist attraction? Will this bored American be the end of our happy and comfortable village? Are we ready for tourists parked on our lawns? Are we ready for the charlatans, the soothsayers, the devil-worshipers that will show up here in our lovely village?

What do you think?

For a full ten minutes, all Jace could do was stare at the newspaper type. The absurdity of what had been written about him made his head spin. Someone had taken a few truths and twisted them into this ridiculous piece of gossip. No, it was stronger than gossip. It was malicious.

With the newspaper in hand, he went downstairs then out to the garage. He wasn't surprised to see Mick standing nearby with his car keys ready.

"Left by the library," Mick said as Jace took the keys from him. "Three houses down on the right."

Jace was so angry that he was off Priory House property before he realized that Mick had been telling him where the newspaper office was. When he reached the center of the village, he stopped at a corner and a man tapped on his window. Jace lowered it.

"I'd make an excellent tour guide," the man said. "I used to work at Priory House until old Mr. Hatch fired me. I could tell people all about Lady Grace on her horse ridin' up the stairs at night. I can be as scary as you want."

"Thanks, but no thanks," Jace said. "I have no intention of making my *home* into a tourist attraction."

"Well, you wouldn't need to, would you?" the man said, his face turning red with anger. "You're already rich, so what do you care about the rest of us that's just tryin' to make a livin'?"

Jace put the window back up and when someone else tapped on the glass on the other side of the car, he didn't answer. At the library, he turned left and parked in front of an old house that had a small brass sign that said MARGATE POST.

Jace ignored the two people hurrying toward him as he went down the flagstone path in four long strides. He didn't bother to knock, but threw open the door. Inside was a room that was furnished like a living room, with a TV against one wall. On the long wall was a window with a desk and computer beneath it.

"You must be Mr. Montgomery," said a short, round, older man just entering the room. "Nigh said I should expect you. She said to send you on down to her."

Jace was confused as to what the man was talking about. He held up the paper, his face furious. "Did you write this about me?"

"Good heavens, no," the man said, walking toward the computer. "I'm more into politics and telling the government how it should run itself. I have no interest in local scandals." He picked up a handful of mail and began to go through it. "No, who you want is Nigh."

"Nigh?" Jace asked.

"N. A. Smythe, the byline," the man said. "But then, with a name like Nightingale, she's wise to abbreviate it."

"Stuart," Jace said under his breath.

The man had been acting as though he wasn't much interested in Jace, but he cocked his head in speculation. "Ann Nightingale Stuart?" he asked in that way the English have of making every sentence a question. "You have been doing some research, haven't you? Are you really going to turn Priory House into a tourist attraction? We could use the revenue in the village."

"No, I'm not—" Jace began, but then shut his mouth. This man was a reporter. "What I do with my house is my business. Where is the woman who wrote this libel about me?"

The man lifted his eyebrows. "Libel? Oh dear, I hope you don't sue us. If you did, as you can see, you wouldn't get much." He waved his hand about the room. "It's just a local paper and not worth much. I'm Ralph Barker, editor, such as it is. I'd be happy to hear your side of the story."

"I bet you would," Jace said. "But the only side you're likely to hear is from my lawyer."

"Oh, my, you Yanks and your lawsuits."

Jace narrowed his eyes at the man. "I want to know where this woman is. I'd like to speak to her."

"You don't have a gun, do you?" When he saw the look on Jace's face, he gave a half smile. "Just having you on. Go back the way you came, past the gate to your house, first house on your left. Nigh should be up by now. Hope you don't catch her in her dressing gown. You'd cause even more scandal, and you don't need that right now."

"More scandal?" Jace said through clenched teeth. "I wasn't aware I had caused *any* scandal."

"And that's what you should tell Nigh. I'll keep next week's *Post* open for you. If you have any recent photos of yourself—"

Jace didn't hear the rest because he slammed the door and got back into his car. He knew he broke the speed limit as he drove toward the house at the end of his property, but as far as he could tell, the English paid no attention to speed limits.

When he came to a small, two-story stone house in the corner of the two roads that were the boundary of his property, he halted so quickly he nearly went through the windshield. There was a short, curved wall with a gate and he flung it open. A blue door was inside a little pointed-roof porch and he pounded on the door.

"It's open," came a woman's voice.

The door hit the wall as he flung it back and strode into a small sitting room. In front of him was a fireplace, to the left a deep window enclosure that contained a desk and a laptop computer. A young, pretty woman with dark hair and dark eyes sat on the desk chair. There was intelligence in her eyes, and something else that he wasn't sure of. If he had to guess, he would have said that she'd seen a lot of things that she hadn't wanted to see.

Jace held up the newspaper. "Every word of this is a lie," he said. He was so angry he could hardly speak.

"Is it? From what I heard, everything I wrote is verifiable."

For a moment Jace could only blink at her. "Everything is twisted and distorted."

She reached for a stenographer's notebook and pen. "So sit down and tell me the truth. I promise to publish your side of the truth this time."

"There is only one side of the truth. What you wrote is nothing but lies."

She looked at him for a moment, then uncurled herself from her chair. "How about a cuppa?" She turned her back on him with all the confidence of a woman who was used to men doing what she asked them to.

In spite of himself, Jace followed her through the doorway, then down three steps into the kitchen. Against one wall were old cabinets and open shelves filled with mismatched dishes and a thousand notes shoved in between. A narrow table was against the other wall and a couple of doors in the corner. When she motioned to the table, he sat down, the newspaper in front of him, his old photo staring up at him. "Where did you get that?" he asked softly.

"Internet. The Big Brother of the modern world. It took a while but I found it. Your family is very secretive about what it owns and who's in it."

Jace didn't answer that. "I have people asking me for jobs."

"I'll print a retraction so the lovely people will forget what I questioned."

She had her back to him, standing at the sink filling the kettle. She had on narrow black trousers that ended midcalf and a long-sleeved, knit black sweater. She wasn't very tall, but she was as thin as a model. When he glanced up he saw that she was watching him in the reflection in the window.

"What do you want?" he asked. "I can't believe you were dumb enough to believe what you wrote, so what do you want?"

She put the kettle on the stove, then turned to him. "We haven't been properly introduced, have we? I'm Nightingale Augusta Smythe—that's with a *Y* and an *E* at the end. My mother was trying to compensate for marrying a man named Smith, so she changed the spelling. Old spelling, but it's still Smith. Mum was born Jane Bellingham, then became Jane Smith. She hated her bland name, so she gave me a rather exotic one."

"Nightingale was Ann's name," Jace said, looking at her.

For a moment she stared at him, blinking in astonishment. "You have been reading," she murmured as she turned away.

With her back to him, she straightened her shoulders. "Will Earl Grey do for you? But then, you Yanks know nothing about tea, do you? Tell me, is it true that you put cups of sugar in it, then add ice? Or is that just one of those American legends put out to make us glad we didn't fight to keep the colonies?"

He could see that she was trying to distract him. She wanted to get information but not give any. "Ann Nightingale Stuart. Any relation to you?"

"Distant," she said. "I have tea bags, will they do? Or do you want loose tea? Or can you tell the difference?"

He refused to let her jibes get him off the subject. "You went to a great deal of trouble, and risked a lot to get me here, so what do you want?"

"I'll use loose tea," she said. "It's what the Queen drinks. Did you know that the Queen Mum never used a tea bag in her life? Now that's a lady."

When she smiled at Jace, he didn't smile back.

"Did you really see Lady Grace in the daylight?" she asked, her pretty eyes wide. "It's all over town that you did. They're saying you saw her on her horse, bearing down on Mrs. Browne, her hair flaming red. Grace's red hair, that is, not Mrs. Browne's."

Jace almost started to explain that he'd made that up, but he caught himself. "What would it matter to you if I did see her? As long as I don't open my house to the public and have helicopters landing on the green, what is it your business what I do?"

Nigh sat down across from him. "You wouldn't have heard of an author called Norah Lofts, would you? No, of course not. My mother read her and I used to sneak the books under the bedcovers. My favorite book of hers was about a house. She told of the people who built it, then took the house to the twentieth century, through being made into apartments, then converted back into a single-family dwelling. That's what I want to do and I want to use Priory House as my prototype."

She was leaning forward on the table and she was batting her thick lashes at him. He could see that she knew she was beautiful and that she was used to getting what she wanted from men. But it was going to take more than a pretty face to distract Jace. "Isn't that called plagiarism? But then, anyone who could write the lies you did wouldn't mind a bit of stealing, would they?"

She started to reply, but the kettle whistled. She got up from the table.

He watched in silence as she poured hot water into a ceramic teapot, then poured the water out and filled it again. She put in several teaspoons of loose tea, put a knit cozy over it, and set the pot on the table. She was lost in thought as she moved about the kitchen and got two cups and saucers.

She got a little pitcher of milk out of a tiny undercabinet refrigerator. "Milk in first or last?" she asked, standing over him.

"Last, like the Queen," he said, letting her know that he did know something about tea.

She gave a sound close to being a laugh, then poured their tea and added milk.

Jace sipped his and watched her, not saying a word. If she wanted to get herself out of the mess she'd put herself into, she was going to have to give him some information.

"I know a lot about Priory House," she said. "I have huge files on it."

"I know. I read your essay in the book."

She sipped some more and seemed to be trying to decide what to tell him. "I know a way to get into the house secretly."

"I'm listening."

"Mrs. Browne has her habits and she's out on Sundays."

Suddenly, Jace understood what she was telling him. "Are you trying to tell me that you sneak into the house when it's empty?" He paused, then opened his eyes wide. "You've been in the tower at night," he said. "It's *your* lights the people see, not the ghost of some criminal."

"Perhaps," she said. "But I've never heard Lady Grace referred to as a criminal before. Most people swoon over the romance of it all."

"Then they have a different idea of romance than I do," Jace said quickly. "Did you know the last owners?"

"No. I've only been back in Margate for the last six weeks. I've been away, working."

"For how long were you away?" he asked, sounding like an interrogator.

For the first time, there was a real spark of interest in her eyes. "From the end of 2001 until recently."

"You're sure of the dates?"

"Yes," she said slowly. "My mother died in November 2001, and I couldn't bear to stay here without her, so I left. Traveling, that sort of thing."

"Alone?"

"Boyfriend, sometimes; sometimes alone. Why?"

"You know all about me, so shouldn't I know about you?" he said, not giving her an answer.

"Mmmm," she said, that sound the English gave in answer to anything they didn't want to answer. She was looking at him hard, as though trying to read his thoughts. "You're searching for something, aren't you?" she said.

"Peace," he said quickly.

She gave a little snort at that and Jace almost smiled.

"I could be a great help to you. I could be your secretary."

"I have a secretary."

"Gladys Arnold," Nigh said in contempt. "Gladys goes to school in the mornings, works for you in the afternoons, and cleans another school at night. And she's shagging Mick every moment she isn't at work, so how much can she do?"

"Gladys and Mick have been good friends to me. I won't have anything bad said about them."

"All right, how about this? Gladys is young and inexperienced; I'm not. I can research. I know the ins and outs of the British library system. Do you? I could be your research assistant."

"To what end? And don't lie to me about some book you could have written long ago," he said, looking down at his cup. When she didn't answer, he looked at her.

She looked at him for a while, her eyes meeting his over the table. She took a deep breath. "When I was nine years old, I had a row with my mother—a common occurrence—and I decided to run away from home. I had fantasies of their missing me and crying about how much they loved me. All the usual things. I slipped out the kitchen window of our house and ran across the fields to Priory House. It was one of the times when it was vacant, the owner having been scared away by the ghost. It was dark and— More tea?"

Jace held up his cup, but said nothing.

"Am I boring you?" she asked as she filled his cup.

Jace's eyes drilled into hers, but said nothing.

"I . . . felt something that night. I couldn't find a way into the house so I curled up under one of the windows and cried my heart out. I'm sure I was a pathetic sight."

"And she came to you," Jace whispered.

"Not the flame-haired criminal, as you call her, but . . . I don't want to sound crazy."

For the first time, Jace gave a tiny smile. "You don't know what crazy is."

"I know enough about being accused of being crazy that I've never before told anyone about this. I did *not* see a ghost, didn't hear one, but I felt as though someone was with me, as though I was being soothed. Does that make sense?"

"More than you know. What happened to you? Did you spend the night in the damp and cold?"

Nigh smiled. "No. After a while I decided that maybe my mum had a right to be angry. My friend Kelly and I had accidentally dumped flour all over the kitchen floor just before her ladies' book club arrived. And we'd eaten all the tea sandwiches and most of the pastries she'd spent the morning preparing. Anyway, at Priory House, when I felt calmer, I went home."

"Were your parents upset that you'd run away?"

"That was the odd thing. My mother *always* checked on me before she went to bed, but that night she didn't. And my dad *always* checked the doors and windows to see if they were locked. But that night he didn't. I slipped through the kitchen window and went to bed. No one ever knew I'd been gone."

"And you've been fascinated with Priory House ever since."

"Exactly," she said. "Over the years, I've done what research I could, and I found the secret entrance when I was twelve—no, don't ask me to tell you where it is. You have to let me in on what you're up to before I reveal that secret."

Jace drank more of his tea. He figured he was now drinking about eight cups a day, but if you asked Mrs. Browne, she would have said he didn't really like tea because he hardly drank any.

"How can I use your help?" he asked. "You're a liar and a blabbermouth. I could never trust you. This . . ." He pointed to the newspaper still on the table. "This may have done irreparable damage to my reputation." Even to himself, his words sounded insincere.

Nigh stood up and went to the sink. She knew he was going to give in. "Since when did you Yanks care about anything except freedom? Say the word 'freedom' to an American and he starts crying."

"Rather like you Brits react to the words 'beef and beer,' " Jace shot back.

Turning, she smiled at him. He didn't smile back, but there was a twinkle in his eye.

"Look at it this way," she said. "If you and I spend a lot of time together, the village will think we're shagging all over the house, so they won't spend their time trying to figure out what you're really up to. Why *did* you make that notorious chintz room up to look like a Victorian movie set? And who's the woman in the portrait over the mantelpiece?"

"I thought you knew all about Priory House," Jace said.

"I only heard about the portrait through the grapevine. I haven't seen her. Describe her."

"Beautiful. Eighteen-inch waist."

"Ann Stuart's cousin. Their fathers were brothers. Ann killed herself rather than—"

"No, she didn't," Jace said quickly.

"And how do you know that she didn't?" she said even quicker.

"I overheard Ann and Catherine talking. Ann *wanted* to marry Danny Longstreet."

At that, Nigh couldn't speak. She just stared at him.

"At last I've silenced that tongue of yours."

"You overheard them? That implies a sort of time travel. Don't tell me—"

"I have no intention of telling you anything, and if you write about this you'll be the laughingstock of the town." He stood up.

She put herself in front of him. "I know everything that's happened in that house and people tell me all the gossip in this village. I know you and Clive Sefton share a secret."

"What secret?" Jace said, his face serious. It was one thing to share information about a ghost, but he didn't want her to know about Stacy.

"I don't know and I'm sure it's none of my business. I'm only interested in the house. Let me help you research whatever it is that you're trying to do."

"What do you really want?"

She looked him in the eyes. "If I told you the truth, you wouldn't believe me."

"Try me."

"There's something there in that house and I want to find it. Call it curiosity or maybe just boredom with writing the same old news stories. Whatever it is, I've been fascinated with that house since I was nine years old and I think you are too. The people who buy that house are a joke in this village. Some of them don't last but six months. The estate agency makes bets on how long the new owners will stay. But you . . ." She trailed off.

"I'm different."

"You certainly don't seem to be afraid of whatever you've seen and heard in that house."

"No, ghosts don't scare me. What *does* scare me is the gossip of this town."

Nigh gave him a puzzled look. "Why would you—" she began, but cut herself off, then smiled at him. "Do we have a deal? You show me yours, I'll show you mine?" When Jace didn't smile, she said, "Sorry. I'll keep this businesslike. No more tasteless jokes."

"Come by tonight and show me the retraction you've written. Have something to eat."

"You mean we'll eat Jamie? Oops, did it again."

"Ah, yes, Mrs. Browne. I'll have to ask her . . . not that she rules me, but she does rule the house. I mean . . ."

"I know exactly what you mean. Don't worry about her. I can handle her."

Jace walked back through the sitting room to the front door, then turned back to her. "What about your boyfriend?"

"He got married six months ago. He offered himself to me but I couldn't bring myself to give up my life and career to be a housewife."

"He wanted you to quit snooping in other people's lives and when you refused he dumped you, didn't he?"

"Flatter than—What is it that you Yanks say?"

"Flatter than a pancake. Flatter than road kill. Flatter than the lies you made up about me."

"I'll fix it," she said, looking up at him through dark lashes.

"Is it the story you're after or something else?"

The tone of his voice was unmistakable. "The story," she said quickly, then smiled. "Don't worry, I find you attractive enough in that brawny, overmuscled American way, but you're not my type."

"Good, you're not mine either." He stepped past her to the outside. "Let me think on this. Depending on how good your retraction is, I'll think about doing some ghostbusting with you."

"You know," she said slowly, "the idea of turning Priory House into a tourist attraction would hide whatever you're really doing."

"I've had enough of people asking me for jobs. Say that I'm a writer. As for interior decoration, that's not anyone's business, is it?"

"You own the big house, so everything you do is newsworthy." She was smiling at him in a way that he was sure had made lots of men desire her, but he didn't smile back.

Turning, Jace got in his car and drove away.

8

Five minutes after Jace left, Nigh was on the phone to her best friend, Kelly Graham.

"Well?" Kelly said as soon as she picked up the phone, not bothering to ask who it was. She'd been waiting for Nigh's call for over an hour. "How did it go?"

"Perfectly," Nigh said.

"Yes? Go on. Tell me every word."

"He was pretty upset about what I wrote."

"I don't blame him. You were OTT. Very, very OTT. What in the world got into you? You accused him of some awful things, and now everybody in the village thinks he's going to make them rich."

Nigh looked down at her desk and couldn't think of anything to say.

"Uh-oh. What's that silence about?"

"Nothing," Nigh said. "I was just looking at my notes."

"No, you're not. Nigh! What's going on?"

"Nothing, really. He was just different than I thought he was going to be, that's all. It's unsettled me a bit."

"Different? Unsettled? What are you talking about?"

"Let's just say that some of the boys down at the pub are going to hear from me. I was told some things that weren't exactly true."

"Such as?"

"That the new tenant of Priory House was a drunk, a lout, a rich boy who'd never worked a day in his life, and generally stupid."

"I see."

"What does that mean?" Nigh asked.

"You liked him, didn't you?"

"I can't say I really *liked* him, but he was more interesting than anyone I've met since I returned here."

"Local boys hold no interest for you? What about David?"

"David is a lawyer, he lives in London, and I've been out with him a total of three times."

"Is that why he called four times while I was there yesterday?"

When Nigh didn't answer, Kelly said, "So help me, Nigh, if you don't talk to me I'm going to wake the kids up from their naps and drag them over there with me. You have never experienced hell until you've been surrounded by three kids who haven't had their naps."

"Yeah, okay, I liked him. Is that what you wanted to hear me say? But he wasn't interested in me. In fact, I think he may hate me."

"After what you wrote about him? How could that happen? So what are you going to do now?"

"Move in with him, I hope."

"Excuse me?"

"Something big is going on at Priory House and I mean to find out what it is. Look, I have to go. I need to talk to some people, then I'm . . . I don't know what I'm going to do next, but I have to figure it out. I'll call you later." She hung up before Kelly could ask another question.

Nigh got into her yellow Mini Cooper and drove into the village. She had a vague plan of confronting Lewis and Ray and telling them just what she thought of their little prank. But the truth was that it was Nigh's own fault. Had she been away from Margate so long that she'd forgotten how the village worked? Lewis and Ray had been the school prats, horrible boys who thought it was funny to glue a kid's homework to his desk, or to put indelible marker on a kid's face. They never did anything really bad, meaning they'd never burned any buildings down, but their idea of a practical joke had caused a lot of tears.

What had made Nigh think that now that they were grown and had kids of their own that they had become upstanding citizens? Two nights ago, she'd sat in the café and listened to them go on and on about the Yank who had taken over Priory House. Nigh had flown in from the Middle East just the night before. She was nearly comatose with jet lag, and she'd listened to the boys—she couldn't think of them as men—as they told her their "fears" for the sweet little village of Margate. At the time, her weary mind had confused the problems in the Middle East with the "problems" in an English village.

Now she was seeing what she'd been told for what it was: revenge served cold. In the sixth grade, she'd seen Lewis taunting a first grader and Nigh had hit him in the nose so hard he had to be taken home. Like the bullies they were, neither of the boys ever again bothered Nigh or anyone else when she was around.

So they got her back at last. It had taken years, but they did it.

When she got to Lewis's house, she slowed down, meaning to turn into his driveway, but she didn't. To bawl him out would give him no end of pleasure.

Instead, she found herself on the road to Aylesbury. Every piece of clothing she owned was worn out and stained. And her shoes weren't much better. And she needed a new tube of mascara, and maybe a lipstick or two. Maybe she'd take a little time off and do some shopping.

Nigh arrived at Priory House at ten minutes to seven. Jace hadn't given her a time for dinner, but she knew that Americans ate early. She pulled into the courtyard and tried to still the butterflies in her stomach. This was, of course, preposterous. Twice in her life she'd been in places where bombs were going off, so why was something like having dinner with this American making her nervous?

She looked down at her dress. It was a deep blue silk, cut on the bias, and fit like a second skin. It was made by some designer Nigh had never heard of, but who the clerk assured her was "famous." And her heels had to be at least four inches high. Her ankle twisted on the gravel as she headed toward the front door, but she quickly righted herself.

As Nigh walked under the archway, she hesitated. Which door should she use? She was an invited guest, so she should use the front door. On the other hand, she was a resident of the village and she'd been there as a child, which made the kitchen entrance more likely.

For a moment she gritted her teeth. Was she insane? She had twice eaten dinner at Buckingham Palace, yet here she was . . . okay, she thought, admit it, Nigh, you're scared of Mrs. Browne.

"I'm not going to be," she said aloud, then started for the front door. Before she reached it, Mrs. Browne appeared out of nowhere.

"Use the front door now, do we?" Mrs. Browne asked. "And all tarted up too, I see. The American strike your fancy? Going after him now, are you?"

"I have been invited to dinner," Nigh said, her nails cutting into her palms. "Mr. Montgomery invited me and—"

"He didn't tell me he was invitin' anybody, but it's not my place to ask. If he'd've told me he'd asked *you,* I'd've told him a thing or two. What a nasty bit you wrote about him in the paper. It's a wonder he didn't use an American gun on you. That's what they do in America, you know. Shoot you. But it's nothin' to me what he does on his own time. Or who he does it with."

"Where is he?" Nigh asked, her teeth clenched, torn between wanting to use her fists on the horrid little woman and running to hide in her mother's skirts.

"Out in the stone round, he is. You do remember where that is, don't you? You used to snoop around here well enough when you were a child, so you should remember. This place was a trainin' school to you, weren't it? I hear you snoop all over the world now."

This is ridiculous! Nigh thought and took the slump out of her shoulders. "That I do. I snoop everywhere, so maybe I'll just tell Mr. Montgomery what happened to the brandy that was supposed to come with this house. You and your old girlfriends still filling the empty bottles with cold tea?"

Mrs. Browne put her nose in the air and stalked away.

"Great, Nightingale," Nigh muttered. "That's two enemies you've made in one day. You should have stopped at Lewis's house, bawled him out, and made it three."

High heels were not made for walking across soft English lawns. After the third time she sunk down to her heels, she took the shoes off and carried them. The "stone round" that Mrs. Browne referred to was the local name for a beautiful eighteenth-century stone gazebo. It had a round floor, columns, and a beautiful domed top. At least it had once been beautiful. The last time she saw it, Hatch was using it to store plastic bags full of greensand.

As she walked through the trees, down the little-used path toward the gazebo, she had a lovely idea. What if Montgomery had set up dinner in the gazebo? Candlelight, a damask-covered table. Would he serve oysters? What delectable thing from Jamie Oliver had Mrs. Browne prepared for tonight? As hateful as the woman was, she was a renowned cook.

Smiling, Nigh contemplated the evening ahead. In spite of the bad that had gone on between her and Jace Montgomery, she'd felt the physical attraction. He was a very good-looking man and she was, well . . . she wasn't bad to look at either. So maybe he had forgiven her about the newspaper, and maybe he was ready for something a little more personal to begin . . .

When Nigh stepped through the trees and saw the gazebo, it wasn't what she'd hoped for. Jace Montgomery was there with what looked like a machete and he was clearing away years of vines and weeds. He was drenched in sweat and what skin was showing from under his dirty shirt was grimy.

When he saw Nigh, he looked startled, as though he'd forgotten their dinner date, but then a slow smile spread over his face. Forgotten or not, obviously, she had misinterpreted his invitation. He'd meant sandwiches and a bottle of beer, while she had taken him to mean a tuxedo in the moonlight. Nigh felt overdressed, foolish, and extremely embarrassed. She wanted to say that she was going to a party afterward and that's why she was dressed up, but she didn't. She did hide her high heels behind her back.

"You brought the retraction," Jace said. "You can put it over there. Sorry if I don't stop, but . . ." He trailed off as he shrugged in the general direction of the mess surrounding the gazebo.

"No, sure," she mumbled, wishing she could sink into the ground and disappear. She should, of course, leave, but she'd have to go past Mrs. Browne's windows. To be seen that she, Nigh, had thought she'd been invited to a real, sit-down dinner but wasn't would be too humiliating. To be fair to herself, usually, when men asked her out they made an effort.

She watched him slash at some vines and pull them off the stone work. "Ann's grandfather built that."

"Did he? Nice man?" he asked.

"No. None of Ann's male ancestors were nice." Jace was tugging on a vine, but she could see that it was caught on a pillar. She thought it was possible that the vines were stronger than the marble. Pull too hard and the whole thing could collapse—on them.

She dropped her shoes into the grass and removed a pair of garden shears from the nearby wheelbarrow. "Wait," she said, then stepped onto the floor in her bare feet and began to cut the vines that clung to the column. Unfortunately, some of them were beginning to take root, so she had to use her nails to disengage them. So much for that afternoon's manicure.

Jace held the vines and pulled as she loosened them. "So what was the grandfather like?"

Nigh thought for a moment. "I think his death tells everything. He drowned when he was just twenty-eight years old. He made a bet with another young man that he could swim across the lake underwater. They all waited for him to come up, but he didn't. Seems he got his foot caught in a pile of old bricks that were buried at the bottom of the lake. His father had thrown the bricks in there so the lake would require less water to fill it. He left everything to his only child, Ann's father, who was only four years old. Not a penny was left to his young wife, yet the will required her to live in Priory House. He didn't want to leave a rich widow behind. Mother and child ended up living in just a few rooms and had only two people to help them take care of this whole place."

"Ah, the English love of primogeniture," Jace said, pulling on the vines as Nigh cut them away from the column.

"Don't knock it. It's kept the big estates intact. Ow!" She sucked at her finger where a vine had lashed back and cut it.

"You're going to ruin your dress if you do that," Jace said. "Why don't you just leave what you wrote, I'll read it later, and call you."

Nigh gave him a little smile. For one thing, she hadn't written anything down. Trying on shoes and dresses, then having wet nail polish precluded writing something she didn't want to write in the first place. Second, she'd rather die than go past Mrs. Browne's kitchen windows and let her see that she had not been invited for dinner after all. "No, that's okay," she said. "It's been a long day and I could use the exercise."

"Yeah, I know what you mean. A truly rotten day. You should have seen what I read about myself in the newspaper this morning."

For a moment Nigh looked at him in astonishment, then she gave a tiny smile. She wasn't about to laugh out loud. His tone was deadpan, so hers could be too. "Yeah, well, I imagine you can handle whatever is dished out to you."

"You're right. At first I was in such a rage that all I could think about was lawyers, but then I calmed down and decided there were other ways to handle the problem. I put up six notices in town that the writer of the article was taking applications and interviewing for the twenty-eight jobs that would be available at the new Priory House Ghost Center."

"You didn't," Nigh whispered.

" 'Fraid so." He smiled at her.

"I think I may be sick," she said.

Jace unbuttoned his sweaty shirt, removed it, and handed it to her. "In that case, you'd better cover up your new dress."

Nigh just stood there looking at his bare upper torso, at what seemed to be acres of sun-bronzed muscles. What did he do all day? Wrestle bulls? That's the only thing that would account for a body like that. He said nothing, but smiled at her in a knowing way. Nigh took his shirt and looked away. She was damned if she was going to let him see what she thought of his six-pack abs.

She put her arms in the damp shirt and hated the way she loved the feel of it, the smell of it. What was more enticing than a warm, sweaty male?

She grabbed a vine and pulled, and when it didn't come away, she cut, then pulled harder.

"Hey!" Jace yelled. "Leave something for me to do. And where did all this energy come from? Was it something I said?"

Nigh had a vision of being followed around the village by people talking to her about their schemes to make money in a "Ghost Center." "So what have you and Dead Ann been up to this afternoon?" she asked with as much sarcasm as she could put in her voice.

"Haven't seen her," he said as he pulled the last of the vines away from the column. "She's angry at me. In fact, she nearly killed me. Took my breath away until I turned blue. Another few seconds and I would have been able to join her."

Nigh quit cutting and pulling to look at him. "Killed you? Took your breath away? I thought maybe you saw her walk through a wall or something. Or heard her. You're having . . . relations with her?"

"I guess you could call it that. Here, do that one next," he said, pointing to a column that was so covered you could hardly see the white marble beneath.

Nigh cut for a few minutes, waiting for him to go on, but he said nothing. "Is that it? Are you going to tell me more or not?"

"Am I going to see it in the newspaper tomorrow? By the way, can you make a living from such a small newspaper?"

Nigh opened her mouth to tell him about her career, but she closed it again. He had secrets; she had secrets. Only hers were pretty public if he'd bother to ask anyone about her. "No, you won't see it in the newspaper. If you did, what would you do to me?"

"I'd do something creative, something to fit the crime."

She waited, but when he again said nothing, she leaned against the column and started cleaning her nails with the tip of the shears.

Jace laughed. "Okay, I saw her under some unusual circumstances and I wanted to see her again, so I decided to . . . well, to court her. Entice her, make her want to visit me again."

Nigh started cutting vines. "Go on. Don't make me beg. Talk!"

"When I saw her in her room, I—"

"Saw her? How did you see her? Is she transparent?"

"You want this story or that one?"

"Both of them. I want to hear every word of all of it. From the beginning."

"That will take hours."

"I have nothing else to do, do you?" she asked.

"Not a thing," Jace said as he pulled on the vine Nigh had cut away. "You aren't hungry, are you?"

"Starving. But then you did invite me to dinner."

"Ohhhhh," he said, and smiled as he looked her up and down. She knew that he saw what she'd been expecting and why she'd dressed up. "So I did. Sorry about that, but I forgot. Today I've had a few other things on my mind. But, anyway, Mrs. Browne has a kitchen filled with food. As soon as we get this done and the whole story told, we'll eat."

Nigh grabbed a handful of vine and pulled hard. "Get busy! Talk! Pull! Any hope of wine with that meal?"

"Whatever's in the cellar."

"If it's not brandy, it'll be great. So start telling me about the very first time you saw Ann."

"Actually," Jace began, "I was right about the history of the lady highwayman. By the way, I was meaning to ask you—"

She held her shears toward him in a threatening way. "Ask me later. Now, I want to hear everything you know, and everything you've done."

She was watching him out of the corner of her eye and she

could tell he was pleased by her words. Yet again she wondered why he'd bought a huge house in England. The Internet said he had a large family. Did he have a falling out with them? Had he done something awful that made them throw him out? Or had one of them done something that he couldn't abide, so he'd left the country? If so, why hadn't he bought a nice apartment in London? Or if he wanted the country, why not a nice little Queen Anne former rectory? Something manageable?

She thought for about ten minutes, then Jace's story began to take over her thoughts. Three times he had to remind her to keep cutting because she was so engrossed in his words that she forgot the task at hand. Hiding in a wardrobe, listening to two women who had been dead for a century? Of course she didn't believe a word he was saying, but he sure did tell a whopping good tale.

9

I can't see my hand in front of my face," Jace said. "I think we'd better go in."

"Sure," Nigh said softly. Her mind was full of the story Jace had been telling her. "She talked to you? Actually *talked* to you?"

"Yes," he said as he put the tools in the wheelbarrow. "You think we can find our way back in the dark?"

"I've been walking these paths in the dark since—"

"I know, since you were nine."

"Right," she said, smiling at him. "Here, you'll need your shirt. It's getting chilly."

"Chilly? Is that what you call it? England has three climates: cold, colder, and coldest."

She had lived in too many places to take offense at his words. "When it's merely cold, we go to Scotland to cool off. Now *there's* cold for you. Wool in August."

Jace chuckled as he put his shirt back on. "Race you to the house."

"You're on," she said, then smiled as he took off running.

Nigh took her time, fumbling around in the grass for her new shoes, then slowly following the dark path toward the house. She listened for a moment, but heard nothing. When she was a child she liked nothing more than sneaking around the grounds of Priory House. She'd always had an idea that Mr. Hatch knew she visited, but until tonight she'd had no idea that Mrs. Browne did also. But then Mrs. Browne made it her business to know everyone's business.

When Nigh got halfway up the path, only yards from the house, she crouched down and went through a thicket of azalea bushes, then she turned a sharp left beside an ancient yew hedge. After another few yards of hurrying across open ground in her bare feet, she came to the old well house. Mr. Hatch stored garden tools in it now, so she hoped she could still find the little door. It wasn't easy in the dark and the latch had rusted. She used to borrow oil from her father's garage to keep the latch and hinges oiled so they wouldn't squeak.

It took her longer than it did when she was a child because there was now a mound of dirt in front of the little door, but she managed to pull it open enough to squeeze through. She had to fight thick cobwebs that grabbed her face as she put on her shoes then stood up in the old tunnel. As a child she'd never worried about the safety of the old timbers holding the earth above her head, but she did now. She fumbled to her right and found the tin box of candles and the matches she'd put there many years before. Would they still light? After all, England had quite a moist climate. Montgomery would probably say it was damp, damper, and dampest, she thought, frowning. "If our climate is so bad, let's compare our gardens with your American 'backyards,' " she mumbled as she lit the candle. "Not too damp, I see."

Cautiously, she made her way down the tunnel toward the house, looking suspiciously at the timbers over her head. What an idiot I am to take this route, she thought. And she'd done it just because some man had challenged her to a race. He'd get to the house quicker than she would, but she planned to surprise him when she walked down the main staircase. "Where have you been?" she'd say, as though she'd been waiting for him. But was such a childish game worth her life?

She stepped on three creepy crawly things, and the beams over her head seemed to creak ominously. As a child she'd loved every sound of the tunnel and never once had she been afraid of it. But back then she had been oblivious to the possible catastrophes. If a child of hers ever went through a tunnel like this, she'd . . .

She broke off when she heard a sound she'd never heard before. She stopped and listened, but she heard nothing unusual. She turned toward the house again. Just a few more feet. What if the old door into the house that was concealed in the paneling now had a heavy piece of furniture in front of it? That had happened once and she'd had to wait until those owners moved out before she could go snooping again. Not that she ever went into the house when people were in residence, but . . . Well, maybe she had once, but that was when she was thirteen and the seventeen-year-old boy who lived there was gorgeous. He—

Nigh almost cried out in relief when she reached the end of the tunnel, then cautiously pushed on the door. Please let it open, she prayed. Please, please. The door swung open with a loud creak, but she wasn't worried because she knew that it opened onto a narrow stone spiral staircase, a leftover from when the house was a monastery. No one inside the house would hear the rusty hinges. The stairs led straight up to the top tower, to a door cleverly hidden in the wooden floor.

When she at last stood on the stone steps, she let out a sigh of relief. She wouldn't do that again. Those timbers were too old to risk it again. The stone steps up to the tower were dirty and cold and Nigh wished she hadn't come through the tunnel. She was suddenly aware that she was very cold, very hungry, and very dirty. She longed for a tub full of hot water and lavender-scented soap.

She started up the stairs, planning to leave the tower at the door that led into the chintz bedroom, when she heard a noise behind her in the tunnel. Did she leave the door open? Had some animal followed her into the tunnel? A dog? A wolf?

"Damn!" she heard and her mouth dropped open. It couldn't be!

Bending, she pulled open the four-foot-tall door she'd entered the staircase by and held her candle inside as far as she could. In the dark she saw movement, then Jace Montgomery came into the light.

"Damned dangerous," he said, scowling. "I think half those timbers are rotten. They're staying up by memory. That was really stupid of you to go through there. And to think that you did that when you were a kid! Your father should have taken a belt to you."

Nigh was too astonished at his presence to say a word. Heedless of what was left of her new dress, she sat down on the stone step and looked up at him while he brushed cobwebs off his body.

"How . . . ?" she began.

"How did I follow you? Pioneer ancestors. But then you made as much noise as a herd of water buffalo. I had an idea that if I challenged you, you'd want to show off and enter the house in your secret way. You seem to want to beat everybody at every game. Damnation, but that was a scary thing. I'm going to have engineers shore that thing up with some good ol' American steel. Forget those old beams." He glared at her. "You should have better sense than to go through something like that. So how do we get out of here? I don't know about you, but I'm freezing and I'm hungry."

"Up one flight," she managed to say, still in shock from her fear of the tunnel and his following her.

He stepped over her, swinging one long leg over her head to reach the step above her. "Well, come on. Don't just sit there. You have the candle. Speaking of which, I think I'll put electric lights in that tunnel."

"Sure, why not?" she said, recovering herself. "How about a bar too? Ice maker, some cut-glass liquor dispensers. What about a barbecue?"

"Not a bad idea, although we have England's weather, so what do we need with an ice maker? Okay, so where's the door?"

"I found it when I was nine, so why can't you find it at your age?"

"Guess I'm not as clever as you are," he said.

Smiling, she reached down about knee level and pressed a little piece of iron that couldn't be seen from above. She'd been able to see it more clearly when she was younger because she'd been shorter.

"Cute," Jace said as the door swung open and they were in the chintz room. Ann's room. He half expected to see her there, but it was empty except for the furnishings he and Gladys and Mick had put in there. Closing his eyes for a moment, he inhaled. He could smell her.

"I've always loved the smell of this room," Nigh said.

Jace looked at her sharply, but he didn't tell her that the lovely fragrance came from Ann Stuart.

"I don't know about you, but I want a shower before I eat." He looked her up and down pointedly.

Nigh looked down at herself. Her dress was ruined. There were three torn places along the hem and there was too much dirt to ever fully come clean.

"You want the master bedroom bath?" he asked, then laughed at her expression. "You can have it all to yourself. I'll use this one."

She looked at him a moment. "Ann's bath."

"Didn't I tell you that she gets in the shower with me?"

He laughed when Nigh frowned. "Go on. Look in the drawers in the bedroom and get some clean clothes. I have some sweats in there that you can tie on. I'll meet you downstairs as fast as possible." With that he half pushed her out of the room and shut the door behind her.

Standing in the hallway, Nigh hesitated. It was really, really stupid of her, but she almost felt jealous of a ghost.

She shook her head to clear it, then headed for the master bathroom. If she remembered correctly, there was a huge bathtub in there. She hoped there was enough hot water to fill it.

"You took long enough," Jace said when she entered the kitchen. "The English love of bathtubs."

"The English love of warmth in any form," she said as she looked at the food spread on the big oak kitchen table. "I see you didn't wait for me." She picked up a black olive and ate it, which only served to reminded her how hungry she truly was. In the next minute she was at the table stuffing herself, and the more she ate, the more Jace piled on her plate.

"Have you tried this?" he asked repeatedly as he ladled something else onto her plate. "What about this?"

"Are you trying to get me fat?"

"You're skin and bones. Do you eat anything besides cucumber sandwiches?"

She started to tell him that she was too often in Jeeps racing across a desert while helping the cameraman haul hundreds of pounds of equipment to be able to eat three squares a day. But she didn't tell him. "Better than fried chicken."

"Touché," he said, smiling and dishing out more buttered parsnips.

"So what do you think Ann wants?" Jace asked as he refilled Nigh's wineglass for the third time.

From the emphasis on "you," she could tell that he had his own ideas of what Ann's restless spirit wanted. "To at last be buried in the sanctified grounds of the churchyard?" she asked. "Isn't that what spirits falsely accused of suicide usually want?"

"So how do we do that?"

Nigh looked down to cover her smile. She liked that he said "we." "If any of what you've said is true, then the important thing is to find proof that she didn't kill herself. If she wasn't a suicide, then she could be buried in consecrated ground. What about you? What do you think she wants?"

"The burying thing was my first idea too, but I don't know . . . sometimes I think it's something else. In the vision I had, when I saw her with her cousin, I got the idea that she was pretty spunky."

"Spunky?"

"Sassy. Cheeky, I guess you Brits would call it. She really seemed to know herself well. She knew what her life was going to be like if she didn't marry, and she was a realist about her future with the philandering Danny Longstreet. I wonder what he was like?"

"Probably like his descendant."

Jace paused with his hand reaching for a piece of bread—homemade whole wheat rolls with honey in them. "You mean there are Longstreets still in the village?"

"Only one. Most of them have moved away."

"So what's this one like?"

"We're the same age and we went to school together. Very handsome," Nigh said, watching Jace intently. "He looks like a short Superman, with glossy black hair, dark blue eyes, and a body that's all muscle. He runs a repair garage. It's down a side street so you've probably not seen it, but it's called 'Long-street's.' "

"Handsome, self-supporting, but I feel a 'but' coming on."

"Right. He's a rogue. Girls love him. Don't look at me like that. I like men who can put sentences together. Girls who like, say, only the physical side of love, go for Gerald in a big way. The real problem with him is that he wants all the women all the time, or at least three at a time."

"Not exactly the faithful type, then?" Jace said.

"Not at all. What about you?"

"Me what?" Jace asked.

"Are you the faithful type?"

"Oh yeah. An absolute bulldog. One woman and that's it."

"I see. And who is the woman?'

"Right now, it's Ann Stuart. How are you related to her?"

"I don't think I am, really. My mother said we were, but I

don't see how. I think she was so horrified at marrying a man named Smith that she gave me the most outrageous name she could come up with, so I got stuck with Nightingale. She probably read it in a book about Priory House."

"The name suits you since you run around in the dark like a night bird."

"Mmmm. You said I made more noise than . . . what was it? 'A herd of water buffalo.' "

Jace smiled and refilled her wineglass. "Maybe not quite that much noise. You can sure slip through some small places! I thought I was going to get stuck in that little door in that little brick building. You think ol' Hatch knows about that place?"

"I think Mr. Hatch knows every inch of this property. He must have seen the ground where the door scraped it when I was a kid."

"I hope he checked those timbers for dry rot."

"Me too." Nigh drained the last of her glass of wine, then pushed back her chair. "It's late, so I'd better go." When she stood up, she had to catch the edge of the table to steady herself.

"Yes, indeed, I'm going to put you in a car and let you drive," Jace said. "Come on, you can sleep in any of half a dozen beds in this oversized, unheated house. Which bedroom do you want?"

"Ann's room, of course." She put her hand to her head. She was dizzy and . . . well, she wouldn't mind if this beautiful man touched her.

"No, Ann's room is mine."

"You're in love with her, aren't you?" Nigh said, still holding onto the table.

"Yeah, that I am," Jace said, his tone sarcastic but amused. "I pine for a woman who died well over a hundred years ago."

"A hundred and twenty-eight, to be precise." Nigh took a step and almost fell. "I do believe I'm drunk."

"Very drunk," Jace said, then moved to put his arm around her shoulders.

"Ooooh, nice," she said, looking up at him and batting her lashes. "You're not bad to look at, Mr. Montgomery."

"You're not either," he said, but didn't look at her as he led her toward the staircase.

"If I like you and you like me, then why don't we . . ."

"I hope you don't remember this in the morning. Put your foot up on the stair. That's a good girl. Now the other foot. That's good. Next one."

"So who *are* you in love with?" Nigh asked. "I mean, someone who is alive, that is."

"I am in love with no one who is alive," Jace said softly.

"But everyone needs someone to love," she said, leaning back on his arm as he guided her up the stairs.

"Yes, they do."

"Then why don't you have anyone?"

"I don't see you with a ring on your finger. So who's the someone for you?"

Nigh gave a great sigh. "Men can't take my career. They're jealous. I'm better at the job than they are. Fearless. That's what they call me to my face. But I hear them. They think I'm crazy. And eaten with ambition. But you know what?" she asked drunkenly.

"What?"

"They only say that out of sour grapes. I won't go to bed with them. I hold myself in very high esteem."

"Do you?" Jace asked, smiling. "We're almost at the top now."

She stopped on the staircase and looked at him. "It's true. High esteem, that's what I have. And I also have a low threshold for jerks."

"I'm glad to hear it. If you'll just—" He was trying to get her to take two more steps, but when she wouldn't, or couldn't, he swept her into his arms and carried her to the landing, then down the hall to the master bedroom, where he set her on a chair while he turned down the bed.

"If I were Ann I'd want someone to love," Nigh said. "I wouldn't haunt a house to get my rotten old body inside the fence of the graveyard. You know what I think?"

"What?" he asked as he pulled down the coverlet.

"I think that it doesn't matter where men put a body or what they do to it while it's on earth. I think it's up to God to sort it all out. Besides, who decides what property is holy or not? Some man, just a mere man, says it's holy here, but over there under that tree it's not holy. Does that make sense?"

"None at all."

Jace stood in front of her. "Can you get up by yourself or do you need my help?"

"Help," she said. "Lots of help."

Smiling, Jace bent down to put his arms around her to help her stand up.

For a moment, Nigh leaned against him—and Jace held her close to him. It was only a second, but it was there and she felt it.

"You do like me, don't you?" she whispered against his chest.

Brusquely, he pushed her to arm's length. "Yeah, I like you. I must be a masochist after what you wrote about me, but I like you."

"Not my fault," she said as she climbed into bed. "Lewis and Ray did it to get me back. I beat Lewis up when I was six."

"Did you?" Jace said, chuckling as he pulled the covers over her.

"Lewis and Ray told me terrible things about you. I believed them. I wrote that for Ralph's paper. He didn't want to print it, but I said the village needed to be saved."

Jace sat down on the bed beside her. "Ralph's paper? You don't work there?"

"No." Her eyes were closing. "Did when I was a kid, but not now. Now I fly."

"You're flying right now," he said as he watched her close her eyes and go to sleep.

He turned out the light and left the room, shutting the door behind him. For a moment he leaned against the door and closed his eyes. He did like her. Liked her very much. She was the first woman he'd met since Stacy had . . . left who he'd liked.

"What are you doing, Montgomery?" he said out loud. He knew that tonight he'd tested her. But tested her for what? he asked himself.

He well remembered that he'd invited her to dinner. At the time he'd done it, he'd wanted to kick himself, but she was the first person he'd met who actually talked to him. Seeing the happy marriage of Emma and George Carew, and seeing the way Gladys and Mick couldn't keep their hands off each other, had made him feel his loneliness of being in a foreign country by himself.

Then he met this beautiful young woman with a smart-aleck mouth and an irreverent sense of humor, and in spite of the fact that she'd just done a rotten thing to him, he wanted to sit in her tiny kitchen all day. It was certainly better than being with Mrs. Browne and her incessant complaining.

Before he could stop himself, he found a reason for her to come to his house and he'd asked her to dinner—without asking her to dinner. He hadn't even given her a time to arrive!

By six, after a day spent reading more about the history of Margate, he'd been so restless that he needed hard physical labor to quiet him, so he'd tackled what Hatch called the "stone round," the gazebo.

When Nigh showed up wearing an incredibly sexy dress and high heels that made her wiggle when she walked, he'd been determined to keep working. He thought that if he stopped and had dinner with her, if he saw her lovely face across a candle-lit table, he'd end up in bed with her. But he wasn't ready to do that now.

Besides, he thought with a smile, after three years of celibacy, if he went to bed with a woman. . . . He didn't like to think what could happen.

Now he went to the chintz bedroom, Ann's room, as Nigh called it. He smiled at the memory of the jealousy in her tone. She made him feel good. He looked in the closet, moved his shoes about, then pried up a floorboard. He'd hidden the photo of Stacy under the board. Holding it, he held it under the light and looked at the face he'd loved so much.

Was he doing the right thing? he wondered. Maybe he should do what everyone had told him to: "Get on with your life." He always said that he had no life to get on with, but in the last hours he'd seen that there were possibilities. He'd seen . . . He hesitated. It was the first time in three years that he'd thought that there could be life after Stacy.

He put the picture back in the hole, then carefully slipped the old piece of wood back over it, then put his shoes back in place.

He undressed, then, on impulse, he took a quick, cold shower, put on a clean pair of sweatpants, and got into bed and turned out the light.

Moonlight was streaming in through the windows over the seat. He looked about the old room, saw the narrow bit of paneling that he now knew held a secret door. The catch was ingenious and well hidden. He would never have found it unless he were imprisoned in the room.

The thought of that made him think about Ann and even the lady highwayman—if she had ever existed. Had they been imprisoned in this room?

"Were you willing to do anything to get out of here?" he asked aloud to Ann. "Is that why you were willing to marry a kid like Danny Longstreet? Half your IQ, probably belched at the table. Was it escape or was it novelty? Or was it just the excitement?" He was quiet for a moment, but he heard nothing. Not that he expected to. He knew Ann was angry that he'd tried to recreate her room. He looked about and saw the little glass bottles on the dressing table, saw the portrait of her cousin Catherine over the mantelpiece. She was smiling slightly, but Jace still felt he saw sadness in her eyes.

"You know, don't you, that the excitement would have worn off. I know men like Danny Longstreet, everybody does. It's the novelty that he likes. He would have been good to you until he got used to you, then he would have gone back to his other women."

Jace was quiet, listening, hoping he'd hear something, but the house was silent. Feeling like a fool, he turned onto his side and closed his eyes. He wasn't drunk, but he'd had enough wine to make him sleepy. Nigh was just a room away and he liked that. Smiling, he drifted into that state of half-asleep, half-awake.

"Loved me," he heard. "Danny loved me."

"I don't blame him," Jace whispered.

Just as he fell asleep, he heard a voice say, "Told me so."

10

Jace and Nigh were sitting at the kitchen table eating the huge breakfast that Mrs. Browne had begrudgingly prepared for them. Jace had gone downstairs first and done his best to prepare his housekeeper for the shocking fact that a woman had spent the night in the house with him. Only not "with" him, but . . . Jace had rolled his eyes in exasperation at himself for his intimidation by the woman.

But Mrs. Browne was not to be placated. When Nigh walked into the kitchen, Mrs. Browne humphed until he thought the plaster might crack. She fried a second plate of bacon and eggs, then she'd left the kitchen, as though she couldn't bear to be in the same room with a woman like Nigh.

"Would she be that way with any woman who spent the night here?" Jace asked. "Or is it just you?"

"Mostly me. She doesn't approve of my job. Thinks it's 'uppity' and not a job for a proper woman."

"Ah. Your job. And just what is it you do?"

Nigh started to tell him, then stopped. "Spelunking."

Jace chuckled. "You'd better eat all of that. We might not get much for lunch."

Nigh ate a piece of fried bread dipped in runny, yellow egg yolk, then asked, "We?"

"Unless you have something else you have to do. If you're going to be my research assistant . . ." He shifted in his seat. "By the way, what salary do you want?"

"None. Finding out things about this house is reward enough for me." The moment the words were out of her mouth, Nigh knew she'd said the wrong thing. What did he think, that she was doing this because she'd fallen in love with him? But she said nothing; she wanted to see what he'd say.

Jace started to say something but stopped. He was frowning as he looked down at his plate. "Nigh," he began slowly. "About . . ." He hesitated. "About 'us.' I can't . . . I mean, I don't want you to think—"

She cut him off. "You don't want me to think that *you* are the prize? Really, Mr. Montgomery, you should get your ego in check. I know I was drunk last night and I'm sure I made a pass at you, but then I make passes at lampposts when I'm drunk— which explains why I'm usually very frugal about drinking. I apologize for whatever I did."

"You didn't do anything," he said quietly. "Actually, it was me who did—or didn't do—anything. I just wanted to say that there are things in my life that . . ." He broke off and said nothing else.

"I'm glad we have that settled," Nigh said, but couldn't keep the anger out of her voice. "I understand that you are off limits.

I'll stay away from the booze from now on. Now, how about we look into our mutual interest, which is the history of this house?"

"Sure, okay," Jace said. He felt bad about what she was thinking, bad about not telling her the truth. If he had any sense at all, he'd . . . what? Go home to the United States and forget all of this?

He looked at the top of her head. "I'm not sure, but I think Ann may have spoken to me last night."

"What did she say? 'Get in an alcohol treatment program'?"

"No, but she did suggest that I send you," he said solemnly.

Nigh tore off a piece of bread and tossed it at his head. He ducked and it missed him.

"Now I know how Lewis felt."

"Lewis?" Nigh said, aghast. "Please tell me that I didn't talk about Lewis last night."

"You beat him up when you were six."

Nigh groaned. "Never again allow me to drink. Please." She took a breath. "What did Ann really say?"

"I was mostly asleep, but I think she said she loved Danny Longstreet."

"Better than all her other suitors? Poor Ann was shut up in this house all her life. When she was a child, the villagers used to wonder about her and thought maybe she was deformed."

"Actually, she's quite pretty. When I saw her—"

"When you were hiding in the wardrobe?"

"Right. When I was hiding in the wardrobe, she was lamenting that she wasn't as pretty as her cousin Catherine. But standards of beauty change. Today Catherine would be ordering diet pills off infomercials and Ann would be a model."

"Hardly a model. She wasn't tall enough. She—" Nigh broke off because a brown pottery bowl fell off a shelf on the dresser and loudly crashed to the floor.

Nigh looked at Jace and he looked back at her. "On second thought," Nigh said carefully, "I think Ann was every bit as beautiful as any model we have today."

Jace gave Nigh a look to let her know she should be careful of what she said. Together, they began to clean up the broken crockery.

"So Ann loved Danny Longstreet," Nigh said as she swept broken shards into the pan Jace held steady. "Actually loved him."

When Jace didn't answer, she looked at him and saw the glazed expression on his face. "What is it?"

"I have it wrong. Ann didn't say that she loved Danny, she said that Danny loved her. And he told her so."

Nigh looked around the room nervously. "Excuse me for saying this, but I don't think so."

Jace dumped the shards in the trash bin, then sat back down at the table. "You're basing your opinion on the Longstreet you know today. Maybe Danny was different."

"I'm basing my opinion on the fact that the parish register says that a village girl gave birth to Danny Longstreet's child a few months after Ann's death. He impregnated her while he was engaged to Ann. Is that true love?"

Jace looked at her with interest. "You have done some research, haven't you? So tell me what happened to Danny."

"He died from a fall from a horse four years after Ann's death. Never married."

"Any more kids?"

"Just the one that I know about. The girl wasn't married to Danny, but she gave the baby the name of Longstreet. Gerald in the village is descended from that child."

"If she gave the baby the name of Longstreet, Danny would have had to agree, wouldn't he? He didn't marry her, but he must have admitted that the child was his," Jace said.

"And maybe supported it as long as he was alive. Danny's father was quite rich."

Jace thought for a moment. "So what happened to Ann's letters? Victorians threw nothing away. Maybe they're in the library and we could—"

"Burned," Nigh said. "After her death, her father burned everything that had belonged to Ann."

"*All* the letters? Maybe he missed something. Maybe in the attic we could find something."

"Arthur Stuart not only burned all of his daughter's letters, he burned all of her possessions. He was in a rage after his daughter killed herself on her wedding day. He had all her furniture, her clothes, everything hauled downstairs, taken out back, and burned. He wouldn't even give it away to charity. The local vicar kept a journal and I've read it. The whole village went to see the bonfire. Arthur Stuart said his daughter was roasting in hell and that's where all her belongings should be too."

"Nice man," Jace said. "No wonder Ann was willing to marry someone with half her IQ just to get away from him."

"And no wonder she loved him. Maybe he would be unfaithful, but he had a generous enough spirit to allow his illegitimate child to have his name. In the 1870s that was an uncommon thing to do."

"Wonder why he didn't marry the mother of his child?" Jace asked.

"Didn't you say he was in love with Ann?"

"I know you're being sarcastic," Jace said, "but it is possible to be in love with one person and go to bed with someone else."

"Speaking from experience?" Nigh asked, teasing.

Jace looked at her hard. "No," he said in a way that made her stop smiling and look away.

There was an awkward silence between them. The food that was left on their plates was cold and unappetizing.

She stood up. "I think I'll go up and . . ." Nigh began, thinking she'd brush her teeth and put on some clothes that fit better than Jace's huge workout suit, but then she remembered that she had nothing with her. "I guess I should go home. Maybe we can meet later and—"

Mrs. Browne came bustling into the kitchen and from the happy look on her face, she had terrible news. "The whole village is looking for you," she said to Nigh, her voice full of joy.

"Me? Why do they want me?"

"To apply for jobs, of course. There are two young people come up from London. They're psychics. Read your mind. Tell you what you're thinkin' and what's gonna happen to you. They said more people from London are comin' today but they had to get their machines ready."

Nigh sat back down. "Machines?"

"Oh, yes. Ghost machines. They have it on the telly. They have little machines and cameras, all sorts of things. They want to take pictures of the lady on her horse. They want to record the hoofbeats on the stairs."

"And they all want to see me?" Nigh said, her mind full of horrible images.

"It's all over town that you're the one to see."

Slowly, Nigh turned to look at Jace, who was standing by the door with a smug look on his face. "You did this."

"No," he said, breaking into a grin. "You did it to yourself. You made up the Ghost Center. I merely told them to talk to you instead of me."

"There's about twenty cars parked in front of that little house of yours," Mrs. Browne said. "Can't nobody from the village drive past. Clive is givin' out tickets. He said that if this keeps up we'll have enough money to repair the library roof. Mrs. Wheeler has been up all night makin' up a brochure about the ghosts at Priory House, and Mrs. Parsons is printin' it out. They're gonna sell 'em for five pounds each."

"Five pounds?" Nigh said, astonished.

"It's the twenty-first century and there's inflation, you know. Well, now, you two gotta get outta here. I got bakin' to do for the tea shop. With all the visitors in the village, they're eatin' everything."

Feeling as though she'd been hit with a bat, Nigh started toward the kitchen door, then turned back. "Mrs. Browne?"

"Yes, what is it?" she asked impatiently.

"If the people are here about ghosts in Priory House, why aren't they here at this house? Why aren't they pounding at the gates?"

"We told 'em the truth, that an American lives here."

Nigh didn't understand what she meant. She looked at Jace, but he shrugged. She looked back at Mrs. Browne.

"Guns," Mrs. Browne said, as though both Jace and Nigh were idiots. "American law says that everybody in that country has to have a gun."

"It's true," Jace said seriously. "It's in our constitution that we have the right to bear arms. The law was specifically written so we could shoot English people."

Mrs. Browne put her hands on her hips. "Well, I never!" she said.

Jace and Nigh ran from the room and were upstairs in the master bedroom before they allowed themselves to burst into laughter.

11

I feel like a clown," Nigh said, and even to herself she sounded petulant, like a pouting child. She pulled up the long sweatpants so she wouldn't walk on them. The bottoms of the pant legs had cuffs on them, and the waist tied with a drawstring, but in between there were about ten yards of fabric that hung about her. The top was just as bad. When she bent over the neckline fell away so you could see all the way to the floor. It was not sexy. As for shoes, all she had were her new, but ruined, high heels. She had on a pair of Jace's gym socks.

Jace glanced at her, nodded, then looked back at the screen of his laptop. "What do we have so far?"

Nigh was sitting on the window seat in the chintz bedroom. It had started to rain outside so Jace built a fire. The room was cozy and warm and altogether wonderful. If circumstances were different, she would be enjoying herself. Maybe it was a bit odd that she and Jace were in a bedroom, but it was the room that had been made to look like Ann's room, so Nigh told herself it was part of the research. But there was something wrong. She couldn't put her finger on it, but it was a feeling. Several times her life had depended on her going with her gut feelings and this was one of those times.

"What is it that you want to prove?" Nigh asked, her tone a bit more aggressive than she meant it to be.

"I think we should start with proving that Ann didn't kill herself," Jace said.

"How can we find out what happened a hundred and twenty-eight years ago? If Ann left a note, it was destroyed by her father. If she wrote letters or kept a diary, they were destroyed too."

"What about who she wrote letters to? Maybe they kept them," Jace said.

"If we read all Ann's letters, what would we find out? That she wanted to marry Danny Longstreet? Maybe we'd find out that Danny wanted to marry her. But we already know these things. How can we find out what happened in those last few minutes before she died?"

"Being in love doesn't stop someone from committing suicide," Jace said softly, then looked at her. "What would we have if we did prove that Ann was murdered? The right to move her bones into the churchyard? I'm not sure, but I'll bet that if you talk to the vicar he'll move them now."

"Probably," Nigh said, looking out the window.

Jace put his laptop on the bed and went to stand by her. "You want me to take you home?" he asked.

"And have people pounding on my door asking me for a job performing séances?"

"Are you really angry about that? It was either you or me and you started it," Jace said. "I think—"

She looked up at him. "No, I can handle those people. It's something else. It's something about this room. I don't think Ann wants me in here. Maybe she's as much in love with you as you are with her."

"I'm not—" Jace began, then reached out to touch her hair, but he drew back. "So where is this tower that used to hold the lady highwayman's clothes?"

"Great idea!" she said, then got off the window—and promptly tripped on the sweatpants. Jace caught her before she hit the floor, but he quickly let her go.

It took them a minute before they could get the old door open. It was easier to open from inside the tunnel. Once they were out of Ann's bedroom, Nigh felt better. She gave a sigh of relief and for a moment leaned against the stone wall. "You can see her but I think I can feel her. She's frustrated about something and I can feel it. I don't think we're doing what she wants us to do." She looked at Jace in the candlelight. "Or maybe Ann is angry that I'm taking up your time."

"If there's one thing in the world a person knows, it's when another person loves you," Jace said. "Not mouths the words, but really means it. I'm sure I'd know if Ann or any other woman was in love with me. She's not."

"So what's this all about?" Nigh asked, looking at him. "Why has she been showing herself to you? In all my research, I've never heard of anyone else seeing Ann."

"But everyone who has lived here has seen ghosts," he said. "They assumed it was the criminal woman and got the heck out. I don't think they were seeing the robber; I think it was Ann. But from all I've heard, the only people who were really able to communicate with her have been children."

Nigh started up the stairs. The stones were cold through the thick socks, but it felt good to have Jace with her. She'd been up the steps a hundred times but always by herself and when she was a child. Had Ann Stuart looked after her when she was small?

"If you're the first adult she's been able to reach and you're not doing what she wants, maybe that's her frustration." She looked back at him. "If you see her again, be sure and ask her what it is she wants you to do."

"My guess is that she wants us to find Danny Longstreet's ghost and get it to her so they can fly off to heaven together," Jace said, smiling.

Nigh didn't say anything for the rest of the way up the stairs and neither did Jace.

At the top was the round turret room, about ten feet in diameter. There was an old chair in the room and the windowsills were covered with small ornaments from outdoors: a bird's nest, three seashells, a striped rock, lots of dried leaves.

Jace knew that these things had been put there by Nigh when she was a child. "The playhouse of a little girl," he said, picking up the items and looking at them. "It's amazing that no one found out you were here."

"I think Hatch knew, but no one else. My parents didn't know. And, of course, the house has been vacant most of my life."

"When was the last time you were here?"

"The day my mother died. Everyone wanted to give me sympathy, but I just wanted to be alone. This was the only place that

I could escape to where no one could find me. I stayed for most of a day, and when I went down, I could face them."

When Jace said nothing, she turned to him. "Has anyone close to you died?"

"Yes," he said, succinctly and curtly, obviously wanting to say no more.

"Does that death have anything to do with this house and why you want to find out about Ann?"

Jace looked down at her and seemed to be debating what to tell her. After a while, he looked back out the window and said, "Yes, it does."

Nigh started to ask more questions, but he turned to her with a scowl on his face.

"That's it. That's all I'm telling you and if you want to keep this so-called job, you won't ask me any more questions. I'm cold. I'm going down." He turned and started down the stairs.

Behind him, Nigh smiled. She felt as though she'd just won an award. She had pierced his armor! It was a tiny hole she'd made in it, but she'd widen it.

If she knew how to whistle, she would have whistled as she skipped down the old stairs, and when she got back into the chintz room, she was smiling.

"I was right. We *must* find Danny Longstreet," Jace said.

"You mean his grave?"

"His last place of residence, or the place he loved. Something about him. But we *need* to find him."

"Good idea," Nigh said. "But what's made you so fierce about it?"

"This." He turned his laptop around so she could see the screen. In big red letters, it said, *Find Danny Longstreet.*

Nigh rubbed her forearms because the hairs had stood up on them. "I guess that's clear enough."

"What do you know about him, other than his death and illegitimate child?"

"That's about it. What I know comes from the vicar's diary. He didn't write anything about Danny until he told of his death, then he backtracked and told about the baby that was being raised in Margate by its mother. It's been years since I read it, so I don't remember if he told where Danny was living at the time. I know that after Ann died, Danny's father didn't buy Priory House." She shook her head. "Sorry. I don't know any more than that."

"Where's the diary?

"Guess."

"In your house, the one that's surrounded by paranormals with machines."

Nigh's head came up. "Did you ever think of—"

"So help me, if you suggest that I allow those charlatans into Ann's room to muck about, I'm going to toss you out in the rain, from *that* window."

Nigh blinked at him. "Good thing you're not in love with her."

"Would you cut that out? You cannot be in love with someone you've 'met' three times."

For a moment they looked at each other, then Jace looked down at the computer.

"I'll call Jerry," Nigh said. "Maybe he'll know something about his ancestor. What?" she asked when Jace started shaking his head in wonder.

"Only in England," he said, "would someone know that far back on his family tree."

"If he knows, it's my guess it's because Danny's father had

bags of money, but his descendants have none. Wonder what happened to it? Gambling? Racehorses?"

"My guess is women," Jace said, then saw one of the glass bottles fall off the dressing table and hit the floor.

"Don't do that!" Nigh said to the room at large. "Maybe he can take seeing ghosts, but I have a weak heart."

Jace picked up the telephone on the bedside table and held it out to Nigh. "If Longstreet's not home, you'll probably reach him at your house."

"Funny," Nigh said. "You're a real scream."

She called information, got the number for Longstreet's Garage, then pushed the buttons. Jerry answered on the fourth ring.

"Jerry? This is Nigh. Remember me?"

"Nightingale, baby, honey, of course I remember you."

Even though she put the receiver close to her ear, Jerry spoke as loudly as if he were standing in the room, and she knew that Jace could hear every word. She turned her back to him.

"I have a question for you," she said.

"Oh, sweetheart, I have some questions for you too. And some ideas about this new business you started. I was thinking of a ghost car. One of those big American things with the fins. I could fix it up for you so it would scream when you sat down in it. Like the idea?"

"Love it," Nigh said. "We'll have to discuss it in detail. What I wanted to ask you about was an ancestor of yours, Danny Longstreet."

"Randy Danny?"

At the derogatory term, she looked back at Jace just in time to see one of the ceramic figures start to slide off the mantel. Jace caught it before it hit the floor.

"Listen, Jerry," she continued, "do you know where Danny was living when he died?"

"Oh yeah. A house named Tolben Hall. It's in Hampshire. It's a B and B now. My mother used to tell us kids that that house should have been ours. Danny's father bought it after he had to get his son out of Margate. Danny left too many bastards behind. It was too hot for them to stay here."

Jace caught another figure before it hit the floor, but he couldn't catch one of the perfume bottles that went flying off the dressing table.

"What was that?" Jerry asked.

"Nothing. Rain hitting the window."

"So, Nigh, honey, when am I gonna see you again? I've missed you. Seen you on TV some, but that ain't the same as a little snog in the backseat, now is it? You still got that heart-shaped mole on—"

"Jerry!" Nigh said loudly. "You've been a really big help, and I can't thank you enough. I'll see you, uh, sometime, I'm sure. Say hello to, uh, whoever your girlfriend is now."

"Ain't got one."

"I know," Nigh said tiredly. "You don't have one, you have a hundred."

"You do remember me, honey bear. Give me a call about that car. I think it'll be a hit at your Ghost Center."

She said good-bye, then hung up—and dreaded the look on Jace's face.

But he was at his computer and didn't look up. "Here it is. Tolben Hall in Hampshire. Shall I give them a call?"

"Sure," Nigh said tentatively, waiting for him to say something. "About Jerry . . ."

"None of my business," he said, concentrating on the screen.

"It's just that we dated in school, and we were friends, that's all. And now because of you and this Ghost Center—"

"You made that up, not me."

"All right, my Ghost Center, then. He's pretty excited about it and, well . . ."

Jace looked up from the computer. "We'll stay at this place and have a look around. Like the idea?"

She held out the bulky gray fabric of the sweatpants she was wearing. "Unless I go back to my house, this is all I have to wear."

He looked at her. "That is a problem. Think you could slip in the back door of your house and get some clothes?"

"And not be seen? Not even in the middle of the night."

"Hey! I know. Why don't you call your landlord and ask him to get some things for you. He must have a key."

She looked at him as though he was daft. "*You* are my land-lord."

"You're kidding."

"Do you really not know that? Why in the world did you buy this enormous house that you obviously know nothing about?" She'd meant it as a rhetorical question, but the look on his face made her know she had made yet another dent in his armor.

Before she could say anything, they heard a sound from downstairs. Voices.

"You don't think Mrs. Browne has let them in, do you?" Jace asked.

"She's probably angry about that remark you made about shooting the English."

"Or she's angry because she thinks you're showing off your heart-shaped birthmark to yet another man."

"I *knew* you were going to badger me about that. Danny is

full of himself, but he can be a lot of fun. At least he knows how to laugh."

"Jerry."

"What?"

"You said Danny."

"No, I didn't."

They stopped talking because they heard footsteps on the stairs. "Someone is coming to get us," Jace said. "One of us is going to have to face the lot of them and confess that you made up the whole thing about the Ghost Center."

"I just asked questions. You made it real when you told people you'd be hiring."

"No, I told them *you* would be hiring."

The steps were getting closer and they could hear more voices.

"You go on ahead. I'm going to get some things and I'll meet you at my car," he said.

"If you can get it out."

"Don't worry. Mick will have the garage open and ready for us to go."

Nigh ran to get the hidden staircase open, then motioned to Jace to hurry up. She wasn't going without him. He tucked his laptop and cord under his arm, then followed her onto the stair landing. It was pitch-black in the staircase with the door closed, and it took minutes to make sure the door was securely closed. They could hear someone pounding on the door of the bedroom.

"I can't see a thing," Jace said. "Where are the candles and matches?"

"At the other end of the tunnel."

"That's clever."

"I was nine when I set it up," she said. "What do you expect? Electricity?"

"I just hope the damned timbers hold for one last dash. Ow!"

"You're too tall. Duck!"

"No, I'm not too tall, the ceiling is too short."

"Take my hand," Nigh said, fumbling behind her as she hurried along the dark, dank dirt tunnel. She felt his chest and even his arm, but she couldn't find his hand. She stopped, then put both hands out to find his. It was a full minute before she realized he was deliberately preventing her from finding his hand.

"I've spent hours locked away in a bedroom with you today and *now* you want to play sex games? Give me your hand and let's get out of here. One of those psychics might be real and tell people where we are."

Chuckling, Jace gave her his hand and they hurried to the end of the tunnel. It was early afternoon, but the rain made the sky gray and fog gave them cover. Jace tucked his computer under his sweatshirt and started running, Nigh close on his heels. They had to stop twice and hide from people who were now swarming over the grounds.

"Don't you people have trespassing laws?" Jace hissed at her once. Before she could answer, he grabbed her hand and started running so fast that she nearly fell, but he dragged her upright and they kept going.

Just as Jace said, when they reached the garage, the door was open and the car running. Mick stood just inside the garage door. "Hatch saw you coming," Mick said, "and he knew where you were going. He told me to clear the way for you."

He looked at Nigh. "Take the old road to the highway," Mick said and she nodded. "I don't know what it's like. We heard some crashes today, so you may have some trouble."

When they got to the Range Rover, Nigh asked politely if she could drive.

"Think you can handle it?" Jace asked.

Mick was on the far side of Jace and he raised his eyebrows at Jace's question. "She can!" he yelled before shutting the door.

"All buckled up?" Nigh asked, her voice calm as she backed the big, heavy car out of the garage.

As soon as the people saw them, they started running. Some of them ran toward Jace's Rover, but some ran back to the front of the house to get their cars to pursue them.

The back road into Priory House was a service road, and it was, at best, full of potholes and whatever had fallen onto it. As Mick had warned, today's rain had brought down several tree branches. The first one that Nigh hit, Jace yelled at her to watch out, but she went over it easily, even if his head did hit the roof.

When they saw a car coming toward them, Nigh didn't hesitate as she turned a sharp right and headed for the steep bank of a stream. She had to move fast. If she slowed down, she knew the vehicle would get stuck.

After his first shout of warning, Jace said nothing but watched where she was headed. "Right!" he yelled one time. "Cut your wheel to the right." He had seen some jagged, tire-slashing rocks that she hadn't. She turned hard and missed the rocks.

When they went up the bank of the stream, they were at a forty-five-degree angle, like sitting in your seat when a jet takes off. "Good" was all Jace said when they were back on flat land.

They came to a fenced pasture and Nigh drove the car through the wire. There were sheep around them, looking up placidly as they chewed.

"My sheep?" Jace asked as he held onto the handle above the window.

"Your pasture, but you rent it to the shepherd."

"Nice to know," Jace said as they banged over a solid rock surface. He drew his breath in sharply when he couldn't see the other side of the rock. For all he knew, it was a sheer dropoff.

But it wasn't. The car bounced when it hit the ground, ran over a bumpy cattle guard, then leveled out onto a gravel road.

The relatively quiet and smooth ride was the calm after the storm. Jace took a few deep breaths and tried to relax. "I guess you learned to drive in your job . . . whatever your job is, that is."

"Right," she said. "You want to take over now?" She pulled the car to the side of the gravel road and got out. For a moment she stood beside the car and took a few deep breaths.

Jace came to stand beside her. When he saw she was trembling, he pulled her into his arms and held her for a moment. "Okay?"

"I'm fine," she said, but she liked being this close to him. He smelled of wood smoke from the fireplace and he was damp from the rain. She wanted to curl up next to him and stay there for a long time.

Jace knew that the hug had turned from paternal to something else, so he pushed her away. "Ready to go? If we don't leave now, one of them will get a divining rod and find us."

She smiled, nodded, then got into the passenger side of the car.

They rode in silence until they reached the highway, then Nigh gave him directions on how to head toward the county of Hampshire.

"Is there a city near here where we can stop?" Jace asked. "I need to call the B and B and we need to get some clothes."

"I don't have my bag so my credit cards—"

"You can pay me back later," he said, cutting her off. He glanced at her. "You did a good job back there," he said quietly. "I've never seen a woman drive like that."

She gave him a look.

"Okay, I've never seen a man who wasn't a professional drive like that. You must have had some training."

"Mmmm," she said.

"You aren't going to tell me?"

"Not until you start revealing secrets to me."

"But I've told you all about Ann," he said in protest. "Every word."

"And I'm supposed to believe that *she* is your secret? You must think I have the intelligence of a doorstop. It's my guess that you didn't know anything at all about Ann Stuart or Lady Grace before you bought Priory House. Is that right?"

"Maybe," he said.

"I know it's right. Fooling with this ghost story is lagniappe, something extra, something . . ." She broke off and looked at his profile. "Dead. You want something from her, don't you? You want something that only a dead person can give you, don't you?"

"It's a roundabout," he said. "You better watch for the signs or we'll end up going around and around it for eternity."

"That one," she said. "The one that says Winchester. You aren't going to distract me from this, you know. I'll figure it out. Did I tell you that I used to date Clive Sefton?"

"You didn't have to. It seems to me that you've dated every male in Margate."

"What's that supposed to mean?"

"I don't know, but they all seem to know where your birthmarks are."

"I'll have you know that—" She stopped, then smiled. "You

are not going to start a row with me just to keep me from asking questions."

She leaned back in the seat and smiled. She had a good nose for a story and she knew she was on the right trail. "So we help Ann, then you hope she'll help you, is that it?"

"Maybe," he said again, but this time there was a little smile at the corners of his mouth.

12

Did you get the reservations?" Jace asked when Nigh returned to the table in the café. He had purchased sandwiches and drinks for them while she called Tolben Hall.

"Yes," she said, then gave a great sigh. "I did, but there's a problem. They had only one room available so we'll have to share. But the owner assured me the room has a very large bed. We can put pillows down the middle. Do you snore?"

"I've never been awake to find out," Jace said, frowning.

"Come on, Montgomery," Nigh said, "don't look so worried. They had two rooms, so I won't disturb your chastity." She sat down across from him. He was still frowning. "Would you stop it!" she said. "I'm not making a pass at you. I was making a joke. Get over it."

When he looked up at her, there was something in his eyes

that made her sit back in her chair. "What has hurt you so much?" she whispered. "Who has hurt you?"

"Nothing and no one," he said, then looked back down.

She couldn't get him to say anything more. They were in Winchester and they had an hour before the stores closed for the day. She was embarrassed to be seen in the huge sweatpants and shirt that she was wearing, and it was difficult to ignore the stares she was receiving from people.

"How do you want to do this shopping?" she asked. "You want to do a *Pretty Woman* and go together?"

"What?" Jace asked, looking up, obviously so distracted he wasn't understanding what she was talking about.

She leaned her head toward his and lowered her voice so the other customers wouldn't hear. "I apologize for making a sex joke, okay? I won't do it again. Are you gay? Is that the problem?"

That question brought a twinkle to his eyes and he smiled at her. "Yeah, that's it. Gay. I don't like women at all. I especially don't like a sassy little woman who looks beautiful even in clothes twice her size. A woman who laughs and enjoys life and is smart and funny and is the first one to take me out of myself in three years. Yes, I'm as gay as you get. Are you finished with that? Let's get some clothes and get out of this town."

With that he stood up and walked out to the sidewalk. Nigh hastily finished her drink and ran after him.

"Pick a store," he said. "Go in, buy yourself a wardrobe, and I'll meet you there in one hour and we'll leave."

"That one," Nigh said, pointing to a high-end boutique that had Prada in the window. "But it looks expensive."

"You snooped into my background, so you know I can afford it."

"And I'm paying you back later, right?"

"Yes," he said, then turned and walked away.

She didn't know what she'd done to anger him, but she had. She couldn't worry about it now. She had a lot to do and little time to do it. She went to the store and told the clerk that she had one hour to put together a wardrobe, then her boyfriend would pay for it.

An hour and a half later, they were back in Jace's Rover and heading toward Tolben Hall. They were dressed in upscale English country, Jace in a jacket and tie with lightweight wool trousers, while Nigh was wearing a dress that looked rather plain but had actually cost a couple of thousand pounds. She couldn't help running her hands down her sleeves.

"It will take me a while to pay you back," she said, glancing at the two suitcases that Jace had brought with him when he'd picked her up. Empty when he'd arrived, they were now filled with new clothes, plus all the toiletries they'd purchased at Boots pharmacy.

"All right," Jace said, "I want the truth. What is it you do for a living?"

"Journalist," she said.

He glanced at her with a grimace on his face.

"No, what I wrote about you is not an example of my work. That was . . ."

"What was it?"

"Jet lag, maybe. And . . . horror. I've had a lot happen in my life in the last couple years and sometimes I have no perspective."

"Tell me about it," Jace said and there was such empathy in his voice that she wanted to tell him.

She told him her parents had died within a year of each other—first her father, then her mother—and it was as though Nigh had had the anchor in her life removed. She suddenly hated everything about her life, and she just wanted to leave Margate and all the memories. She wanted to get *away*.

"So you went to London," Jace said.

She laughed. "Exactly. Where all Englishmen and -women go when they want to find themselves—or lose themselves. I got a job in a newsroom, mostly getting coffee for the bosses. I didn't know what I wanted to do and they didn't know what to do with me. But one night the news presenter didn't show up. Later we found out she'd fallen down a flight of stairs in her house and knocked herself out. She lived alone, so there was no one to call in sick for her."

Nigh told Jace how they'd looked around at the people who were in the studio and Nigh had been the only person there who, as they said, wouldn't "frighten the viewers," so they sent her to hair and makeup and put her on the air. The only instruction she was given was to read what she saw on the teleprompter.

No one knew it at the time, but it had been an audition. Nigh had done an excellent job in the reading and she photographed well. The next day she was given a real job.

It was a month later that she heard that a news team was being sent to Egypt to report on a tourist bus that had been shot at, and Nigh asked to be allowed to go.

"Foreign correspondent," Jace said.

"Yes. For the last eight years I've never been in any one place for more than four days at a time. I live on airplanes and in hotels." She looked out the window and said no more.

"But now you've come home. Is it for *good*?"

"I don't know. I know that I'm tired. I know that I've seen too much bloodshed and too much horror in the world." She took a deep breath. "Eleven months ago I was in Iraq and my cameraman, Steve, was blown up. He was standing three feet away, film-

ing me talking to some women and children. I had a translator
with me and I was asking them about the horror in their lives. I
was near to tears as I heard what they had to say. In the next second, I heard a sound and suddenly there was blood and metal
fragments everywhere. A mortar or a missile, something, I don't
know what, had directly hit my cameraman, a man I really liked,
a man with a wife and three kids. His body exploded over us and
the camera equipment blew into tiny pieces. Many of the children I was talking with were seriously injured. I was wounded
too, but mostly I was in shock."

Jace reached over, took her hand in his, and held it.

"I don't remember too much after that. Medics came and the
kids were treated."

"And you?"

"Airlifted out, stitched up, given some pills, and told that if I
wanted to talk to someone, they'd listen."

"Did you?"

"No," Nigh said softly. "I couldn't talk because I didn't know
what I would say. I wanted to help the world, but I don't think
I'm cut out for death and destruction. I can't seem to disconnect
myself from what I see."

Turning, she looked at him and smiled. "I thought I was
someone who could fight, but I seem to be a coward."

"You don't sound like a coward to me," Jace said. "What happened to you would traumatize anyone."

"You don't know the news world. The real news people have
something like that happen to them, they have a couple of
Scotches, then they go right back to it."

"But you couldn't," Jace said.

"No. I've done some reporting since then, but not much, and
I taper off more and more. I thought I might . . ."

"Might what?"

"Write about what I've seen. I thought I might write about the people I met, what I heard and what I saw. I came back home to be still and to listen to my own thoughts, and think about what I want to do with the rest of my life."

"And you thought your little village was being invaded by a big, bad American."

Nigh smiled. " 'Fraid so. Sorry. I'm used to hearing two sentences of information and within six minutes changing it into a headline-grabbing story. I can't tell you how many news reports I've written in helicopters."

"So have you made any decisions?" Jace asked.

"Turn here," she said. "So far, not a one. My idea of spending my days alone and taking long, thoughtful walks has been superseded by ghost hunting with an American who keeps more secrets than all the Middle East."

"Small secrets. Personal ones. Not important except to me. Not earth-moving like your secrets, or your life."

"There it is," Nigh said, pointing to a sign that said Tolben Hall.

Jace pulled into the long driveway and the house came into view through the trees. It was lovely, a huge Victorian house with a turret on one end, and a pointed roof. There was a deep porch with a swing and several round windows.

"I can see why Longstreet bought this instead of Priory House."

"There it is again," Nigh said. "You hate your house. You think it's dreadful, but you paid an enormous amount for it. Why?"

"Didn't I tell you that I'm a masochist?"

"Great! I brought my dominatrix gear. We'll tie you up later."

Jace was laughing as he got out of the car and opened the trunk to get the suitcases.

"I'll check in," she said, then ran up the steps to the front door.

A few minutes later, Jace entered carrying the two suitcases. Nigh was talking to a short, thin, gray-haired woman who introduced herself as Mrs. Fenney. "I was just telling Miss Smythe," she said, "that you'll have the whole house to yourselves. We're usually full on the weekends but not so busy during the week. And you'll be staying how long?" She looked at Jace.

"Three days," he said quickly.

"Oh, that's fine then. Let me show you your rooms."

They followed her up the stairs to a long corridor with several doors along it. She opened one to reveal a large, pretty room done in pink and green chintz. There was a round sitting area at one end. "Mine!" Nigh said.

"Yes, it is our prettiest room," Mrs. Fenney said with pride. "And now you, sir," she said and Jace followed her.

Nigh walked to the window and looked out. Below her she could see the surrounding acres of trees that the hotel owned and she looked forward to walking among them. In fact, she wanted to explore the town and every shop of the little village.

She leaned her head against the cool glass and thought about what she'd told Jace in the car. When she'd returned from that nightmare, from when she'd seen death at such close range, she'd been a brilliant actress, telling no one how traumatized she'd been. She'd walked out of the hospital with nearly a hundred stitches in her, but other than wincing a few times, she'd let no one see her pain.

She'd even gone to Steve's wife and talked to her. The woman had cried, but Nigh didn't. She thought that if she began crying, she'd never stop. Steve had been a great guy, funny, always able to look on the bright side of life. He was never pessimistic; he never lost hope. He was sure that he was doing something good in the world and he never let other people forget that.

Nigh didn't cry for seven months, but then, one day, she couldn't seem to stop. TV commercials made her cry, children laughing, old couples who looked at each other with love. Whatever she did or said or thought or heard made her cry.

Her editor, a man in his sixties, was the only one who saw Nigh's deterioration. "I wondered when you'd start coming apart. I want you to take some time off and think about this job. Some people are made for it and some aren't. Based on forty years in this business, I'd say that you should get out of it. But that's just my opinion."

"I have some assignments."

"Yeah, get them done, then go home to that place where all of you come from. Some village or other where everybody knows you."

"Margate," Nigh whispered.

"Right. Marwell or whatever. Go there and think about what you want to do with the years you have left. Call me when you decide."

Nigh nodded and turned to leave, but he stopped her.

"Smythe?" She turned back to him. "You're lucky. You have heart and you feel things. But best of all, you can write. Use it."

Now there was a knock on the bedroom door. "Come in," she called, and turned to see Jace standing there.

He looked at her sharply. "You okay?"

"Perfectly. Just a bit of the blues. So how's your room?"

"Dark blue, mahogany bed. A gentleman's room. I asked her about the Longstreets and she has a couple boxes of old papers.

She's going to dig them out of the attic and we can look at them tomorrow."

"That's great," Nigh said, moving away from the window and wiping a tear away.

"Hey," Jace said as he put his hands on her shoulders. "You don't look so good."

She looked up at him. "I'm fine. Just thinking too much. It's better if I stay busy and don't think."

"You and me both. How about dinner? I was told there's a great restaurant in town."

"No, I think I'll . . ."

Jace moved his hand to under her chin, then lifted her face to his as his eyes searched hers. "I know how you feel," he said softly. "I know what it is to lose someone close to you, and I know how it feels to be eaten alive with the question of 'why?' Why did it happen? What was the sense of it? I know—"

He broke off as he bent and put his mouth on hers for a long, sweet kiss, a gentle kiss, but one of such longing that chills went down Nigh's spine.

Abruptly, Jace broke away and stepped back from her. "I didn't mean to do that."

"It's all right," she said. "It's fine to kiss someone. I'm fine with—"

"No," Jace said. "I meant that I didn't mean to do that."

Nigh was confused. "You said that."

He ran his hand over his face. "Look, you and I both know that we're attracted to each other. From the moment I first saw you my palms have been sweating. I should have been furious with you for what you wrote about me. I could have sued you, but what did I do but sit down and have a cup of tea with you? And since then I haven't spent more than ten waking minutes away from you—and don't want to. It isn't a question of whether or not I want to kiss you, snog you, or shag you, as you English say, but I'm telling you that *I didn't mean to do that.*"

He had given her so much information that all Nigh could do was blink at him. From his attitude toward her she'd begun to think that he actually was gay, but . . .

"So who kissed me?" she asked, swallowing. "Sweaty palms," he said. "And how do you know the difference?"

Jace started to say something, but instead he pulled her into his arms and kissed her with the passion he'd been feeling since he met her. His hands ran over her back, up her neck, through her hair, then back down again, while his mouth overtook hers, his tongue touching hers, invading her mouth.

He released her as abruptly as he'd taken her, and when he broke away, for a moment, they both stood there panting, staring at each other with heaving chests.

"Did you mean that one?" Nigh managed to say.

"Oh yeah." He took a step toward her, but then stopped. The next moment he was at the door to her bedroom. "Look, Nigh, I have things—"

"Don't say it again," she said. "You have issues in your life. Me too. Right now I want to take a bath. I'll meet you downstairs in an hour. We'll have dinner with no liquor, or none for me anyway."

Jace nodded but said nothing, then left the room.

Alone in the room, Nigh thought that she should be angry at him. She should tell him what she thought of him and his on again/off again, hot and cold attitude toward her, but she didn't feel that way. Instead, she started waltzing about the room humming the words to "I Could Have Danced All Night."

She spent nearly a half hour soaking in the tub, smiling the whole time, then she spent a long, leisurely half hour applying makeup and dressing in a black silk cocktail dress, black hose, and high black heels.

When she went downstairs, she also had a letter ready to fax to Ralph, who owned the newspaper that had caused so many problems. She asked him to print a retraction saying that there would be no Ghost Center, that everything had been a mistake. There would be no jobs. Priory House was a private residence and would remain so.

She showed it to Jace, and he practically ran to find Mrs. Fenney and a fax machine. Ten minutes later, he returned, took Nigh's arm, and said, "It's done."

They laughed together in relief.

13

Jace and Nigh drove into the village and went straight to the restaurant. By silent mutual agreement, they didn't talk about the Longstreets or the Stuarts, but only about themselves. Jace wanted to hear more about what Nigh had done in her life and where she'd been. She wanted to know about him. She quickly saw that he'd talk and answer questions as long as it didn't involve recent history. She could get him to tell anything about himself until about six years ago. After that, he grew silent.

True to her word, Nigh drank only half a glass of wine. After dinner, they went back to the hotel and separated to go to their own rooms. There was no kissing, no hand-holding, no awkwardness. But when Nigh closed the door to her room, she leaned against it for a while, her eyes closed. It didn't happen often, but sometimes you met a man you could talk to, laugh with, tease, and . . . well, maybe you could love.

She went to bed smiling.

The next morning, she met Jace for breakfast at 8:00 a.m. and wasn't surprised to see him chowing down on a "fry-up."

"Not many people want these anymore," Mrs. Fenney said, sliding fried tomatoes onto Jace's heaping plate. "I think it's a shame. My husband had a fry-up every morning for forty years and it never hurt him."

Nigh leaned across the table and whispered, "But he's not here now, is he? That stuff is going to kill you."

"Can't help it," Jace said. "Mrs. Browne spoiled me." He bit into a blood sausage.

After breakfast, they walked into the town. "I like this village," she said. "I like it better than Margate."

"I got the idea you loved Margate."

"They know too much about me there."

"Like where your birthmarks are?"

"Like when my parents died and what I've seen and done and who I know. I think it would be nice to move somewhere else and start over. Clean, fresh."

"What about your job?"

"Maybe I'll write murder mysteries and sell them to Americans and make millions."

Smiling, Jace said, "There's the church, and I think that's the vicar going in. Come on, let's catch him."

"You go on. The day's too pretty to be inside. I think I'll stay out here."

"I'll meet you . . ."

She waved her hand. "Go. You're not going to lose me. I'll be around."

He smiled at her, then hurried off to the church. She followed him at a slower pace, looking about her as she walked. What she'd said to Jace about starting over, clean and fresh, had just come out of her mouth, but she liked the idea. It wasn't as though she'd grown up having a burning ambition to be a journalist. It was something that had just happened to her. On the other hand, she'd been told she was good at it, so maybe she had wanted to do it. The question was, could her being a journalist make a difference in the world?

The church was enclosed by an iron fence, old and rusty in spots, but intact and kept in good repair. To the left was the cemetery, and Nigh knew she should go there and look for Danny Longstreet's grave, but she didn't want to see any tombstones. Right now, she didn't want to think of death.

To the right of the church was a lovely border of flowers and a pretty wooden bench. She sat down on it and looked at the stonework of the church. For a moment she closed her eyes and almost went to sleep. A sound startled her.

A young man wearing riding clothes was walking past her, obviously trying to be quiet, but he'd stepped on a twig. "I was trying to be quiet," he said, "but I didn't make it." He looked at her in speculation. "Do I know you?"

"No," she said, looking at him. He looked a bit like Jerry Longstreet, only more handsome, more refined, not so . . . oh dear, her class system was intact. This young man looked to be of a higher class than Jerry. "Your name isn't by chance Longstreet, is it?"

His eyes widened. "You're either a soothsayer or a distant cousin. I do hope it's the latter and not the former."

She smiled. "Neither. I'm a research assistant to a man who bought a house in the village of Margate. It's—"

"Priory House," he said.

"Yes. Do you know of it?"

"Only where it concerns my relatives. In the 1870s a man named Hugh Longstreet wanted to buy it."

"So much so that he tried to force a marriage between his son and the daughter of the owner of Priory House," she said, testing him to see how much he knew.

"What I was told was that 'force' isn't the right word. I heard it was a love match."

Nigh sat up straighter on the bench. "That's what I heard too, but what was your source?" She couldn't very well tell him her source was a couple of ghosts.

He smiled at her in a way that made her smile back. "That would be revealing family secrets, wouldn't it?"

Nigh looked toward the front of the church, but there was no sign of Jace. "Are you busy right now? I'd love to ask you a few questions."

"You sound like a reporter," he said as he sat down beside her.

"Guilty." She turned to face him, her back to the front of the church. "I'd love to hear everything you know about Danny Longstreet and his father and Priory House, and anything else you can tell me. Oh, by the way, my name is Nigh Smythe."

"And 'Nigh' is short for . . . ?"

"Nightingale," she said, and as always felt a bit embarrassed by the name.

"Like Ann Nightingale Stuart?" he asked softly. "Are you related to her?"

"My mother said we were, but I don't know how we could be. My mother came from Yorkshire."

"But that's very possible. Didn't you know that Ann's father sold Priory House after Ann . . . died, and he moved north and remarried? I think it may have been Yorkshire where he went, but I'm not sure of it. I think he had more children as his second wife was quite young."

Nigh blinked at him for a moment. She'd never been much interested in genealogy and so hadn't asked her mother much about her grandparents. They were dead by the time Nigh was three, so she didn't remember seeing them. It was interesting to find out that it could be true that she was related to the Stuarts.

"I think it would be too much of a coincidence that a descendant of Arthur Stuart's second marriage would end up in tiny Margate," she said.

"Unless she went there on purpose," he said. "Was your mother interested in family history? Maybe she went to Margate to do some family research."

"That's highly likely," Nigh said and felt a wave of guilt wash over her. Her mother had been very interested in family history, but her daughter hadn't been. In fact, Nigh remembered groaning and being a pest when her mother got out her "box of the old ones," as Nigh and her father called it.

She turned her attention back to the man. A reporter learned to focus on the person he was interviewing rather than himself. "I'm staying at Tolben Hall."

"Beautiful, isn't it? Hugh bought it after Ann's death, but he didn't live long enough to enjoy it."

"Why did Hugh Longstreet want Priory House so much?"

"It was his life's dream. Actually, it's what fueled his life. His wanting Priory House was what drove him into becoming a millionaire." He paused and smiled at her. "I think I'm boring you."

"Not at all," she said honestly.

"Is that your young man?"

Turning, she saw Jace standing at the corner of the church, talking to the vicar. She raised her hand to him and he nodded, then she turned back to her new friend. "Why was the house Hugh's lifelong dream?"

"His mother had been a housekeeper there. It was said that . . . no, I'll bore you."

"I promise you won't."

"It's just a silly story, a bit like Dickens. When Hugh was a young man, it was said that he found out that his mother was much more than just a housekeeper to the owner of Priory House. It was possible, even probable, that the owner was his father. It was also said that on the day he found out, Hugh stole half the Stuart family silver and ran away to America. I was told that Hugh dedicated his entire life to one thing, and that was to owning Priory House."

"But Arthur wouldn't sell it to him," Nigh said.

"Correct. Arthur had been a little boy when Hugh lived there and Hugh had . . . shall we say, been unkind to him."

"Tortured him mercilessly, did he?"

"Without letup," he said, smiling. "So Arthur wanted to get him back. Besides, Arthur was an angry, bitter man. His father had told him to marry for money, but Arthur had married for love, to a penniless daughter of a vicar. She died less than a year later."

"Giving birth to Ann," Nigh said.

"Yes. Arthur could hardly stand the sight of his daughter."

"He kept her so imprisoned when she was a child that the villagers thought she was deformed," Nigh said.

"Exactly."

"Then Hugh Longstreet and his handsome son came along and they made a deal."

"Yes. It was a deal that took months to negotiate. Arthur was going to continue to live at Priory House after the sale, but Hugh didn't care who lived there. He just wanted to own that house that should have been his by birth because he was Arthur's older brother."

"What about Ann and Danny?"

"Ah," the man said, smiling brighter. "There are sometimes true wonders in this world. On the surface, there were no more mismatched people in the world than Ann Stuart and Danny Longstreet. She was all refinement and quiet graces, while he was—"

"Wild and devil-may-care. A descendant of his lives in Margate and I know him well."

"Does he?" the young man said with interest. "He must be descended from . . ."

"Danny's illegitimate child."

"Ah, yes, that," he said, ducking his head for a moment. "Danny was rich and handsome, and women old and young adored him."

Nigh laughed. "Sounds like Jerry, but maybe Danny was a bit brighter."

"He wasn't stupid, if that's what you mean," he snapped.

"Sorry," Nigh said. "I meant no offense."

"I am the one to apologize. Danny's mother was from an impoverished but upper-crust Boston family, and his father was half aristocracy with a working-class mother. Danny had a lot of different blood in his veins, and Ann brought out the best in him. While their fathers spent months haggling over who owned what furniture, Danny and Ann were free to be together. Their knowledge of the world overlapped on no points, so there was no competition between them. She taught him poetry and flowers, and he taught her . . ." For a moment, he closed his eyes as he thought.

"Raw, rough sex," Nigh said, laughing.

The man turned to her with a face full of anger. "Don't say that! Danny respected Ann. He never touched her except for a few chaste kisses."

Nigh sat up straighter, moving away from the young man a bit. She was glad it was daylight and that she was in public and that Jace was nearby. She glanced over her shoulder. He was no longer with the vicar but standing by the corner of the church, leaning against the wall and watching her. She thought of motioning for him to come over, but she feared that the young man would quit telling her about Ann and Danny. But she was glad Jace was close.

She turned back to the man. "I apologize. I guess I'm confusing our low morals with their high morals."

"I'm sorry. Again, I'm the one to apologize. I've had a long time to think about all this and the injustice of it still angers me."

"I agree. I, we, don't think Ann killed herself."

"Of course she didn't. She was in love with Danny and he with her. They were longing to get married."

"Then who killed her?"

"My guess is it was the girl in the village."

"Ah. The mother of Danny's child."

The young man grimaced. "Too much gin, too much song, too much of loving a woman he couldn't touch. An accident. The result was unfortunate."

"And you think she killed Ann."

"Yes, I do. There was no proof, but her cousin Catherine said that a piece of candy was found on the floor of Ann's room. The woman in the village worked in a candy factory."

"How awful," Nigh said. "Poor Ann. She was believed to be a suicide and buried outside the churchyard."

"Yes," he said, his mouth in a tight line. "Absolutely no one could believe that a lady like Ann could love an American lout like Danny Longstreet. No one questioned that she'd killed herself rather than marry him."

"Poor Danny. Do you know what happened to him?"

"Stayed drunk for a week, then left Margate with his father and never returned."

"But he supported his child," Nigh said. "And he let it carry his name." Turning, she glanced at Jace, still standing against the wall, still watching her with unblinking intensity. She couldn't read his expression. Was he, in some odd way, jealous that she was talking to another man? Why didn't he come over to be introduced?

Nigh looked back at the young man. "I didn't get your first name."

Abruptly, he stood up. "Your young man is getting impatient, and I must be off. Did you know that you look a bit like Ann?"

"How do you know that? I thought all likenesses of her were destroyed by her father."

"Danny had one and it stayed with him."

"Is it at your house? Do you have it here? I'd very much like to see it."

"Look in Tolben Hall. You'll see it." He glanced over Nigh's shoulder. "The vicar comes. I must go."

Nigh looked back and saw the vicar standing with Jace, his hands full of papers, and looking at her. She lifted her hand to him, then looked back at the young man, but he was gone. Rats! She'd wanted him to meet Jace so they could exchange information. She hurried after him, running to the gate, but she didn't see him. She looked up and down the street, but he wasn't there.

Shrugging, she went back to Jace and the vicar.

"You must be Miss Smythe," the vicar said. "And my name is Innis. I'm told you're researching the people who used to own Tolben Hall."

"Yes," Nigh said, smiling and shaking his hand. "I just met— Ow!" she said when Jace's fingertips bit into her arm.

"Ankle," Jace said when the vicar looked concerned about her yelp of pain. "Father Innis was telling me that no Longstreets live here. Danny and his father came, bought Tolben Hall, then both of them died without issue."

"But I was just—"

"I do thank you for all this," Jace said loudly, cutting Nigh off. "The photocopies will help us a lot, I'm sure of it."

"As I told you, most of what little there is left is at Tolben Hall."

"Yes, Mrs. Fenney said she'd get the box of papers and we could see them today after lunch. By the way, I wondered if there was a place we could get takeout. We'll go back to Tolben Hall to eat."

Nigh said nothing to any of the plans Jace was making without consulting her. It had taken fingertips in her arm and a rude cut-off, but she now realized that Jace didn't want her to mention the young man she'd been talking to. He was a Longstreet, but the vicar said that no Longstreets lived in the village. Was he visiting? On the other hand, the young man had run away as soon as he saw the vicar. What in the world was going on?

She only vaguely listened as the vicar gave Jace directions to a couple of shops where they could get food to take back to the B and B.

As soon as they were out of earshot, she turned on him. "What was that about? Why did you cut me off like that?"

"I didn't want you to talk to the vicar about the man you were talking to."

"But why—? Oh, I see. Secrecy. Keep what we're doing to ourselves, that sort of thing."

"Sort of," he said, not meeting her eyes.

Minutes later, they were walking back through the village and stopping in the different shops and loading up on fruit and chicken pies and bottled juice. They also got some little chocolate cakes filled with cream.

"We're going to get fat," Nigh said, smiling, feeling good because she had lots of information to tell him.

"I think we're going to need the chocolate," he said under his breath. "Endorphins. We'll need them. I think I'll get a bottle of wine—or two or three. Maybe some whiskey. Do you like single malt?"

"No. Too strong for me. What in the world is wrong with you? I mean, I know you're the moodiest person on earth, but—"

"Moody? I'm not moody!"

"No? So tell me why you bought Priory House."

He opened his mouth to speak, then closed it again. "How about gin? Do you like that?"

"Why are you trying to get me drunk?" She wiggled her eyebrows suggestively at him.

"Not for that reason. I just want to calm you down."

"Calm me down from what?"

"Nothing. Forget I said that." He handed his credit card to the wine merchant. "So who were you talking to at the church?"

"A very nice young man. You were rude. Why didn't you come over to be introduced?"

"I didn't want to interrupt you. Who was he?"

She waited until they were on the sidewalk again. "A Longstreet. He's a descendant of Danny Longstreet, and he lives near here."

"Didn't the vicar say that no Longstreets lived in the village?"

"Yes, and I thought that was odd. Even odder was that when the young man saw the vicar he jumped up and ran away. It was almost as though he was afraid of him."

"Or of holy water," Jace mumbled.

"What?"

"Nothing. What did you two talk about?"

They were walking down the road toward Tolben Hall, Jace carrying the heavy packages, Nigh with the lighter ones. "Sex," she said.

Jace didn't smile, but kept his head down, as though he was listening intently to every word she said. "What else? And sex in what context?"

"I believe the term we used was 'raw, rough sex.' "

"What else?" Jace asked solemnly.

Obviously, she thought, she wasn't going to make him jealous, so she gave up. It was nearly a mile walk back to the B and B, and Nigh talked nonstop, telling Jace everything she could think of that the young man had said.

"But you didn't get his full name?"

"I meant to, but I was so fascinated with what he was saying that I forgot to ask. I did ask him if he was a Longstreet and he said yes. I'm sure that if we used the directories on the Internet we could find his address."

"I think I know exactly where he lives," Jace said.

"And how could you know that?"

"It's in the papers I got from the vicar. He photocopied some registers for me that show some deaths."

"What does that have to do with this young man?"

"He, uh . . ." Jace trailed off, not answering her question. "Poor Danny Longstreet. I bet he tried to tell people that Ann had been murdered, but what could he do? Tell them the person who killed Ann was the mother of his child?"

"True," Nigh said. "If he'd sent the woman to the gallows, what would have become of the child? If Danny had taken the child, he might have been in the same situation as Ann's father. The child would remind him of Ann's death."

"There wasn't any good part of any of it," Jace said.

"Poor virgin Ann, and miserable Danny. All because Danny got drunk one night."

"I think everyone except Ann was at fault. She was the only truly innocent person in all of it."

They could see Tolben Hall through the trees.

"So this Longstreet guy said you look like Ann?"

"Yes, and that there's a picture of her somewhere in Tolben Hall."

Jace groaned. "Hidden under floorboards in the closet? Move the shoes, take a screwdriver to the board?"

Nigh looked at him curiously, and when he turned his head away, she was even more curious. "I hope it's hanging on the wall. I saw lots of little Victorian knickknacks around."

"Yes, there are a lot of Victorian things around," he said. "Things *and* people."

14

I don't believe you," Nigh said, glaring at him.

They were in her bedroom at Tolben Hall and spread on the little table were the contents of the box Mrs. Fenney had lent them. There wasn't much in it, just a few business letters from Hugh Longstreet, and a ledger of the cost of running the place for one year. There were no personal papers, no delicious letters of love sent by Ann to Danny.

The only thing of interest was on the very bottom of the box. It was a photo of a young man, leaning against a tree, and looking at the photographer as though he thought the whole world was for his enjoyment.

"That's him," Nigh said, picking up the photo. "I mean, it's not *him,* I know this has to be Danny, but he's a dead ringer for the man I talked to today. The Longstreets have strong genes if they can pass down their looks so completely. It's as if the women of the last few generations had nothing to do with the children."

She handed the photo to Jace. "That looks like him, doesn't it?" When Jace said nothing, Nigh frowned. "You saw him and it looks just like him, doesn't it?"

"I would imagine it looks just like him," Jace said quietly.

"And what is that supposed to mean? You would imagine? What did you *see*?"

Jace smiled at Nigh in a way that she didn't like. "I forgot to ask Mrs. Fenney about Ann's picture. Maybe we should wander about the house and see if we find a picture of someone who looks like you." He got up from his chair and headed for the door, but Nigh didn't move.

"What are you hiding now?" she asked.

Jace looked like he'd rather do anything on earth than sit back down and answer her question. But he sighed, then sat down across from her. "I didn't see anyone," he said, his head down, not wanting to face her.

"You what?" she asked, then she stood up and went to the window. She took a moment before she looked back at him. "I don't like what you're trying to say. Is it possible that you're telling me that I was talking to no one?"

Jace looked up at her and gave her a crooked smile.

"I don't believe you," she said. She advanced on him. "You know what I think? I think you're so obsessed with this whole ghost story that you're desperate to have someone else in it with you. I think you made up the whole thing about seeing Ann and her cousin talking, and now you're trying to make me think I too saw a ghost. I can assure you that the man I talked to at length today was as real as you are. I think—"

"Do you have a reason why I'd do something like that? So I could drum up business for the Ghost Center you made up?"

Nigh started to say something, but could think of no reason why he would make up the ghost story. But then, she knew he was filled with secrets. "I don't know why you'd do such a thing, but I think—"

She broke off as he looked through the papers and pulled out one, then he went to the telephone and dialed a number.

"Who are you calling?" she asked.

"The vicar. If you don't believe me, maybe you'll believe him."

Seconds later, Jace was speaking to Father Innis. "Sorry to bother you again so soon, Father, but my assistant has some questions she'd like to ask you." He handed the phone to Nigh.

With a look of defiance, she took the phone. "Check your sources" had been drummed into her head since she first started as a journalist.

"I wanted to ask you about what you said about there not being any Longstreets in the village," she said. "I read somewhere or heard that there were some Longstreets living in the area."

"Not any that are alive," the vicar said, laughing. "We've had a number of reports that a young man fitting Danny Longstreet's description has often been seen in the churchyard. I didn't want to say anything as I don't like to perpetuate such myths, but now that you've found out . . ."

"I see," Nigh said, and her knees were feeling weak. "Why do you think Danny Longstreet is hanging around here?"

"I have no idea. He only lived at Tolben Hall for a few years, but the locals say that their grandparents told them that he was the unhappiest young man on earth. They say he used to ride his horse up the stairs of Tolben Hall. In fact, the legend is that that's how he died. He got to the top of the stairs on his horse, then fell off, rolled down the stairs, and broke his neck. Dear me! Here I am carrying tales. What was it you wanted to ask me?"

"This morning I was talking to a young man while I was on the bench by the flowers. He left before I could get his name. I wondered if you knew him." Nigh glanced at Jace, but he had his back to her as he looked out the window.

The vicar was silent for quite some time, and when he spoke, his voice was exaggeratedly calm. "I saw you sitting on the bench, your back to us, but I saw no one else." His voice lowered. "Were you talking to Danny? We've had a couple people report that they've talked to him."

"No, of course not," Nigh said. "You're right. I was talking to no one. I, uh . . . thank you so much, Father Innis, you've been a great help. Thank you," she said again, then hung up the phone.

Jace turned to look at her and Nigh stared back. Every moment of that morning, of sitting on the bench with that good-looking young man and talking about his ancestors—and maybe hers too—came back to her. But it hadn't been real. Had he been a ghost? Was that what she was supposed to believe?

She looked at Jace, saw his eyes widen in alarm, then the next second, everything went black.

When Nigh awoke, she was on top of the bed, the cover folded around her; the curtains were drawn and there was a cold washcloth on her forehead. As she tried to sit up, the door to the bathroom opened and Jace came out with another washcloth.

"Be still," he said, coming to sit by her on the bed as he changed washcloths.

"I don't want this," she said, pulling the thing off and trying to sit up. But she was woozy and dizzy and she fell back onto the bed.

She looked at Jace. "How long have I been here?"

"About four hours," he said, and when she tried to get up again, he put his hand on her shoulder to stop her. "The vicar sent the local doctor and he gave you a sedative. You're going to be out of it at least until tomorrow morning."

"Doctor? Sedative?" Slowly, she began to remember what she'd been told just before the world turned black. "Danny Longstreet," she whispered. "I sat and talked to a ghost." She put her hands over her face and began to cry.

Jace pulled her into his arms and stroked her back and hair as she cried.

"Why aren't *you* afraid of ghosts?" she asked, sobbing into his shoulder. "And why can I handle bombs but not ghosts? What do they want of you? Of me?"

"You look like Ann and you're related to her," Jace said softly. "I would imagine Danny wanted to be near anyone who was part of the woman he loved."

"But they never contacted me in all the time I was in Margate," Nigh said. "I was in that house many, many times, but I never saw a ghost."

"I think you felt Ann. I think she took care of you, looked after you."

His words and the truth of them made her cry harder for a moment, then the tears began to lessen. Jace gave her a handful of tissues from the box by the bed.

"Do they want us to do something for them? Find out something?" Nigh asked as she blew her nose. "Why are they appearing to us?"

"And why are they giving us information?" Jace asked. He put her back on the pillows, but stayed sitting by her on the bed. "Does it seem odd to you that you and I are together? I mean, I own Priory House, and you're a descendant of Ann Stuart. And now we're together and we've both seen ghosts."

"At least you dreamed them," Nigh said, "so you can stay sane. I was talking to a dead man in broad daylight."

"What do we know about ghosts?" Jace asked. "How do we find out more?"

Nigh blew her nose again. "We don't know anything because ghosts don't exist. I see those shows on TV and all people have are feelings, they *feel* ghosts. If they see one, it's just as a light. They do *not* sit on a bench and chat with them. You saw me there, talking away to nobody. You must have thought I was insane."

"I had an idea of what was going on. It was a been-there-done-that situation. My concern was if something bad happened."

"You mean like Ann did to you, of nearly killing you?"

"Exactly."

"I guess Danny could have carried me off on his horse." For a moment she put her hands over her face again, then looked up. "This village should have danger signs posted. 'Warning! You might be accosted by a ghost seeking his long-lost love. In case of terror, see the doctor.' "

Jace gave a snort of laughter. "In Margate you put a bogus article in a tiny local newspaper and we were deluged by people wanting in on it. Imagine what it would be like if you told a . . . excuse me . . . reporter that you'd sat on a bench and had a long conversation with someone who wasn't there."

"I don't want to imagine it," she said. "By the way, thanks for not letting me blurt out all that . . . that Danny and I had talked about."

"You're welcome. I don't think the people here want more

ghost sightings spread around. It seems that so many people have seen Danny that the local GP is often called in."

"And he has barbiturates at the ready. Rather like keeping snakebite venom in a herpetarium."

Jace smiled. "I think you'll be okay if you have your sense of humor back. I spent some time with the doctor and the vicar and—"

"Who else knows?" she asked. "Did you call my editor in London? Is it on CNN that a war correspondent was felled by the sight of a handsome ghost in a village in England?"

"You didn't tell me he was handsome," Jace said as he moved to stand at the foot of the bed, then smiled when she started to defend herself. "I have orders from the doctor to give you what you want to eat for dinner and to talk about what you saw or not talk about it, depending on whatever you want to do."

"Anything to keep me from going insane, is that it?" She looked at him in speculation. "It seems to me that *I* reacted in a normal way after seeing a ghost."

"If passing out is normal, then I hope I'm never around another person who sees a ghost," he said.

"My point exactly," she said as he poured her a glass of water. "I'm normal. I reacted with hysteria and totally collapsed. But you didn't. You saw a ghost but you didn't freak out. Why?"

He handed her the glass of water, but when her hand trembled, he sat by her and held it to her lips. When she'd finished, she again asked, "Why?"

Jace walked to the window and opened the curtain a bit. It was dark outside. He turned back to her. "I think maybe I'm closer to death than you are," he said softly.

Nigh's eyes widened. "You're ill, aren't you? Is that your big secret?" Her eyes again filled with tears.

"No," he said, smiling. "I'm not ill, but thanks for your concern." He paused for a moment, as though debating about what to say. "I had someone I loved very much die, and since then, I haven't really rejoined the living. Maybe these spirits feel that."

She blinked at him. "You want to contact the person who died, don't you?" she asked softly. "That's why you made the room to look like Ann's. You wanted to, as you said, entice her to come back because you wanted to ask her questions. Is that it?"

"Yes." He smiled in a way that made Nigh think that he was relieved to have told her so much.

"I think maybe you're assuming too much," she said, and she could feel the investigative reporter in her rising to the surface. "When I meet people in other countries I'm often asked if I know so-and-so in England. They'll say, 'I met a man from England once, maybe you know him'."

"I get that about the U.S. So what's the point?"

"Do all the ghosts on this planet know each other? Do they know everyone who has died?"

"I don't know," Jace said, anger rising in his voice. "I don't know any more about this than anyone else. What I do know is that I can't hurt a ghost. I wish I could fall in love with Ann Stuart. I wish I could wed her and bed her and have children with her. I wish I could fill that huge house with little spirit children who would live forever and never die."

With his anger spent, he sat down on the end of the bed, his face ragged from his emotion. Nigh tossed back the covers and went to him and put her arms around him, her head on his shoulder. "I'm sorry for whatever has happened to you," she said. "I'm deeply and truly sorry."

He patted her hand. "Look, I think I'd better go. I apologize for my outburst. There are sandwiches on the table and Mrs. Fenney said she'd bring up a pot of tea in about a half hour."

"What about you?" she asked.

"I'm fine," he said as he stood up. "I may go into the village to get something to eat. I don't know."

"You're going to go to the church, aren't you?" she said. "You're going to go sit on that bench and ask Danny Longstreet to come to you."

"I . . . uh," he said as he moved toward the door. "I think you'll be fine now. The doctor said you'd be weak for a while, but you'll be all right. After a good night's sleep, maybe all this will seem like a dream. Maybe you won't remember much of it. Good night," he said, then left the room.

As soon as he was gone, the room seemed huge and very dark and very empty. If Jace was gone and Mrs. Fenney was in the opposite side of the house and there were no other guests, she was alone. It took some strength on her part to get out of the bed. Her legs were wobbly and weak, but she managed to go to the bathroom, then to turn on every light she could find. She didn't want to be in the dark.

She ate half a chicken sandwich, drank a bottle of water, took a quick bath, and changed into her new nightgown. Mrs. Fenney didn't show up with the pot of tea and that made Nigh worry that the woman was as afraid as she was.

It was still early when Nigh got back into bed. She felt as tired as if she'd climbed a mountain. She wanted to go to Jace's room to see if he'd returned, but she didn't think she had the strength.

She got into bed, all the lights still on, and images came to her. Talking to a man who'd died over a hundred years ago. "What did he want?" kept going 'round and 'round in her head.

Over and over. What *do* they want? By "they" she meant Ann and Danny and Jace. What did Jace want? To say good-bye to the person he'd loved so much? To talk to her—and Nigh was sure it was a "her"—one last time?

It was difficult for her to fall asleep with all the thoughts in her mind and with all the lights on. She saw headlights through the curtains and her heart jumped into her throat. The bright lights moving across the room seemed ghostly, eerie. She squeezed her eyes tightly shut.

She didn't know what time it was when she awoke, but the lights were out and the room was dark. Immediately, she was afraid, but a big, strong hand stroked her cheek. "Ssssh," a voice she'd come to know well said. "Everything is all right. Be still and rest." She felt the warmth of a strong body near hers, felt strong arms around her. She smiled and went back to sleep.

When she awoke in the morning, the curtains were open and sunlight was streaming into the room. She remembered what had happened yesterday, but it no longer seemed so clear to her, and certainly not terrifying.

She took a shower, washed her hair, dried, dressed, put on makeup, and hurried down the stairs. She felt like she could eat one of Mrs. Fenney's fry-ups.

Jace was at the breakfast table. He looked clean and he'd shaved, but his eyes looked haggard and worn.

"You look like you're the one who saw the ghost," she said brightly, but her joke fell flat because Jace didn't smile.

"I think you should leave here today," he said over his teacup. "I think you've seen more than enough."

In spite of what she'd been through, she didn't want to leave. "We haven't found Ann's portrait," she said. "Danny said it was here."

Her eyes widened as she looked at Jace in wonder. "Did I just say that? Dead Danny told me where a picture was and I mention it as though I'd just talked to him on the phone."

Jace reached across the table and picked up a folder. In it was a photograph of a pretty young woman wearing a dark dress with a bustle, à la the 1870s. Her hair was pulled tightly back from her face and piled in shiny loops on the back of her neck. She was a slender woman and looked to be tall. As Jace said, if she were alive today, she could have been a model.

"I am flattered that anyone thinks I look like her," Nigh said.

"We see her as beautiful today, but I don't think she was considered beautiful then. She was too tall and too thin. And her face wasn't demure enough."

"You mean that Ann looked much too sexy."

"Yes," he said, taking the picture from her.

Nigh went to the sideboard and filled a bowl with cereal and added milk. She sat back at the table and poured herself a cup of tea. "Where did you get that picture?"

"Mrs. Fenney had a box full of old photos. After Danny died, the house and contents were sold, but no one bothered with emptying the attic, so a lot of things stayed in the house."

"What happened to the money from the sale?"

"It all went to pay Danny's debts." Jace was pushing his eggs around on his plate. He hadn't eaten much of Mrs. Fenney's full English breakfast. "I think Danny knew he was going to die so he gave away a lot of money to charities, then he lived on credit for four years. Last night I talked to some man who is the village historian and he said the money worked out almost perfectly. The sale of the house and furniture exactly paid off what Danny owed."

"You think he committed suicide, don't you?" she asked softly.

He looked up at her. "I think that after Ann died, Danny didn't want to go on living. He knew that her death was his fault. If he hadn't been drunk and impregnated some village girl, she wouldn't have killed Ann. How do you live with the knowledge that you've killed the person you love most in the world?"

His words were so heartfelt that she reached out to touch his hand, but he pulled back.

"Nigh?" he said.

"Yes?" She sensed that he had something serious to say and she held her breath.

"You've been a great help to me in these last days and a great companion, but from now on, I need to work by myself. I checked and there's train service from here to Margate. You only have to make one transfer. You can be at home, safe in your own house, by this afternoon."

She didn't know whether to be angry or hurt by his words. Anger won out. "I freaked out in a normal way about having talked to a ghost, so now I'm being thrown out."

He looked directly into her eyes. "Yes," he said. "That's it exactly. You aren't much use to me as a research assistant if I have to call a doctor because you've had a fainting spell, and if I have to sit up with you all night. I wanted someone who could actually help me with what I'm doing, but you're much too cowardly to be of any use. I want you to go back to Margate and I want you to stay away from Priory House. No more snooping in my house.

I'll have the entrance to the tunnel sealed shut. Am I making my-self clear?"

"Very," Nigh said, then she got up and left the dining room. Ten minutes later, she was packed.

Mrs. Fenney was downstairs and ready to drive her to the train station. "I'm so sorry about this," she said. "Our village ghost hasn't appeared to anyone in years, so we thought maybe he'd gone to his heavenly reward, but the vicar said you spent some time with him."

All Nigh could do was nod. She was too angry to do much more.

They drove the four miles to the station in silence and when they got there, Mrs. Fenney handed her the tickets. They were for first class.

"Mr. Montgomery said I was to ask if you needed anything and I was to give you this." It was an envelope that she knew contained cash.

"I don't want—" she began, planning to refuse the money. She'd eat when she got home.

Mrs. Fenney took Nigh's hands in hers. "You shouldn't be angry at him, dear. He's been sick with worry about you. He stayed out late last night and I was told that he talked to the doc-tor about you, and the vicar, and he visited our local historian. When he got back I had to unlock the front door for him and I happen to know that he stayed in your room last night. He looked after you. He must love you very much."

"No," Nigh said. "He—" She broke off. She didn't want to tell this woman her private problems. "Thank you," she said. "Thank you for everything. You have a lovely home and the food was excellent."

"I'm glad you enjoyed part of your visit," she said, starting to shout because the train was pulling into the station.

Nigh hefted her bag onto her shoulder and started toward the train. "Take care of him, will you? And keep those blood puddings away."

Mrs. Fenney smiled. "They never hurt my husband," she said.

"Ah, but where is he now?" Nigh asked as she climbed onto the platform.

"He's in Alaska working on an oil rig," Mrs. Fenney called as the train started to move.

Nigh laughed and waved, then went to find her seat.

15

Nigh got the greengrocer's son to give her a ride from the train station to her house. He didn't shut up for the whole ride.

"I tell you, Nigh, you are the most exciting thing that has ever happened to this village. I know that people think it's Priory House and all the ghosts those people see, but my money's on you. First you run off the day after your mother's funeral, and the next time we see you you're on the telly reading the news and the next time we see you're in—Where was it?"

"Afghanistan."

"Right. I knew it was some place really foreign. You know how some places are more foreign than others? Australia is foreign but not really foreign. You know what I mean? Maybe it's the language. And the States are foreign, but not really. Although, ol' Harris at the butcher's says that the States are the most foreign of all. You know what I mean? But, anyway, I think anybody would agree that Afghanistan is about as foreign as you get. You know? So, anyway, there you are and there you've been and everybody's lost count of all the places you've been. So then this rich American shows up and first thing we know, you and he have run off together. 'But how could they?' everybody says because you wrote that awful stuff about him in the paper. No offense, Nigh, but if my girlfriend wrote anything like that about me, she wouldn't be my girlfriend no more. You know what I mean? But maybe Harris is right that Americans are the most foreign because you two run off God only knows where to together just like you was regular lovebirds. Mrs. B. said the two of you spent a whole day together in that haunted bedroom, didn't even come out for lunch. Then you run off together and the next thing we hear is you made up the whole thing and there's not gonna be any industry in the village and we could have used some industry here, if you know what I mean. So where'd you and that American go, if you don't mind my askin'?"

They were at last at her house. Nigh opened the car door, said thanks for the ride, and got out.

"If you get tired of foreigners, you know where I live," he called to her through the open window.

"Yeah, I know what you mean," Nigh said, gave a wave, then hurried into her house and shut the door behind her. She paused only a second to listen to the quiet, then she went into the kitchen to put the kettle on. It hadn't even come to a boil when she heard her friend Kelly's voice. The only thing in the world she wanted at that moment was to be alone to collect her thoughts.

Nigh managed to put a smile on her face as Kelly came into the kitchen. "Kelly, dear, how nice to see you."

"Don't give me that crap!" she said, tossing her bag on the kitchen table. "I could wring your neck! Everybody in town has been asking me what you're up to and I've had to say—truthfully, mind you—that I have no idea. When you were in Afghanistan, you sent me a video letter telling me everything. When you were in Saudi, you sent me twelve postcards. You've called me from some places that I couldn't find on the map. But now you return home and what happens? You disappear. And not only do you disappear, you do it with some man nobody knows anything about. Where the *hell* have you *been*?"

The answer to Kelly's question was so long and complicated that Nigh didn't know where to begin—or if she even wanted to. She was silent as she filled the teapot, got some digestive biscuits out of the cupboard, and put them on a plate.

While Kelly poured the tea and put in the milk, she kept glancing at her friend. When she spoke again, her voice was calmer. "You look like you've been to hell and back."

"To hell, but certainly not back," Nigh said.

"So where is he?"

Nigh shrugged. "In a village in Hampshire."

"You spent the night together? What happened? Did you quarrel and split up?" She put her hand over Nigh's. "I'm sorry. But maybe it's for the best. Maybe—"

"Could you think a little higher than below the belt?" Nigh snapped. "First of all, I didn't run away with him. If you remember, the whole village was going crazy because they thought a Ghost Center was going to be opened and they wanted in on it."

"But that's what you wrote, isn't it?"

"At the time, that's what I thought he was going to do. It's what I was told."

"Who told you that?"

Nigh shook her head. "That doesn't matter now. That was so long ago I can hardly remember it."

"It was three days ago," Kelly said.

"Three days can be a lifetime."

Kelly drank her tea and ate a biscuit as she looked at her friend. "So tell me everything."

"No," Nigh said. "I can't." She put up her hand when Kelly started to speak. "It's not that I won't tell you, it's because I don't know anything to tell you."

"Are you trying to make me believe that you spent days with this man and didn't ferret out every secret he had, including the whereabouts of the secret box he had when he was a kid?"

"I don't know anything more about him now than I did before I met him. Oh, I know where he grew up and the names of some of his cousins. I know lots of unimportant things, but I don't know what's driving him. I don't even know why he bought Priory House."

"For the ghosts. Mrs. B. has told everyone how he made up the haunted room to look like a Victorian set. Of course everyone says Americans know nothing about history because they have none of their own, or he would know that Lady Grace did *not* live in Victorian times. Somebody should help him get his time periods right."

"Stop it!" Nigh said, her hands over her ears. "I am sick of hearing gossip! I am sick of people making up stories about something they know nothing about."

Kelly didn't say anything and when Nigh looked at her she was serious.

"You're right," Kelly said. "I've become one of them. I've sunk so low that I've begun to listen to that harridan, Mrs. Browne. I apologize. If you talk, I will listen, and what you tell me won't go any further than this room. If you want, I'll even spread false rumors so people won't know the truth. Come to think of it, I might enjoy that."

Nigh took her friend's hand. "You're a good friend to me, and I want you to continue to be a good friend."

"That means you plan to tell me nothing."

"Right," Nigh said. "But I want you to give me some information."

"On one condition."

"What?"

"You get me George Clooney's autograph. And it has to be made out to Kelly. I don't want just an anonymous signature."

"Are you crazy? I don't do celebrity interviews."

"I saw on TV that George Clooney and his father went to some country like you go to and—"

"Okay, I promise that if I'm in some war-torn country and I happen to bump into Mr. Clooney and Mr. Clooney, I will ask George to sign a piece of shrapnel to Kelly. Satisfied now?"

"Perfectly. So what do you want to know?"

"Everything you know, and can find out, about Clive Sefton."

Kelly's face mirrored her disappointment. "That's it?"

"What I really want to know is what to do to make him reveal secrets to me. I'll do anything except have sex with him. I'll even cook for him."

"I'm sure that will make him talk," Kelly said in sarcasm.

"You know what I mean," Nigh said, then laughed.

"What?"

"The greengrocer's son drove me back from the station."

"Oh," Kelly groaned. "That boy can talk, can't he?"

"The last time I saw him, he was just a kid."

"You've been away a long time."

"I feel like I've been here longer than I've been away." Nigh ran her hand over her face. "Mr. Montgomery is so afraid of something or someone in this town that I can't get a word out of him. I really need to know what it is."

"It's ghosts," Kelly said. "Anyone in their right mind is afraid of ghosts. If I saw one I'd—"

"Pass out, and a doctor would come and administer a sedative that would keep you flat on your back for most of twenty-four hours."

"Tell me you're not saying that from experience."

"I won't tell you," Nigh said. "Now, would you mind going to find out what you can? I'd ask questions myself, but . . ."

"The sight of you would cause a riot. People are torn between being furious and being glad that Margate isn't going to become famous for its lady highwayman ghost. What's funny?"

"It's just that I'm not sure there ever was a lady highwayman ghost. However, I know for absolute certain that there're a couple of Victorian ghosts running around loose."

"Then your American isn't so uneducated after all."

"No," Nigh said, smiling, "he's not uneducated or dumb, and he doesn't want to turn Priory House into a place for tourists." Her head came up. "Kelly? Do the MacFarlands still have that dreadful little dog that pees on people?"

"Yes, but they keep it penned up in their back garden."

"Would you like to do something really awful for me?"

"Love to."

"Do Lewis and Ray still have lunch together every day outside the fire station?"

"Haven't changed in ten years that I know of." Kelly and Nigh had been best friends since they were three years old and there were many times when they could read each other's minds. "Wait! Don't tell me. They were the skunks that told you lies about the American. And you believed them?"

Nigh shrugged in embarrassment.

"Okay. I'll take care of them. I'm sure the MacFarlands would love to lend me their dog. I assume I get to tell them why. A truck full of Londoners ran over one of Mrs. MacFarland's flowerbeds, so she'll be glad to help."

"Sounds good to me. Now go so I can do some work. I have some things to figure out. Call me the minute you find out anything."

"I'll unload the kids onto James tonight and come over with everything. I'll bring dinner."

"Perfect," Nigh said as she ushered her friend out the door.

The house was quiet once again and she planned to spend the rest of the day writing down everything she could remember about Jace Montgomery. He hadn't told her much, but she might be able to piece together something. It had been on the train that she'd realized that the only reason he would send her away was if he was afraid for her. Since she knew that he wasn't afraid of the two ghosts who had been in love with each other for over a century, it was something else and Nigh meant to find out what it was.

16

Kelly called at seven and said she couldn't get away, but that Emma Carew knew "everything."

"What does that mean?" Nigh asked.

"I don't know. George said that Clive and your Montgomery had their heads together for nearly an hour one night and they were talking very seriously about something."

"What led up to their getting together?" Nigh asked.

"George said he couldn't remember, but you know George, if it isn't politics, he isn't interested. He said Emma and Clive were in some argument, then Montgomery dragged Clive off into a corner. George said to talk to Emma."

"I hope you didn't tell them it was me who wanted to know."

"Certainly not! I told them I hadn't seen you. Sorry, but I have to live here and your name is mud right now."

Nigh hung up the phone, wondering why she had left the relative peace of the Middle East.

She'd made a list of all she knew about Jace Montgomery's activities since he arrived, and was trying to figure out the real reason he'd bought Priory House. She was certain of two things. One was that he hadn't bought the house because he loved it and wanted to live there forever. The second was that he wasn't there for the ghosts. For him, the ghosts were a means to something else, the something that had made him say he was "close to death."

She made an outline of where he'd been and who he'd met, as best she could. Jace had told her some things and she'd heard the others. She'd been told that he had met "the three," Mrses. Browne, Wheeler, and Parsons. Growing up, the children of the village had outdone themselves in adding to the names. Terrible Three. Horrible Three, etc. Kelly won by calling them the Three Gorgons.

Whatever their names, the women thought they were the rulers of Margate. They had known each other since they were children and had been fast friends, equally involved in telling everything there was to know about everybody else—all while keeping their own lives secret. Not that they had much that people wanted to know about, but what there was was private. Mrs. Browne's husband had been killed in some war—some people said it was WWI—and she'd come back with a baby and needed a job. She'd been at Priory House ever since. Her daughter had fled the town when she was eighteen and had never been seen or heard from again.

Mrs. Parsons's husband had died only last year, and he had the reputation of being the most henpecked man on earth. She used to boss him about in the stationer's shop as though he were a slave. Mrs. Wheeler had been born in Margate as Agnes Harkens. She'd left with her parents when she was sixteen and returned when she was twenty-three with the title of Mrs. Wheeler. She had no parents, no husband, no children, but she did have enough money that she bought a house on the main street and opened what she called a "historical library." She was as formidable at twenty-three as she was at her present age, and no one had dared ask her what had happened to her parents or her husband.

The three women had renewed their childhood friendship and had reigned over Margate for half a century. There wasn't anything that went on that they didn't tell each other and the town about.

Nigh found out that Jace had been subjected to the New House Treatment by the three. He'd been sold a lot of expensive notebooks and pens by Mrs. Parsons and had been lent the Priory House box by Mrs. Wheeler.

As Nigh looked at her list, she had an idea that maybe Jace had seen something disturbing at the library.

Yawning, she went to bed. For a while she lay awake, fearful that she'd see Danny Longstreet again, but all was quiet and she closed her eyes. She dreamed of Jace, saw him laughing as he pulled vines away from the stone round. She seemed to see him laughing everywhere.

When she awoke it was 8:00 a.m. and the sun was out. Her energy had returned and she was more determined than ever to find out what Jace Montgomery was hiding.

She drove her Mini around the back of Margate, not wanting to drive down the high street, and parked behind the library. She knew that it wasn't open until nine, but she also knew that Mrs. Wheeler was there at seven. She knocked on the back door.

"I'm not open yet," Mrs. Wheeler said in her imperious voice as she opened the door, ready to tell the person what she thought of him. "Oh, it's you."

"Yes, it's me. Do you mind if I do a little private research? I won't bother you." Subservience often worked with Mrs. Wheeler.

"All right," she said grudgingly, but Nigh could see that she was pleased. After all, Nigh was the local celebrity. "I don't have much on the Middle East, if that's what you want." She lowered her voice. "I do have some things on Cornwall."

Nigh was puzzled, then she looked at her in conspiracy. "Are they smuggling down there again?"

"That's not for me to say," Mrs. Wheeler said, but she let Nigh know that she knew something no one else did.

"Is that where you lived in those years you were away from Margate?" Nigh asked innocently as she got her pad and pen out of her bag, as though she was going to record whatever the woman revealed to her.

As she knew she would, Mrs. Wheeler backed off. "What can I help you with?" she asked coldly.

"I'm researching our newest resident, Mr. Montgomery."

"Ah," Mrs. Wheeler said, and began to warm up. "Now there is an odd man. Not that I carry tales, but Mrs. Browne tells me of the very strangest things that go on with him." She looked Nigh up and down. "But then you should know. You've spent a great deal of time with him."

"A true reporter must make sacrifices," Nigh said.

"Ah, yes, I see what you mean."

Nigh worked to keep from grimacing. She knew that yet another gossip story would soon be all over town. Would it be told that Nigh had just been trying to get a story out of Jace? "What I want to know is if Mr. Montgomery looked at anything besides information about Priory House when he was in here last week."

"Actually, he did," Mrs. Wheeler said. "As you well know, for years, that man Hatch has refused to enter anything from Priory House in the annual garden competition. Mrs. Browne and I, as well as Mrs. Parsons, think it's irresponsible of him. Mr. Montgomery seems to want to change that."

"Change the garden contest?"

"At least make Priory House enter it. I know that the entire village is tired of hearing how Hatch's plants would win over everyone else's. I think there should be a fair competition and—"

"Could I see the article Mr. Montgomery was looking at?" Nigh asked, interrupting what was sure to be an hours-long tirade. She didn't know what Jace had been reading, but she'd put money on it that it wasn't about the local garden contest.

"Here it is," Mrs. Wheeler said, handing Nigh the roll of microfilm.

There was a lot on one roll of film and since Nigh didn't know what she was looking for, it took her nearly two hours to find it. It was a small article that took up little space compared to the pages of news about the coming garden contest, which was the biggest event of the year in Margate.

It was a report of a suicide of a beautiful young American woman. Had it been the suicide of a local, it would have been given the front page. But the people of Margate didn't like to think that an outsider would come to their village and use it for unpleasant purposes. There was a time when Margate wasn't as clean and "pure" as it was now, and people wanted to forget that time. The old pub, with its unsavory characters, was gone. The

Carews had bought the pub and made it for families. Everyone was embarrassed that such an awful thing had happened in their village.

Nigh punched the buttons to make copies of both entries about the suicide, then paid Mrs. Wheeler for them and left the library. She had to promise to talk to Mr. Montgomery about making Hatch enter the contest. "He can make Hatch do things about as well as he can make Mrs. Browne do them," Nigh muttered as she went to her car and left the articles. Then she walked to the pub.

As she hoped, Emma Carew was there alone, getting ready to open for lunch at eleven. When she saw Nigh, she unlocked the door and put the kettle on.

"I know this couldn't be a social call, so how can I help you?" Emma asked.

"Am I that transparent?"

"The whole town has been abuzz with your running off with that gorgeous Montgomery. So how is he in bed? Fantastic, right?"

"I haven't been to bed with him."

Emma looked at Nigh in disbelief. "But everyone said—"

"What do they know? He's been doing some research and I've been helping him. It's all business."

"Too bad. And I'm disappointed in you. A big-city girl like you, I would have thought that you . . ." She trailed off, then shrugged. "Sometimes my imagination gets the better of me. So what can I help you with?"

"Is this between us?" Nigh asked.

"Sure. I like to hear the gossip, but I don't spread it. For instance, I won't disappoint all the women in this town and tell them you haven't been to bed with that beautiful man. They wanted to hear details."

Nigh smiled. "It's kind of you to keep my secret. I was told that Mr. Montgomery and Clive Sefton spent some time together here talking. Do you know what it was about?"

Emma looked over her shoulder to see if anyone was behind her, then leaned toward Nigh and lowered her voice. "I can't let George hear me because he'll go ballistic. He's threatened to ban Clive if he mentions the incident again. Well, not incident, but the death."

"The suicide," Nigh said.

"Exactly. Clive thinks it was murder, but that's impossible. We were here in the pub, working, and the woman took sleeping pills and killed herself. I told Clive that she'd been crying and I think she was miserable. Besides, her mother and sister came here and showed us papers about the girl. She'd had a lot of mental problems."

"So why does Clive think she didn't commit suicide?"

"Two things," Emma said in disgust as she poured two cups of tea. "One is that she looked happy as a corpse, and second, she tripped on the stairs."

"Tripped on the stairs?"

Emma told Nigh Clive's theory about how the stairs had been changed, so he knew that the young woman had been to the pub before.

"What if she had been here before?" Nigh asked. "Maybe she was unhappy, wanted to die, and this was a familiar place."

"That's exactly what I said!" Emma said.

"But Clive didn't believe you."

"Hardheaded, he is. And I think he deeply disliked the girl's mother and sister, who came over from the States. He didn't like that they showed up with papers saying the girl was mentally unwell, but I thought that was wise of them. It took away any doubts the rest of us had about why she'd done it."

"The newspapers said she'd had a fight with her boyfriend. Did you meet him?"

"He didn't show up at all. I heard he was in London. Couldn't have cared too much about her, could he? He was in London but didn't bother to come to Margate, but her mother and sister flew in from the States. That told me what he was like. She should have put pills in *his* drink, not her own."

Emma sipped her tea. "Why this sudden interest in this? Clive has never stopped talking about it, then this man Montgomery comes in here and says he wants to write English murder mysteries and did we know any. Clive starts on the suicide and they move to a booth and talk for an hour. Is it true that Montgomery wants to write?"

"Yes, I think so." Nigh was thinking about the suicide and wondering what else she could find out about it.

"He should write about the lady highwayman," Emma said. "Did you know that when that movie came out it was the most watched movie in English history?"

"No, I didn't know that," Nigh said, uninterested. She cared as much about Lady Grace as Jace did, which was not at all.

"So how is he?"

"Who?" Nigh asked.

"Mr. Montgomery. The man who is the topic of all conversation in the village. Him. You know, the man you spent days with but didn't bed. That man."

"I haven't seen him in days."

"The greengrocer's son said he brought you back from the station late yesterday afternoon."

"He's grown, hasn't he?"

"His mouth has grown. I can see that you don't plan to tell me anything."

"Sorry, Emma, but I have a lot on my mind. I have to go."

"If I were you, I'd hide out for a while. People in town are a bit angry with you over the Ghost Center thing."

"Big mistake on my part. Sorry. Thanks for the tea."

Nigh left the pub and went to the parking lot behind the library. She sat in her car for a while, looking at her notebook, reading what she'd written. She reread the copies she'd made of the facts about the suicide.

She wasn't sure and had no proof, but she felt sure that Jace was the boyfriend mentioned in the article. Is that what he was so sad about, that he'd caused a woman to commit suicide? Or had he tried to save her and failed? Had he tried to save her even though she'd had a history of mental problems?

Nigh leaned her head back and closed her eyes. She remembered how Jace had taken care of her after she'd found out she'd been talking to a ghost. He'd taken charge and known exactly what to do. She knew that he'd spent the night with her. She was sedated but she knew she hadn't dreamed him beside her.

If Jace was such a caring man, maybe he'd taken on a mentally disturbed woman and tried to keep her from harming herself. But he'd failed. She'd killed herself anyway.

But Clive didn't think she had committed suicide.

"Read between the lines," she'd heard her editor say a hundred times. "Read what they're not saying."

She looked back at the two articles taken from the newspaper and read them again. Emma had raised a good question. If her fiancé was in London, why wasn't he called? Nigh smiled because she realized that it was all right there. Ralph had written the story, and now he might be the editor of only a village newspaper, but before he retired he'd worked in Edinburgh on a big paper for all his working life. He knew how to report the facts.

The fiancé in London wasn't called because they didn't have his name or number, Nigh thought. They had called whomever Stacy Evans listed in her passport as who to call in an emergency. Nigh imagined Jace in London, looking for his fiancée, being frantic about her, while her mother and sister were flying in from the United States.

So why didn't *they* call Jace? He was never seen in Margate. Clive had never met him, so he was never connected with Miss Stacy Evans.

As Nigh went over the articles again, she began to get a clearer picture of what had happened. If there was one thing she knew about Jace Montgomery, it was that he wasn't hard to talk to. A man who was open to ghosts and the extraordinary things that had happened to him since he'd arrived in Margate wasn't a man who'd force some woman to marry him.

Nigh would like to go to Ralph's house and ask him questions, but he'd taught her that when it comes to reporting there is no such thing as "off the record." If she expressed doubt about a suicide, Ralph would probably report it in the next issue. And worse, Ralph would probably figure out that there was a connection between the suicide and the man everyone in Margate seemed to think Nigh was having an affair with.

"I wish," she said out loud as she turned the key in the ignition. She glanced in the rearview mirror to see if anyone was behind her, then froze. Standing on the grass, on the other side of the pavement, was Danny Longstreet. He was smiling at her, and when she looked at him in the mirror he raised his hand in a wave. He had on his riding clothes, an outfit that hadn't changed much in many years, but she could see now that it was different, old-fashioned, out of date.

Quickly, she turned to look out the back window. She saw

nothing. There was no one there, just the grass, a wire fence, then the pasture beyond.

She put her hands over her face and sat there for a moment. Danny Longstreet had followed her to Margate. Would he follow her to her house? Haunt her? Was she going to live in fear of seeing ghosts everywhere she turned?

She took a deep breath, then opened her car door and got out. She marched across the parking lot to the grassy patch where she'd seen Danny. "I'm not going to stand for this," she said out loud. "I am *not* Ann Stuart! Do you hear me? I may look like her and be a distant cousin, but I'm not her. Ann is at Priory House and I suggest you go there *now!* Do you hear me? Oh!" she said. "Good morning, Mrs. Vernon. Looks to be a nice day."

The woman scurried past Nigh as quickly as she could.

"You heard me and I mean it!" she said under her breath, then got back in her car.

Jace wandered about Priory House for most of a day. After he sent Nigh to the train station yesterday, he'd gone to the local library and tried to find out more about Danny Longstreet, but there was nothing. Everywhere he turned, he was told that Mrs. Fenney and Tolben Hall had everything. At last he had to face it: There just wasn't much about Danny or his father.

He spent another night at Tolben Hall, but left early the next morning, without having Mrs. Fenney's fry-up. He stopped at a roadside restaurant and had a bowl of sticks and twigs cereal and whole wheat toast, but ate only half of it. When the pretty waitress asked him if he'd like something else, he almost told her to fry the bread, but he didn't.

He drove back to Margate, arriving just as the sun was coming up, and the sight of the ugly old house depressed him. He'd never liked it, never wanted it.

He managed to bypass Mrs. Browne and get to the chintz room without being seen. But as he looked about the room, he suddenly hated the way it was a reproduction of Ann's room. He hated the wallpaper that had cost him so much, hated the Victorian furniture. In fact, at the moment, he seemed to hate everything.

He went to the closet, unscrewed the floorboard, and took out Stacy's photo. For the first time since her death, he didn't feel as close to her, didn't feel as though she was in the room with him.

He looked out the window toward the village and thought he saw a streak of yellow. Maybe it was Nigh's outrageously bright Mini Cooper that she drove at breakneck speed, careening around corners.

For a moment he smiled at the memory of being with her while she drove his Rover across rocks, a fallen tree limb, down a creek bed, then back up the side of it at an angle that had made his stomach clench. When she'd first started driving, he'd been terrified, but when he saw that she knew what she was doing, he kept his fears to himself. He held on and gave her the respect that such driving deserved.

Last night at Tolben Hall he should have been going back through the papers in the box about the Longstreets. Maybe he'd missed something. Maybe there was something important in there that he hadn't seen.

But, instead, what did he do? Hooked his computer up to a land line and went on the Internet to read about N. A. Smythe, the reporter. He saw a short video of her in the Middle East, and winced when a bomb went off not far from her. He read half a dozen accounts of the cameraman who'd been killed while standing beside her. After that happened, there were few articles about her or by her. She'd been quoted as saying that she needed to take some time off, then there was nothing.

He'd gone to bed at midnight and dreamed of the kind of things Nigh must have seen. He awoke at four, dreaded the long wait until breakfast was served, but then decided not to wait. He left Mrs. Fenney a note and crept out at five.

On the long drive back to Margate, Jace thought about how much he'd enjoyed the trip down when Nigh was with him. He was sure she'd noticed that he refused to talk about the time he'd known Stacy.

There was a part of him that wanted to talk about Stacy, wanted to ask Nigh her opinion. But he knew he couldn't do that. If he was right and someone had murdered Stacy, that person could still be living in Margate. The person who had sent Stacy the note to meet him at Priory House could still be in the village. He hadn't met anyone who she might like, but—

He had a thought so startling that he nearly ran off the road. What about Jerry Longstreet? Maybe he was the reason his ancestor, Danny, had appeared to Nigh. Maybe Danny knew that Jerry had killed Stacy. Maybe—

So many thoughts went through Jace's head that he had to make an effort to watch his driving.

When he got back to Priory House, he was bursting with questions, but who to ask? If he asked Mrs. Browne, he was sure she'd say that it was none of her business—then she'd call one of her awful women friends and tell them that Jace was asking about Jerry Longstreet. Jace couldn't imagine what kind of gossip would follow that tidbit.

Hatch wouldn't know and if he did, he wouldn't tell. Gladys and Mick were too interested in each other to notice anyone else. The maids were . . .

Jace well knew that the only person he wanted to talk to was Nigh.

At lunchtime he went downstairs and ate in silence while Mrs. Browne fussed about his actions of the last few days.

"Driving an expensive car like that," she said. "I never! If you had any sense—"

Jace had had enough. He picked up his plate and went to the door. "From now on, Mrs. Browne, I'll eat in the dining room."

He heard her usual "hmph!" but he also thought he heard a "yes, sir."

At 3:30, it started to drizzle outside. He'd jogged for an hour and even taken a nap, but it was now only the middle of the afternoon. He was in the small sitting room off the kitchen that no one used, a room he had never before spent any time in. A fire was burning and the rain was streaking the windows. He should have been content to read more of the books about the history of Margate, but he couldn't seem to sit still.

"Excuse me, sir," came a voice and he turned to see Daisy the flirt standing there. He really hoped she wasn't going to make one of her little come-ons to him. "Mick gave me this to give to you."

"What is it?" he asked cautiously.

"A note." She looked both ways down the hall to see if Mrs. Browne was anywhere near. "I think it's from Nigh," she whispered.

Jace was on his feet in seconds, but Daisy's knowing smile made him slow down. When she stood there watching him, waiting for him to open the envelope, he gave her a look to go away. She left, giggling.

Jace closed the door, then went to stand by the fire to read the note.

Sorry to bother you, but thought you'd like to know. I saw Danny Longstreet this morning.

Nigh

A grin so big that it almost broke the skin spread across Jace's face. "Very serious problem," he said aloud, then nearly ran to the telephone in the hall.

Nigh answered on the first ring. "Hello?"

Jace took the smile off his face. "You weren't hurt, were you?" he asked solemnly. "By Danny, I mean."

"No," she said, sounding a bit breathless, as though she'd run to get the phone.

"Were you scared?"

"Actually," Nigh said, "he made me angry. I got out of the car and bawled him out."

"Good for you."

"Maybe," she said, "except that old Mrs. Vernon was walking her dog and I think I may have given her a real fright."

Jace laughed. "I'm glad to hear *you* weren't frightened."

"I was still too embarrassed after the first time to collapse again. I do apologize for that. I certainly wasn't keeping up the British tradition of stiff upper lip."

"I think even the Queen would have been frightened by what happened to you."

"I do hope you're not talking about *our* queen! After all her relatives have put her through, do you think a little ghost would do her in? I think not!"

Jace laughed. "You aren't hungry, are you?"

"Starved. I've had nothing but my own cooking since Tolben Hall. By the way, how is Mrs. Fenney?"

"Good. She said we were her favorite guests she's ever had."

Nigh laughed. "I'm sure she did. Maybe we were her most exciting."

"So how about tea?"

"You mean with you?"

"Unless you'd rather . . ." He trailed off.

"Eat here alone? No, thanks. I'll go to your house. Except that it's raining."

"Excuse me, I forgot. You're English, so you don't know how to deal with rain."

"I thought maybe I should take some dry clothes with me, that's all."

"Oh," Jace said. "Yes, by all means. Bring some. Maybe after tea you could show me those sheep or my property boundaries. It might be good to know what I own. I'd like to see it at under sixty miles an hour."

"I think that's a great idea. I'll be there by four. See you soon."

Jace put down the phone and the grin came back on his face. They'd not said so, but she was coming for a sleepover, he thought, thinking he sounded like a first-grader. He found Daisy in the big downstairs sitting room. He hadn't been in the room since the first day he'd been there. "Please build a fire in here," he told her, "then I want you to put fresh sheets in that bedroom . . ." He had to think. "Isn't there a blue bedroom somewhere? One with a bathroom attached?"

"The lady's bedroom," she said, her face wearing a know-it-all smirk. "It's across from the master bedroom."

"Good," he said. "And put clean sheets on the big bed in the master bedroom please."

"But you sleep in the chintz room."

He gave her a look that made her erase the smirk. "Master bedroom and the blue bedroom. Got it?"

"Yes, sir," she said and came close to bobbing a curtsey, then she hurried down the hallway and out of sight.

He went to the kitchen to give Mrs. Browne instructions for a weekend of wonderful meals to be prepared.

"Havin' guests, are we?" she said, but he didn't answer.

"And today at four I want a tea served that would make Edward VII proud. Got all that?" He started to leave, but turned back. "And Mrs. Browne, if you say one derogatory word to my guest, there will be consequences."

Her eyes widened and she said nothing, but she nodded. It was the most he could hope for.

He went upstairs to change out of his running clothes, and when he saw Daisy and Erin changing the sheets in the room across from his, he told them to tell Mick that he wanted the rooms full of flowers from the garden.

"Yes, sir!" Daisy said, smiling.

"Maybe this old house will come back to life," he heard Erin say as he went into the chintz room to shower and change. He looked around it and again thought that he'd made a mistake in trying to re-create what Ann had had. And he'd been mistaken to sleep in that room.

On his way downstairs, he stopped by Daisy and Erin and told them to move his things into the master bedroom.

This time, their laughter made him smile.

17

ovely," Nigh said, her feet propped on the big round ottoman before the fire. At tea she'd told him every word about seeing Danny Longstreet in her rearview mirror, the telling of which had taken all of about ten minutes. He'd told her all about what he'd done in Tolben Hall, which took another ten minutes. After that, they'd talked about—

She wasn't sure what they'd talked about, but they'd never run out of things to say. After tea, they'd walked in the rain, both of them in tall rubber boots, and looked at the boundaries of his property.

At the southwest corner, he looked down at a small house. "That looks familiar." It was Nigh's house.

She shook her head. "Didn't the estate agent show you what you were buying?"

"I'm sure he told me everything, it's just that I don't remember what he said."

"Yet you bought the house anyway. Imagine that."

"Mmmm," he said. "Imagine that." He changed the subject. "So I own your house. How often are you there?"

"Seldom. You rent it to me very cheaply, so I mostly use it for storage. I have a bedroom in an apartment in London with two roommates, but it doesn't matter since I'm gone most of the time."

"I saw."

She looked at him in question.

"On the Internet. I looked you up." When she said nothing, he said, "So what are you planning to do with your life?"

"I don't know. Ask me a year from now."

"Is that how long you plan to take off?"

"I haven't had any time off since I started and it's almost ten years now. I have to figure out what I want to do. What about you?"

"Same here. My degree is in history, but all I've done is buy and sell things for my family's business. All done under my uncle's supervision."

"That sounds modest. You must have had some ideas of your own."

"A few," he said. "Now and then. But I'm like you and have no idea what I want to do."

"You could live here," she said, smiling.

"In Priory House?"

"Right. I forget that you bought a terrifically expensive house that you detest. And why did you do that?"

He wouldn't meet her eyes. "On impulse."

She knew she should just let it go, but she couldn't. She

wasn't going to bring up Stacy; he had to do that, but she wanted to let him know that she would listen. "You bought a house that you don't like on impulse. On a whim."

"Yes," he said, still not looking at her.

"You must have had a powerful reason for doing that."

"Very powerful," he said, then hesitated before he spoke again. "What if you had been falsely accused of something horrible? What would you do to clear your name?"

"Anything that I could," she said.

"Then you understand why I bought this house."

"Actually, I don't, but have you made any progress in clearing your name?"

He shook his head. "None whatever. All I've done is get entangled with a bunch of ghosts, a smart-aleck female, and a bunch of employees who think I'm a great source of entertainment."

Nigh smiled at his joke. "I'm not going to push on this, but if you want help in clearing your name, I'm willing. You would, of course, have to tell me what happened to dirty it."

"I'll keep that in mind, and thank you," he said, smiling at her. "You ready to go back? Mrs. Browne is making roast lamb for us tonight. And we're having it in the dining room."

Now, hours later, they were both full of food and drink and warm from the fire.

Jace was sitting in the chair next to her. "I enjoy your company," he said softly.

"And I yours," she answered.

He was quiet for a while and Nigh did her best to not let him know that her heart was pounding hard. It seemed that each man had *that moment,* the moment when he seemed to make up his mind about a woman. Some men had shown the decision by inviting her to meet his parents, some with a ring. Nigh knew that all that was much too early for her and Jace Montgomery, but what she was hoping for was that he'd tell her what was ruling his life.

"I want to tell you something," he said after a while. "No, I don't *want* to tell you, but I need help. I find that I can't do what I set out to by myself."

She didn't say anything, just sat there quietly, willing him to go on, to tell her all of it.

He did. He told her about Stacy, but she could see that it wasn't easy for him to speak of the woman he had loved, and when he told of her death, she felt his anguish. After an hour and a half, he wound down and turned to look at the fire.

He hadn't added much to what Nigh had already read and figured out, but she didn't tell him that. He mostly told her facts, not of his pain, but she saw it in his eyes.

"Do you have the photo with the note on it?" she asked.

"Upstairs in Ann's room," he said and she followed him up the stairs.

The room had become familiar to her over the years, since the entrance to the secret staircase was there, and the new decoration of it had become known to her in the last week. Had it only been a week since she'd met Jace?

She watched as he went to the Victorian wardrobe he'd bought in London, opened it, and took out a box from the bottom. She couldn't resist saying, "Quit hiding the things under the floorboard in the closet, have you?"

She enjoyed the shocked expression on his face, then he smiled and his eyes twinkled. "You do listen, don't you?"

"A must in my job."

She sat down on the bed beside him and they went through

what little evidence he had. She held the photo of Stacy and said how pretty she was, even though it made her feel jealous to say the words—which was stupid, but emotions rarely had logic.

"Ours again. Together forever. See you there on 11 May 2002," she read aloud.

"She died the next day," Jace said.

He stood up and went to the cold fireplace. "I need to know what happened," he said. "Can you understand that? Until I know what happened, until I've cleared my name—if it can be cleared, that is—I can't do anything else with my life."

She looked at him with understanding. "You don't want to talk to Ann because she's a ghost but because she was here that night."

"Yes," Jace said. "You thought I wanted a séance, didn't you?"

"It makes sense."

He ran his hand over his face. "None of this makes sense. Why are Ann and Danny showing themselves to us? Danny to you, Ann to me. Or she did until I made her angry." He looked at the ceiling. "I was just trying to do something nice," he said. "I didn't mean to offend you or make you feel worse than you already do. If there's anything I can do to make you feel better, you know, like help you get to the white light, let me know."

When he looked back at Nigh, her face was pale. "What?"

"I wouldn't tempt fate, if I were you," she said. "You take ghosts in stride, but I don't. Haven't you heard that they're always looking for bodies to take over?"

"A month ago, I would have said that they could have my body."

"You loved her so much that you can't ever get over her?" she asked.

"Yes," Jace said. "And no. I've grieved for Stacy until I can't grieve anymore. But my grief has become selfish. I need to know about myself. Her mother and sister said I drove Stacy to suicide. They said that I was such a tyrant that I wouldn't let her out of the wedding. But that makes no sense. If she felt free enough to tell me just days before our wedding that she didn't want to have children, then she could have told me that she didn't want to get married."

"I can see you as a lot of things but not as a tyrant," Nigh said. "I think there was a lot more going on and you knew, know, nothing about it." She looked at the photo of Priory House again, read what was written on it. "Someone somewhere knows about this."

"Mrs. Browne," Jace said flatly.

"I'm sure of it, but she's a mean-spirited old woman and she'd put splinters under her own fingernails before she told what she knows. If Stacy clandestinely met a man here, Mrs. Browne would think it was right and proper that she paid the ultimate penalty for doing so."

Jace winced, then sat on the bed beside Nigh. "This afternoon I had an idea. Maybe Danny Longstreet has appeared to you because his descendant is involved in this."

Nigh looked at him questioningly. "Jerry? You think maybe Stacy was meeting Jerry Longstreet here in Priory House?"

"I can tell that you don't think so."

"No, I don't. For one thing, look at her. She looks like one of those disgustingly healthy California girls that you Americans sing about. Jerry isn't as tall as me and he's always had a belly on him. He's cute in an obscure way, but not to outsiders."

"*You* like him," Jace said.

"I grew up in Margate, went to school here. The pickings were slim. Now that I've been out in the world, Jerry Longstreet is a joke. I think your Stacy would think he was too. Besides, where would she have met him?"

Jace stood up again. "Now that is the question," he said. "I've wracked my brain until it's depleted. Stacy told me her life story. She went to England with her mother, and when she was in college, she took a couple trips to Europe, but she was always chaperoned. She complained that she never got to see anything or meet anyone."

"I think you can fall in love with a person in a very short time," Nigh said quietly, looking at Jace.

He didn't turn away from her, but met her eyes. "So do I." He held her eyes for a moment, then looked away. "But I can't think about my future until I clear up my past."

Nigh couldn't help sighing as she looked back at Stacy's photo, then put everything back in the box. "I think you should keep all of this hidden. I don't think you should let anyone in this house see any of this."

"You think she was murdered, don't you?"

Nigh stood up and looked down at the box for a moment, then up at him. "I think that any woman who would leave you . . ." She didn't finish the sentence. It was too maudlin, too sentimental—and it revealed too much about her.

"It's late and I'm tired," she said. "I brought my hiking boots, so why don't we take a walk tomorrow, somewhere away from this house and Margate? Let's go over what you know and see what we can figure out," she said, then before he could respond, she said "good night" and left the room.

She hurried across the corridor to the blue bedroom, the "lady's bedroom." She smiled to see that it was full of fresh flowers and that her clothes had been unpacked and put away. The first time she'd visited Priory House with Jace, the maids and

Mrs. Browne had been an insolent lot, but he seemed to have done something that was working.

She filled the bathtub and soaked for a while before putting on a flannel nightgown and going to bed. The sheets smelled of sunlight. She felt good because Jace had told her what was eating at him, told her his most private secret. Now all they had to do was solve the mystery.

She fell asleep smiling.

18

L et's go," she heard Jace say.

Sleepily, Nigh rolled over in the bed and looked toward the uncurtained windows. It was still dark. "Go away," she said.

Jace sat down on the side of the bed. "I've been up for two hours and Mrs. Browne has already started frying things. Get up, get your boots on, and let's go. There's a trailhead twenty miles from here and we're starting there."

"Trailhead?" she muttered. "Is that an American word?"

"Up!" he said, then, when she didn't move, he stretched out beside her, the thick coverlet separating their bodies. "You smell good," he said, putting his face into her neck.

Nigh smiled and moved so her backside was closer to him. "I love morning sport."

"Me too. And it looks like Ann and Danny do too." He nuzzled her neck under her warm hair. "I guess that's why they're here."

"What?" Nigh said, turning over to look at the room.

There was no one but them in the room. Jace got off the bed and smiled at her. "No ghosts, just us. Get up and get dressed. Let's go! We're burning daylight."

"What a disgusting turn of phrase," she muttered as she sat up. "I was thinking of a leisurely walk near here, not some mountain trek."

"I need the exercise," Jace said. "I need a lot of exercise. In fact, I need to run up a mountain."

She couldn't help giving a giggle as his meaning was clear. "Where's my early morning tea? Every good hotel serves early morning tea."

"Sure," he said. "Tea from Hotel Priory House coming up. In the dining room, that is. See you downstairs, and if you take more than fifteen minutes I'll go without you."

At that, Nigh flopped back on the bed. "A reprieve!"

With a serious look, Jace went to the bed, scooped her up, covers and all, and stood her up outside the bathroom. "Fifteen minutes," he said, then left the room.

Yawning, but smiling, Nigh pulled on layers of clothes that she could peel off as the day got warmer. On the bottom was an old T-shirt that had been washed a hundred times and was so tight that it left little to the imagination. Over it went a long-sleeved cotton shirt, then a sweatshirt. She pulled on jeans, then put on her heavy socks and boots. She thought about makeup but she had an idea she'd be sweating it off, so she didn't bother.

Ten minutes from the time Jace had left the bedroom, she was in the dining room and eating part of one of Mrs. Browne's fry-ups.

"You'll get there yet," Jace said, meaning that she'd eventually be able to eat a whole one of the enormous breakfasts.

"I hope not," Nigh muttered, but his good mood was infectious.

Thirty minutes later they were piling heavy backpacks into Jace's Range Rover and heading north. It was a gorgeous, sunny Saturday and in spite of a lack of sleep she was looking forward to the day.

"Today we have a rule," he said as he pulled onto the highway.

"And what is that?"

"Today we only talk about us, you and me. No one else."

He didn't have to say who they were not to talk about, but she knew. Thinking that, for the first time, there would be no ghosts—old or new—between them made her feel wonderful.

"I've been awake most of the night," he said, "and I've been thinking about something."

"Oh?" she asked. "And what is that?"

"I like England." He glanced at her. "It's wet and cold, and eccentric doesn't begin to describe the people, but there's something about this place that appeals to me."

She was looking at him hard.

"My grandmother has been saying for years that someone should write the history of our family. We go back a long way and there have been some unusual characters in our family. We know all this by word-of-mouth tradition and through some old trunks full of letters and uniforms and family documents. But no one has ever written a complete story about my ancestors."

She waited for him to continue, but he was silent. "You mean you're thinking of writing your family history?"

"Maybe," he said.

"And living in England while you do it."

"It did go through my mind."

"And you'd live in Priory House?"

"Heavens no!" he said. "I thought I'd buy a little house some-where. Something old and nice, but something that could be heated."

"A Queen Anne former rectory," she said, her voice dreamy.

"Sounds great to me," he said. "In fact, it sounds perfect. But it would have to have a garden."

"And a conservatory. It must have a conservatory. You know something? Writing has been something that I thought I might like to do too."

"Really? What would you write?"

"About what I've seen. And I'd do some ghostwriting." She gave him a quick glance. "Not *that* kind of ghost, the other kind. I've met some old reporters who had fantastic stories to tell. There was one old guy who'd seen everything since World War Two, and what he could tell wasn't to be believed."

"Tell? He didn't write it down?"

"Not a word. To him, every word he did write was a chore. He could dictate a thousand words over the phone, but he couldn't sit and write anything. And all the good stories he knew couldn't be told—at least not then, that is. Now he could tell what he saw during the many wars he's been through."

"Does he want to write his memoirs?"

Nigh snorted. "What do you think reporters live on if it isn't ego?"

"Bourbon?" he asked innocently and she laughed.

They talked all the way to the trailhead, then kept talking while they got their packs and started walking. They talked a great deal about their dream houses and what they had to have, but never once did they speak of the house as belonging to the two of them and of their living in it together. Nor did they speak of the fact that they were thinking of changing their lives in a way so they could live together.

At noon they sat down on a rock by the side of the trail and ate the ham sandwiches Mrs. Browne had prepared and drank their Thermoses of tea. Nigh had peeled off her sweatshirt an hour before and it was tied around her waist. She leaned against a tree as they ate in companionable silence, the sun warm on them.

"The Raider," she said. "That sounds like my kind of man." She was referring to the story Jace had told her about one of his ancestors. During the American Revolutionary War a young man had disguised himself and fought for the freedom of his country. It didn't bother her that he'd fought against the English.

Jace kept looking ahead at the forest. They were surrounded by trees, the birds singing. They were alone. "Besides men wearing masks, what is your kind of man?"

Nigh had to take a drink of tea to keep from saying *you.* "Big, brawny, rugby player," she said. "Or polo. I really like polo."

"I have a cousin who plays polo."

"What's his name? Maybe you'll introduce us."

"Lillian."

They laughed together and minutes later they picked up everything and started walking again. They went about a mile when Nigh called a halt. "I don't know how you stand this," she said, looking at his heavy shirt as she put her pack on the ground. "I'm about to burn up."

"This is nothing. You should spend a summer in the American South. How did you stand the Middle East if you don't like hot weather?"

"Dry heat," she said, pulling her long-sleeved shirt over her head. "And—" She broke off because Jace was staring at her chest with wide eyes and open mouth. She had worn the tiny T-shirt to get his attention, but this was ridiculous! Hadn't he ever seen . . .

She looked down at her shirt and realized he was staring at the logo on her T-shirt. "What is it?"

"That," he whispered and raised his hand to point at her chest. "Where did you get that?"

"It's from Queen Jane's School," she said. "It's a posh little public—to you, private—boarding school about two miles from Priory House. It's astronomically expensive and I don't know anyone in Margate who has ever gone there. Gladys Arnold works there."

"Stacy had a shirt like that," Jace whispered.

"So does everyone who lives within thirty miles of here. The school puts on fund-raisers and sells things with the logo on them. We used to buy things from them until—"

Jace was still looking at her with wide eyes. "You don't think Stacy went there, do you?" Nigh asked. "She could have bought the shirt in several places. They sell them in a few shops in London."

"I don't know," Jace said, "but it's a lead. We have to go back. We have to find out if she did go to that school. We have to—" He stopped talking and started going back the way they'd come at double speed.

For a moment Nigh stood where she was. "So much for a romantic day out," she said, then hitched up her pack and ran after him.

It took them only forty-five minutes to get down the trail and back to the car, then Jace drove back to Margate as quickly as he could.

"Turn here," Nigh said and Jace took the turn so quickly

Nigh grabbed the handle over the window. "I'm assuming you want to see Queen Jane's School."

"Yes," was all Jace said, which was the most he'd said the whole way back.

"Turn up this dirt road," she directed and he followed her instructions. When they came to a dead end, he stopped the car, got out, and looked down over the house and grounds below.

Nigh stood beside him. The school was in an enormous old Victorian house, rather pretty, with manicured, treeless lawns that were divided into various playing fields. There were girls of high school age running about with balls or hockey sticks, all wearing the school colors of green and white.

"So how do I find out if Stacy went there?" Jace asked.

"I guess we could go and ask them. I'm sure they have records. But . . ."

He looked at her. "But they must have heard that a Stacy Evans died in a pub not ten miles from their school and if they didn't say anything then, they aren't going to want to get involved now."

"My thoughts exactly," she said.

"Maybe we could try the Internet. They may have an alumni association."

"They do, but it's sealed. You have to be an alumni to get into the thing."

Jace looked at her as though to ask how she knew that.

Nigh shrugged. "Sometimes the girls deign to come into Margate to see how villagers live. The locals always want to know which one is the daughter of a duke, or an earl, so we used to look them up. The school found out about it and sealed the records from outsiders. And now the girls are rarely allowed into Margate, so that's why you didn't see the logo around town. It's become very much a separation of them and us."

"So how do we find out?" Jace asked. "You're the journalist. How do we see if Stacy went to this school?"

"Short of breaking into the records office, I have no idea." When she saw Jace's face, she took a step backward. "I was joking. You can't break into the school. Maybe if it weren't in session you could do it, but there are three hundred girls living there now."

Jace stared at her a moment, then started back to the car, Nigh right behind him. When they were inside, she asked him what he was going to do.

"Contact some people, namely Clive and Gladys."

Nigh's mouth fell open. "You're going to ask Clive to help you? He's a policeman!" When Jace's look didn't change, she started getting upset. "You can't do this! You absolutely can*not* do this! And you especially can't get a policeman to help you do this."

"Do you know anything about Clive Sefton's background?"

Nigh knew all about the young man's troubled past. He had been arrested so many times it was a joke. Drugs. Gambling.

"You can't do this," Nigh said again, but this time her voice was weaker.

Jace backed the car up, turned around, and headed back to Priory House. Twenty minutes after they arrived, he called Clive and Gladys and invited them to dinner, along with Mick. Jace had ordered Mrs. Browne to prepare a feast, then he'd headed for the shower.

Nigh went to her bedroom and debated whether or not to get in her Mini and go home. In her profession she'd seen the consequences of illegal behavior too many times. On the other hand, she'd seen the consequences of legal behavior. All in all, she didn't know which was worse.

She took a bath, then dressed in plain black trousers and a pink cashmere sweater. Dinner was in an hour.

🌿

"I can't so much as see the yearbooks without a search warrant," Clive was saying, his mouth full.

"Why in the world is this school so secretive?" Jace asked, spearing another slab of rare roast beef. "The public has more access to prisoners than to these girls. You'd think that Margate was a den of sin and that the virtue of the girls had to be protected from us."

As he spoke, the heads of Nigh, Clive, Gladys, and Mick got lower and lower. By the time Jace finished, their noses were almost touching their plates.

"Okay," Jace said, "out with it. What happened to make the school hate Margate?"

"Mutual fascination," Nigh said.

"That's a good one," Clive said. "Mutual fascination. I'll have to remember that one."

Gladys looked at Jace. "About four years ago a local boy impregnated a duke's daughter. There was a bit of a row, but the story was hushed up. The duke threatened to call the parents of every student if what he called 'the Margate scum' weren't banned forever from the school."

Jace nodded. "So I take it that the daughter wasn't allowed to marry the kid from Margate."

That made the others laugh.

"All I want to know is if a Stacy Evans went to school there or not."

"Begging your pardon, sir," Gladys said, "but I think you also want to know the names of all her classmates. If your young lady did attend the school, you'll want to call them and ask who she knew."

Jace smiled at her, then looked at Mick. "You'd better keep her," he said.

Mick put his hand over Gladys's and said, "I intend to."

An hour before, Jace had dismissed Mrs. Browne, watched as she left the kitchen to go back to her own apartment, then he'd briefly told Gladys and Mick about Stacy having been his fiancée and that he believed she'd been murdered. He told them she'd met someone at Priory House the night before her murder and he wanted to find out who it was.

"Gladys?" Jace asked. "Do you have keys to the school?"

"Not to the records office," she said quickly and firmly.

"But you do have keys to get into the buildings?"

Both Nigh and Clive shouted "no!" at the same time.

"I can't help on this if it's to be a break and enter," Clive said. "Sorry, Mr. Montgomery, but I can't risk my whole future for this. If some other bloke on the force was caught, they'd forgive him, but not me. Not with my past record."

Jace leaned back in his chair. "I'm open to ideas."

"All right," Clive said, then leaned forward and lowered his voice. "I think I have a plan."

"Mr. Montgomery," the headmistress of Queen Jane's School purred. "I do believe we can accommodate your niece."

"Our family doesn't usually send children to boarding school, but Charlotte wants to go, so who are we to deny her? The child wants to play field hockey."

"Oh, good, then she's an athlete."

"Yes, she's a real jock."

The woman kept her smile even through Jace's slang. She handed him a fat sheaf of papers. "Our brochure is in there and an application to the school."

"Thank you so much," he said, taking the papers.

In the next second, a screaming alarm filled the room and their ears.

"What in the world?" the woman said. "I don't think this is a real emergency," she shouted above the din, "but I must go and see about my students." She quickly moved to the door and waited impatiently for him to leave her office.

Jace caught his sleeve on the chair, then had trouble extricating it, then he tripped over his shoelace.

The woman was looking anxiously at the girls who were beginning to gather in the central hall. Her keys dangled impatiently in her hand.

"So sorry," Jace shouted as he stood up and started toward her. But he dropped his papers, then went on one knee to pick them up.

"Mr. Montgomery!" she shouted. "I must see to my girls!" She gave him a look of disgust, then ran from the room.

In one quick motion, Jace took the yearbook for the year 1994 from the bookshelves by the door and slipped it under his jacket. Last night he'd done some hard thinking and he realized that the only year Stacy could have gone to the school was in 1993-94. Her mother died the summer of 1993, and her father had just married a woman only a few years older than his daughter. It was Jace's guess that her stepmother would have shipped her off to an English boarding school to get rid of her. Jace knew that Stacy had graduated from a school in California, so if she had gone to Queen Jane's, she hadn't stayed all year.

The alarm was still screeching as he left the office with the papers the headmistress had given him in his hands. She was standing but a few feet from the office door, directing her students as they filed out of the building. Jace made a show of turning the knob on the door so it would lock behind him, and she gave a nod as though to tell him she approved.

Jace left the building smiling—while the girls around him hooted and yelled.

"Are you what's in Margate?"

"I can see why we're not allowed to go to the village if you're what's there."

"My room's on the southeast corner. I'll throw you down a bed sheet."

"Ha! You'll throw down the mattress and jump on it."

By the time Jace got back to his car, his face was red. He handed the yearbook to Nigh, then pulled out of the parking lot. "Girls weren't like that when I was young."

"Of course they were. Girls have always been like that," she said, flipping through the book. "Bingo! Stacy Elizabeth Evans."

Jace paused a second to glance at the photo in the yearbook, then drove back to Priory House with a smile on his face.

"Now all we have to do is find out who she met in this area," Nigh said, "then we'll know who sent her the invitation." She leaned back against the headrest. "Jace?"

"I know," he said. "You're going to ask me if I'm prepared for what I might find out. I've heard it all before from my uncle Frank. You should meet him. You two think alike."

"I'll take that as a compliment."

"You should. He's a self-made billionaire."

"Ooooh, *that* Frank Montgomery."

Jace laughed as he pulled into the driveway of Priory House. It was Sunday, Mrs. Browne's day off, and she'd gone wherever she went on Sundays, leaving them alone in the house. Clive's plan to get the yearbook had been so simple that Jace wasn't sure it would work. Gladys often went to the school on Sundays to catch up on her cleaning, so it was easy for her to pull the alarm at an agreed-upon time. The rest had been up to Jace.

Once they were in the house, Jace and Nigh bent over the yearbook, their heads nearly touching. He was determined to not let her or anyone else see his shock and hurt that the woman he'd loved so much hadn't told him that she'd attended a boarding school in England. Maybe it had been for only a few months, but Stacy had been there long enough to fall for someone. All he'd had to do, years later, was to send her a postcard with a date and Stacy had shown up. To see him again, she'd begged the man she was planning to marry to accompany him to England, and she'd picked a fight so she'd have an excuse to run away.

"See anyone you know?" Jace asked Nigh.

"Several, but only from the society columns. Let's get on the 'Net."

An hour later, they had done a great deal of research, but how did they contact these young women and ask them questions?

"You can't just call Chatsworth and ask about a school chum of one of the daughters of the house," Nigh said.

"Why not?" Jace asked. "You have to remember that I'm an American and we fought a war to do away with your class system."

"Give me a break!" Nigh said. "Can just anyone call your sister and ask her questions?"

"First of all, they'd never get through to her. She has three kids and not a moment to—"

She narrowed her eyes at him.

He laughed. "Okay, I get your point, but I have an idea. There is one woman I know who can get put through to the Queen if she wants to."

"Ha! Only a horse person could get through to the Queen."

"But we don't need the Queen, do we?" Jace asked. "We just need someone who can get through to these rich English girls, and there is one woman I trust more than any other in the world."

"Who is that?"

"My mother."

Nigh laughed. "You'll turn it all over to her?"

"Every bit of it. You think Gladys bought a color copier?"

"From what Mrs. Parsons said, Gladys bought every machine known, and Mrs. P. didn't buy any of it for her. Which means that Gladys got it all for half the price Mrs. Parsons charges."

"Let's go copy these pages, then send them to my mother. She'll charm her way into their houses."

19

Jace and Nigh spent the day trying to pretend they weren't nervous. They played Scrabble—Nigh won—and they wandered about the garden, with Nigh giving opinions about what she'd do to the garden if the house were hers.

"You like this house, don't you? If you had a choice, you'd live here, wouldn't you?"

"No," she said honestly. "The house is cold, drafty, and it's full of ghosts. And I'm not talking about just Ann Stuart. I think my mother's spirit is here and maybe my father's. Or maybe it's just me and my memories that are here." She shivered. "No, I wouldn't like to live in this house. There's something else in it too, but I don't know what it is."

"I think it's the ghost of that damned lady highwayman. I think she did live here and I think her presence is here."

"Maybe you're right. Shall we check the machines again?"

All day long they'd checked the fax machine, the answering machine, and Jace's e-mail. His mother kept them posted every step of the way, of who she'd called and what she'd found out. So far, there had been nothing about who Stacy met outside the school.

They had found out that Stacy had been a very, very unhappy student and mostly kept to herself.

"I guess that's why she never told me that she'd spent most of a year in a boarding school," Jace said. He was doing his best to understand why Stacy had kept such a big secret from him.

Mrs. Montgomery had called Jace three hours ago and told what she'd found out from the woman who had been the headmistress of the school when Stacy was there. When Stacy entered the school, she had been a newly traumatized person. Her mother had died just months before the term started and she had been sent to live with her father, a man she'd rarely seen in her life. He had just remarried. The man didn't have time to take care of his expanding business and two needy females. His new wife won out, and Stacy was sent to school in another country.

"One of the girls I talked to," Mrs. Montgomery said, "told me that no one knew much about Stacy. She spent the few months she was there in her room."

"But there was a man—" Jace began.

"I'm getting to that, dear," she said, "but you must be patient. But first of all, I want to know who is there with you. I can hear her breathing on the phone."

Nigh jumped away from the telephone as though she'd been burned.

"It's the gardener's boy, Mick," Jace said.

"You never could lie well. Who is it?"

"Got a pen?"

"Of course."

"Look up N. A. Smythe on the 'Net. Spelled S-M-Y-T-H-E. You'll see all about her. She lives here in Margate, when she isn't globetrotting, that is, and she's been helping me with . . . well, with whatever I need help with."

"You sound much better than you did when you left, so tell her thank you from me."

"I will," Jace said, smiling at Nigh. "So now tell me what else you found out."

"About three months after she arrived, one of the girls I talked to said that Stacy had changed. She was as secretive and as separate from the rest of the girls as ever, but they saw her smiling now and then. One of the girls said she thought that sometimes Stacy wasn't in her room all night."

Jace raised his eyebrows at Nigh, as he knew she could hear.

Nigh nodded, yes, this was possible back in '94.

"Was she sneaking out to see someone?" Jace asked his mother.

"They thought so. I think the security of the school was rather lax at that time, which is why the headmistress was dismissed the next year and the current one hired. Is she lax?"

"Airport security could learn from her," Jace said. "Can you keep calling and find out what you can? I need the name of the man she was seeing."

"Jace, honey, I'll ask you again: Are you sure you want to find out all this information? You might find out some things about Stacy that you won't like."

"I'm sure. In fact, the more I find out, the better I feel."

"I'm not sure I agree with that. Oh! My goodness! I just pulled up your N. A. Smythe. She's beautiful! And she looks to be intelligent. Well done!"

"Mom," Jace said, laughing and embarrassed at the same time.

"What does the 'N. A.' stand for?"

"Nightingale Augusta."

"She should fit right in with our family. Okay, I have to go. I'll call you when I know more. Or I may send a fax with a name. I love you."

"Me too, Mom," Jace said softly, then hung up.

The phone didn't ring again until 1:30, just after lunch. It was his mother and she was yawning. She'd been on the phone and fax and Internet all night, compensating for the time difference in England.

"I have a name and an address," his mother said without preamble, "and you're to go to her house to have tea at four. Her name is Carol Heatherington, and she was Stacy's roommate."

"Her roommate!" Jace said, looking at Nigh in triumph. "Did she give you a name?"

"No. Carol wants to talk to you personally because she feels very bad about Stacy. She was out of the country when Stacy died or she would have come forward."

"She knows that Stacy didn't kill herself."

"No, quite the contrary. Carol thinks that Stacy did kill herself and she thinks she knows why."

"That's what she said?"

"Yes. Jace, darling, I did warn you that you might find out things you didn't want to know. You should leave now. I told Carol that you'd be bringing a friend with you. Jace?"

"Yes," he said, still reeling from being told that someone who knew Stacy believed that she'd killed herself.

"I know you have your own mind, but I suggest that you listen to what this young woman has to say. Really *listen*."

"Yeah, okay, sure, Mom," Jace said listlessly. "I better go. I'll call you when I get back."

"Make it twelve hours from now. I need some sleep."

"Thanks for this, Mom. Love you."

Mrs. Montgomery gave a jaw-cracking yawn. "Me too. Give my best to Nightingale."

"Nigh," he said. "We shorten it to Nigh."

"I look forward to meeting her." She hung up.

Nigh looked at Jace. She'd heard enough of the conversation to know what it was about. "I think we should put on our best clothes and go to tea," she said. She looked at the address Jace had written down. "It will take us a couple hours to get there."

Silently, Jace nodded, then went upstairs to change. He didn't want to give himself time to think about what he was finding out. The reality that Stacy'd had a life that he knew nothing about was at last coming through to him. He knew that from now on, what he found out was going to be difficult for him to hear. Part of him wanted to stop where he was, but the bigger part knew he had to go on.

"I asked you here today mainly to assuage my own guilt," Carol Heatherington said. She was young, not very pretty, but she had that English skin that was flawless and she had a presence that only money and breeding could give a person. She had a pretty house set near a river, surrounded by thirty acres of land. Her husband commuted every day to London, leaving her with her horses and dogs and a young child. She seemed utterly content with her life.

Carol poured the tea into Herend cups. "I'm afraid I wasn't

very kind to Stacy when we were at school. You see, I had requested that I be put in a room with my best friend, but instead I was put in with this angry, sullen American girl. I'm afraid I took out my disappointment on her."

Jace grimaced and had to clamp his mouth shut to keep from telling her what he thought of someone who would be unkind to a girl who'd just lost her mother.

Nigh took the cup of tea. "We're all bitches at that age," she said calmly.

"The irony is that years later I found out that my so-called best friend had asked her grandfather to call the head of the board of the school and ask that they not give me as her roommate. I took my anger out on Stacy when I should have been angry at my sister-in-law."

"Your sister-in-law?"

Carol smiled. "I married her brother, which is just what she didn't want me to do."

"Did Stacy meet anyone that year? Probably a man?" Jace asked.

"Yes," Carol said. "Back then—it does seem long ago, doesn't it?—we were still allowed to go into Margate on the weekends. All of us girls stayed together. I'm afraid we were frightful snobs. We traveled in little packs, each of us belonging to one pack or the other."

"But Stacy wasn't part of the group," Jace said.

"No. She was American and . . . I'm not defending my actions, but truthfully, Stacy never made an effort to be a part of us. Sometimes we asked her to go with us, but she always refused. It didn't help that she said she hated England and that her father was going to send for her any day. We all thought boarding school was perfectly normal, but I think Stacy looked on it as a punishment. I think she thought it was a jail and that it was her duty to try to escape."

"With someone?" Nigh asked.

"Yes. At least I think so. Stacy was a very secretive person. You could talk to her but she told you only what she wanted you to know. She never really revealed any confidences. Did you find this to be true?" she asked Jace.

"I wouldn't have said so, but I found out that that was true. Even though we were engaged to be married, I didn't know that she'd spent a year in an English boarding school."

"I think Stacy looked on it as most people would think of having served a term in prison. She was probably too embarrassed to speak of it. I could see that she'd keep it a secret. I'm curious as to what happened with her father and his young wife."

"Stacy told you about them?" Jace asked.

"Only in the most sarcastic manner. She used to make us laugh with her black humor. One time a little girl, about twelve, came into the dining room, and we all wondered who she was. Stacy said, 'She's my father's new wife.' "

"That sounds like her," Jace said, looking away for a moment. "You said that you think Stacy did commit suicide and it was your fault."

"I've been haunted by Stacy since I heard of her death. I wish I'd been kinder to her, made more of an effort to include her in our gatherings."

"Why would you think she committed suicide?" Nigh asked, trying to steer the woman onto the path of what they needed to know.

"For Tony, of course."

"Tony?" Nigh asked.

"Tony Vine. He was the man she was in love with. At least I think she was in love with him."

Nigh and Jace looked at each other. "Could you tell us all that you know about Mr. Vine?"

Carol took a sip of her tea. "The first time I saw him, I was in Margate with half a dozen other girls. It was a Saturday afternoon and I thought Stacy had stayed back at the school. I asked her if she wanted to join us, but she said she had to study for a chemistry exam. Hours later, I was with the girls and there was a street market that day. I was looking at the things in the stalls when I looked up and all my friends were gone. I didn't see them anywhere, and I'm afraid I panicked. I started running back toward the school, but as I passed a side street I saw a flash of bright red. I stopped where I was. Curiosity overran my fear of being without my herd of girlfriends."

"Was it Stacy?" Nigh asked.

"I thought so. She had a beautiful red silk scarf—we all envied Stacy's American clothes—and I thought I saw that scarf going around a corner. I looked to see if anyone could see me, then I went down the little road toward where I'd seen the scarf.

"When I got to what looked like a garage, I saw the scarf again and turned the corner. There was Stacy wrapped about a young man. Oh, excuse me," she said to Jace.

"No, that's all right. I'd like to hear everything."

Carol put down her cup of tea. "You have to understand that almost all of us girls were virgins. We talked about sex all the time and we all made out as though we had the sexual experience of a woman of the streets, but actually we knew nothing. But there was Stacy, the quiet American who kept to herself, entangled with a man in a way that most of us girls had never even imagined. She had one leg up about his waist and—"

She broke off after a look at Jace's face.

"You saw them in Margate," Nigh said. "Do you know where else they met? And how did you find out who he was?"

"I was afraid they'd see me, so I left, but I went back to the market. My curiosity was stronger than anything else, so I wanted to see if I could find out more about this man Stacy was with."

"Man?" Nigh asked. "Not a boy?"

"Oh, no! He was thirty if he was a day, and we were only sixteen then. I think Stacy was seventeen."

"A thirty-year-old man," Jace said softly.

"Did you see them again?" Nigh asked.

"Not that day. I went back to the school and there was Stacy, curled up on her bed with her chemistry book. You would never have guessed that she'd been out of the school, certainly not that she'd been twined about a man nearly twice her age."

Carol took a bite of a cucumber sandwich. "After that, I can tell you that I began to watch Stacy. I never let her know and I never even hinted at what I saw, but I watched her."

"And what did you see?" Jace asked.

"Secrets and lies," Carol said. "She was a great liar. Sorry again. I mean no disrespect to Stacy's memory, but I saw her lie directly to Matron and never so much as blink an eye."

"What did she lie about?"

"Where she'd been and what she'd done. Stacy used to sneak out of our room at night. I've always been a sound sleeper, so it was hard for me to stay awake to watch what she was up to, but I managed it on three nights. She'd listen for me to go to sleep, then she'd tiptoe out of the room. Twice I looked out the window and saw her running across the green. She stayed away from the outdoor lights, but I could see her."

"Do you know where she went?"

"Toward the back, to the hill. One day I climbed the hill and there's a dirt road up there. I saw candy bar wrappers and some soda cans, rubbish along the edge of the woods."

"Very non-U," Nigh said.

Carol smiled. "I haven't heard that term in ages. Yes, it was very non-U, and I felt sure that Stacy's boyfriend had left them there." She looked at Jace. "Sorry for the snobbery. Non-U means 'not upper class.' "

Jace didn't tell her that the term was used in the States, too. "You think Stacy met the man at the top of the hill?" Jace asked.

"I'm sure of it. It was a steep climb, but it could be done. I did it. The second night that I was able to stay awake to see what Stacy was doing, I thought I heard the sound of a motorcycle. I think he was waiting for her up there on his motorcycle and they rode away together."

"When did she get back?" Nigh asked.

"She was always there when I awoke in the morning. Stacy never seemed to need much sleep," she said, looking at Jace for verification.

"No, she didn't. Insomnia was a problem for her," he said. "It's why she always had prescription sleeping pills with her."

"I never saw her yawn," Carol said. "I never saw her look sleepy in class. If I don't get a full eight hours, nine if I can, I'm incoherent during the day. But not Stacy."

"So why do you think Stacy's death was suicide?" Jace asked.

Carol looked at Jace. "I must apologize for that statement. I said it before I knew all the facts. I knew nothing about you or that Stacy had been engaged to someone other than Tony Vine. All I knew was what I'd seen in the papers, and I didn't see them until months later. I thought Stacy had returned to Margate to get back with Tony. After all these years she was going to at last be with him, but maybe he turned her down. Stacy was always an intense person and I could imagine that once she loved someone, she'd love them forever. I could see that if she went back to him and found he was maybe married to someone else, she'd be extremely unhappy about that."

"Who is Tony Vine?" Nigh asked. "Or did you not find out who he was?"

"About a month after I saw him and Stacy together, I saw him walking down the street in Margate. He was a very handsome man, but he wasn't my type."

"What do you mean?" Nigh asked.

Carol shrugged. "Everything about him was too . . . shiny. My father hates new clothes. If he puts on something new, he'll spend the day riding and doing his best to break the clothes in. That's what I was used to, so Tony was a shock to me. There was something about him that . . . please don't think I'm being melodramatic, but it was dangerous. He seemed like a dangerous man."

"A thirty-year-old with a seventeen-year-old girl?" Jace said. "He should have been locked up."

"Anyway," Carol said, "I asked someone who he was. I think it was a woman in a tea shop. She said, 'That's Tony Vine,' and the way she said it made me think that everyone in town knew him."

"Do you know where he is now or what happened to him?" Nigh asked.

Carol got up and went to an antique cabinet behind the sofa and took a piece of paper out of a drawer. "About a year ago I was in London and I saw a man on the street. I knew I knew him but I couldn't remember where I'd seen him. That night I remembered that he was the man Stacy used to sneak out to meet. Tony Vine. It hadn't been too long since I'd heard of her death in Margate so I wrote down the name of the building that I'd seen Tony come out of." She handed the paper to Jace, who looked at it, then passed it to Nigh.

"I was very sorry to hear about Stacy," Carol said to Jace. "When I heard, I thought, She killed herself over that awful Tony Vine. There was a point when we were at school that I thought about going to the headmistress and telling about Stacy. I was afraid for her, and worried about her, but then, her father came to school and got her and took her back to California and I never heard from her again. Until I was told of her tragic death."

There was silence after that and no one spoke for a while.

"I think we've taken up enough of your time," Jace said, standing up. "I cannot thank you enough for your help."

Carol and Nigh also stood up. "I only wish I hadn't been so passive when we were girls," Carol said.

Nigh took the woman's hand. "I don't think any of this is your fault."

"And I don't think that Stacy committed suicide," Jace said.

"But if she didn't kill herself—" Carol's eyes widened. "You think Tony killed her?"

"If he didn't, I think he may know who did. Thank you so much for this. I cannot begin to tell you how much you've helped me."

They exchanged more pleasantries, then they left Carol's house and got into Jace's car. For a moment he leaned back against the seat, his eyes closed. Nigh didn't disturb him. She knew how he felt. It was a lot of information to take in. Secrets and lies. Carol had said that Stacy was full of them. Nigh would never say so to Jace, but she agreed. Stacy hadn't told the man she was to marry about her year at an English boarding school or about a man that she was probably in love with. In normal circumstances, this would have been understandable, but Stacy seemed to have been still in love with this Tony Vine many years later. She loved him so much that she'd gone to a lot of trouble to get to see him just before her marriage. All he'd had to do was send her a picture of Priory House with a few words scrawled on the back, and Stacy had jeopardized her future with Jace to meet Tony.

What had happened in that meeting? Nigh wondered. Had she told Tony that he'd always been the one? That she wanted to marry him and no one else? That she'd dump Jace if Tony would have her back?

Did Tony say no? Did he say that he already had a wife and kids and didn't want her? Is that why Stacy went to the pub and took a bottle of sleeping pills?

Nigh glanced at Jace as he started the car and wondered what he was thinking. To Nigh's reporter mind, it was becoming more and more clear that Stacy *had* killed herself.

As far as Nigh could piece together, when Stacy was a girl she'd been worried about getting her father's love. He was the only parent she had left, and he'd chosen his new, young wife over his daughter. From Carol's polite description of Tony Vine, he seemed like a real sleazebag. Girls didn't get the approval of their fathers by marrying men who wore shiny suits and dated schoolgirls.

Nigh looked at Jace and wondered if Stacy had agreed to marry him because he was the kind of man a father would approve of. Jace was everything that a father dreamed his daughter would marry.

"Comparing me to Tony Vine?" Jace asked.

She didn't want to lie. "Yes."

"You're beginning to think that Stacy killed herself because her high school boyfriend told her he no longer wanted her, aren't you?"

"Yes," Nigh said, dreading what he'd say to that.

"Good," Jace said, smiling. "If you think that, then you'll be more curious to find out the truth."

When they reached Margate, Nigh said, "I guess I'd better go back to my house."

"But your things are at Priory House," Jace said.

"I can get them later. I have another toothbrush and nightgown, so I'll be okay."

"If that's what you want to do," he said.

"It's not what I want to do, but—" Her temper got the better of her. "You and I have practically lived together since we first met. I'm sure that the entire village is talking about nothing else. And the worst part is that not a word of what they think is true. You and I are just friends and we're working together. That's all."

Jace stopped the car in the courtyard of Priory House and turned off the engine. "Friends? Is that what you think we are?"

As he got out of the car, he was chuckling. Nigh sat in the passenger seat and frowned at him, but then she smiled and got out of the car and went into the house. She went in by the front door, not the kitchen door.

They spent a quiet evening "at home," as Nigh was beginning to think of it. Like two old married people—except that every time Jace got near her, her heart started beating wildly. She refused to let him see how she felt because he didn't seem to feel the same way. Was he interested in her the same way she was interested in him? His pulse didn't seem to quicken when his arm brushed hers. His breath didn't seem to catch when her face came near to his.

They talked about their futures in a roundabout way that made her happy and insane at the same time. She wanted to know if he truly meant to include her in his future. And she wanted to know what he planned to do after he found out about Stacy. Would he put Priory House up for sale and leave England forever? But then he'd said that he liked England. "In spite of all its faults" was how he'd generally put it.

The more she thought, the less she could figure out.

Mrs. Browne put dinner on the table, and Jace and Nigh ate, saying little, each of them lost in their own thoughts.

After dinner they went to the drawing room and sat there in silence.

"We haven't found out why Ann and Danny have been appearing to us," Nigh said.

Jace was sitting in a chair staring at the fire. "I'm afraid we may never find out," he said. "I think I'll go to London tomorrow."

Nigh wanted to yell, "Without *me*?" but she said nothing. It was his decision. No doubt he was embarrassed at her having heard so much about his former fiancée.

She gave a yawn. "I think I'll go to bed," she said. When Jace said nothing, she stood up and started for the door. As she passed his chair, he caught her by the wrist, then held the back of her hand to his cheek.

"I'm sorry that I'm not very good company. I haven't been myself since Stacy died. But I want you to know that you're the first person who has managed to make me think that life may yet be worth living." Still holding her hand, he looked up at her. "I promise that when I get this settled, I'll make up for lost time."

She smiled down at him, then he released her hand and looked back at the fire. Feeling partly happy and partly frustrated, she left the room and went upstairs to the lady's bedroom. A fire had been laid and it was warm and cozy in the room. But not as warm and cozy as it could be, she thought, looking at the empty bed.

She took a bath, put on her nightgown, and went to bed. She didn't turn off the light until she heard Jace come up the stairs and go to bed. There was a shadow under her door, and she held her breath.

When the shadow moved, Nigh cursed, turned out the light, hit the pillow with her fist, and settled down to sleep. In spite of her annoyance at Jace Montgomery, she was asleep in minutes.

20

Nigh was awakened by music. It wasn't loud, but she could hear it coming from far away. At first she was disoriented, not knowing quite where she was. As she awakened more fully, she listened. It didn't seem to be coming from downstairs but from just outside her door. Was Jace awake and playing music? Big band–era music from the sound of it.

She got out of bed and went to the door and opened it. Jace was just coming out of his bedroom. He had on jeans and a heavy wool sweater and a pair of leather boots. He put his finger to his lips for her to remain silent. The music was coming from the chintz room, Ann's room. The haunted room.

Nigh's first instinct was to run back into her bedroom and crawl under the bed. Better yet, maybe now was the perfect time to get in her car and go home.

But Jace's next gesture made up her mind for her. He gestured for her to go back into her room, close the door, and get back in bed. No doubt he thought she was too cowardly to face whatever was going on in Ann's room.

His lack of belief in her gave her courage. She gestured for him to wait for her while she put on some clothes. It was bad enough to face ghosts, but she couldn't do it in a nightgown. She ran back into the room and put on the same as he was wearing: jeans, a thick sweater, and boots. Four minutes later, she was back in the hall and tiptoeing behind Jace toward Ann's room.

The door to the room was open and the lights in it were on. That wasn't how they had left the room. Jace pushed Nigh behind him as he peered inside, looking all around, but no one was in there, no one either dead or alive.

Nigh bucked up her courage enough that she stepped out from behind him and started into the room. Still, neither of them spoke.

As soon as they were inside, they saw that the hidden door to the tunnel was open and the music was coming from inside it.

Again, Jace pushed Nigh behind him as he looked into the dark recess of the stairwell. He pointed down, toward the tunnel. The music was not coming from the secret room upstairs, but from the tunnel itself.

Nigh touched Jace's arm and made a gesture to ask him who knew about the passage and who could be playing music inside it at two o'clock in the morning. Jace shrugged to let her know that he had no idea.

He started into the stairwell, meaning to go ahead of her, but she caught his arm and shook her head no vigorously. She didn't like whatever was going on. It could be that Hatch, who she was sure knew about the tunnel, had left a radio on, but she didn't think so. Her true thought was, What the hell is Danny Long-street up to now?

When Jace shook his head, letting Nigh know he was going into the tunnel no matter what she said, she held up a finger to him: Wait a minute.

She went to the fireplace and got two candles off the mantel and some matches, part of the authenticity of Ann's room. Jace smiled at her, and mouthed "good girl." If she could have talked, Nigh would have asked if he was also going to throw her a bone.

Jace struck the match and lit both candles, handed her one, then he started down the old passage, Nigh about three inches behind him. She was trying to act brave, although she felt any-thing but.

The music was very loud. Whoever had started it had used an old-fashioned boom box. It was Woody Herman playing now, a jazzy tune that made her think of swing dancing, the boys throw-ing the girls up in the air, then pulling them down to slide them across the floor between their legs.

She smiled at the image, then remembered where she was and what they were doing. She clamped her hand onto the back of Jace's sweater and followed him as he cautiously made his way forward.

They were in the middle and on the floor was a big boom box. Bending, Jace turned off the music. The silence it left be-hind was almost deafening.

Jace turned to her and motioned for her to stay there.

Did he mean that she was to stay without him? She knew her fear was silliness. She had spent a lot of her childhood in this an-cient place and it was as familiar to her as her own bedroom. But back then part of her security had been that she was sure no one knew she was there. How could a bad man get her if he didn't know where she was?

But what they'd seen and heard tonight—music blaring, bright lights, the secret door open—frightened her. She knew without a doubt that it was Danny Longstreet's doing. He had probably greatly enjoyed his little joke of sitting by her on the bench and chatting in broad daylight. And she knew he was in Margate because she'd seen him.

Again, Jace told her to stay where she was, and again, she shook her head no. She knew that he wanted to check the rest of the tunnel, check the outside entrance, but she didn't want to stay there alone. Someone had been in the tunnel and it had been recently. When they'd gone to bed the lights hadn't been on in Ann's room and there was no music playing.

Jace smiled at her in a way that she was sure was meant to make her relax, but it didn't. He nodded his head. Yes, she could go with him.

He clasped her hand in his, then took a step away from the huge, battery-powered stereo that was at their feet.

But that one step was all he took because in the next second they heard a rumbling that Nigh had heard twice before in her life. Bombs!

"Get down!" she screamed. "Down!"

The rumbling was coming from both ends of the tunnel, so they couldn't run in either direction.

Jace understood. He grabbed Nigh and pulled her under him, then he bent his body over hers and hit the cold, hard earthen floor.

Under him, Nigh put her hands over her ears and Jace did the same. She had no hope that they were going to live another minute. The old tunnel would collapse under bombs put at each end of the passage. If the falling beams didn't get them, the caving walls would.

She held onto Jace as the sound drove out all thoughts. Dust, debris, timbers, dirt that had been packed solid for hundreds of years all hit the floor and threatened to crush them.

The two explosions happened quickly, but they seemed to go on forever. Jace held Nigh under him so that not much dust hit her. They stayed that way for long, fearful minutes, expecting at any second that the roof over their heads would come down on them. But it didn't.

When the noise stopped, and even the echoes had quieted, Jace moved off of her. "Are you okay?"

Nigh could only nod. Her ears were ringing.

The candles had gone out and they were in absolute darkness. She felt Jace fumble about, feeling the floor, looking for them. When he found one, he pulled the box of matches out of his pocket and lit it.

Nigh sat on the floor by the stereo and watched Jace move about what was left of the tunnel. Both ends had collapsed. What was left was about ten feet of space to their right and another fifteen or so to their left. That meant that there were yards of packed dirt between them and the world.

She watched Jace examine their surroundings. He looked at the wall of dirt, pulled some of it away, then stopped when the ancient beams over their heads began to creak. He lifted the candle to look at the barricades, and Nigh followed the light. The old beams were finally giving way. They were bowed, and about ten feet from where she was sitting she could see a fresh crack in one.

"So who knows about this tunnel?" Jace asked, sounding as though it weren't of vital importance.

"More people than I knew," she said. "Whoever put this stereo in here knew about it."

Jace looked down at her. "I'm sure half the village heard this explosion and they're probably getting . . . what do you call them? Digging machines out."

"JCBs."

"Right. Backhoes. They're getting the JCB backhoes out right now. Think Hatch will let them cut into his lawn? I can hear his saying that owners come and go, but lawns are forever."

She didn't smile at his joke. She'd been in situations like this and she'd seen worse. They weren't going to get out alive. In all likelihood, it would take a week before anyone realized they'd disappeared. The villagers knew that Jace and Nigh were often running off someplace and staying for days.

"I don't think we should lie to each other, do you?" Nigh said softly. "They won't miss us and if they did, they wouldn't have any idea where to look."

For a moment Jace didn't look at her, then he turned slowly. "This is my fault," he said, his voice heavy. "I knew there was danger. Stacy was killed and her murderer has done this. I meant to protect you. I meant to . . ."

She looked up at him and there were tears in his eyes. She opened her arms to him and he went to her and she held him.

"I'm sorry," he said over and over. "I'm sorry. I so wanted to share with you that I lost my caution. I should have protected you."

She stroked his hair and soothed him, holding him tightly to her. "Whatever happens, I'm glad you told me about . . . about yourself," she said. "But why . . . ?"

"Because I love you," he said, as though that was a fact known to the world.

"You what?" She pulled back from him to look at his face. "You what?"

Jace sat up and leaned back against the cold dirt wall beside her and wiped his eyes. "Sorry about that. I've tried to keep my emotions reined in, but sometimes—"

"I'm British, so don't try to talk to me about emotions that are kept in. I want to hear about the love part."

He looked at her as though she were daft. "I fell in love with you that first time I met you. I thought you knew that."

"Excuse my stupidity, but, no, I didn't know that."

"Hmph!" he said in amazement. "I went to your house—uh, my house—ready to sue you, but I ended up inviting you to live with me." He waved his hand. "More or less."

Nigh wanted to hear what he had to say. She wanted to argue with him, to do anything in the world rather than think about where they were and how they were never going to get out. Would lack of oxygen be the first thing that killed them?

"All right," she said, calming herself. No reason to go sooner than was necessary. Conserve air. "So why haven't you touched me?"

Jace was looking about the walls. He picked up the candle and went down the long passage. "Do you hear something?"

"No," she said. "I want an answer to my question."

"You'll laugh at me," he said.

"I don't think that anything in the world could make me laugh right now."

"For a year after Stacy died, I was afraid to so much as speak to a woman who wasn't a relative. I was afraid I'd say something that would make her so despondent that . . ."

"That she'd kill herself?"

"No, I was never that bad. But I was sure that Stacy had secrets and I was afraid that there was something wrong with me because she hadn't confided in me." He was inspecting every surface of the tunnel.

"We all have secrets," Nigh said. "And Stacy had a lot of awful things in her past. She had survived the death of her mother and her abandonment by her father all in the same year. She was one strong lady."

Jace looked back at her. "I'm beginning to think she was."

"So what about the touching? You and me touching, that is."

Jace bent to look at the pile of dirt at the end of the tunnel that led to the outside. "By the second year after Stacy's death and I hadn't touched a woman, I sort of made a vow to Stacy's spirit that I wouldn't until I found out the truth about her death. Good or bad, I was going to find out about it."

It took Nigh a moment to understand what he meant, then she smiled. He had taken a vow of celibacy. She didn't know why the idea pleased her so much, but it did. She wondered how many men were capable of love to the point where they'd give up sex.

Years before, Nigh had been somewhere horrible, surrounded by men as she always was, and they were waiting to tell the American TV-viewing audience in three minutes all about the horror they were seeing. One of the men—who'd been leering at her for days—asked her what she wanted in a man. Knowing how selfish he was and what a lecher, she snapped out, "I want a man who is capable of love." It had been a spur-of-the-moment statement, but she'd thought about it later and she knew it was right. A man who was capable of true love, deep love, love that put others above itself.

She watched Jace as he put the candle down and began to dig at the dirt. She knew it was a futile act, but she liked that he was trying. He was a man who had loved so completely that he'd stood up against what everyone told him they thought and had remained true to his own conviction. He didn't believe that Stacy had killed herself and he'd dedicated his life to proving that she didn't. He didn't want the false accusation against her or himself.

"I think you should sit down," Nigh said softly.

He turned to her and looked as though he was going to make some cheery statement about their getting out soon, but he seemed to change his mind. "Yes, we should conserve oxygen."

He sat down beside her and pulled her into his arms, her head on his chest. One candle was almost gone and the other one wouldn't last for long. But then, neither would the air.

He held her, stroking her hair, and they didn't talk. Nigh thought about telling him that she loved him too, but she knew that he knew. They had been inseparable since the first day they'd met. If they had run off and eloped that day they couldn't have been more together.

She didn't know she was crying until she felt the wetness of his shirt under her cheek.

"Sssssh," he said, stroking her face. "Be quiet. We need to be still and quiet and breathe as slowly as possible."

She nodded. There was no use doing anything else. Anger would be futile. Talking was unnecessary.

She didn't know how long she lay there, her body close to his, feeling his warmth, her face against his heart, hearing the steady rhythm of it, before she fell asleep.

She didn't know how long it was before Jace woke her. "Quiet," he said hoarsely and she could feel how he was breathing deeply. There wasn't a lot of air left in the tunnel. "Listen."

She tried to raise her head, but it seemed to be too much effort. She put it back down on Jace's chest.

"Do you hear it?" he asked.

She could hear nothing.

With effort, Jace moved her away from him, then stood up, using the cold, earthen wall for balance. He put his ear against the wall.

"What do you hear?" Nigh whispered, then took a few deep breaths, searching for oxygen.

"I don't know." He moved to the other side of the tunnel and put his ear against that wall. "Maybe it's nothing," he said, then pointed. Whatever he heard, it was coming from the wall that Nigh was leaning against.

Bending slowly, Jace helped her to stand, both of them gasping for air. He helped her to move to the far wall and toward the end of it, as far away from where they had been as possible.

She could hear it now, and looked up at Jace with wide eyes. What is . . . it?" she asked.

He took a breath. "Machine," he managed to get out, then pulled her down to sit beside him on the floor, his big arms wrapped around her protectively.

They waited, listening for any sound, then they felt it. They could feel a great rumble, a vibration coming from the wall. Nigh envisioned another explosion, or one of the ancient roof beams coming down and bringing the ceiling with it, but she was too light-headed from lack of oxygen to be concerned. She put her head on Jace's arm and started nodding off to sleep.

When the big bucket of the backhoe tore into the ceiling, she wasn't prepared for it, but Jace was. He had figured out what was going on and he knew that when there was a hole made in the tunnel, the roof would collapse. He had to be ready!

When the bucket came through the ceiling, he looked up, meaning to spring into action, but he was too depleted of air to be able to move. But he didn't have to worry. There were a dozen faces peering into the hole and they were ready to work. Before the hole was fully open, two men had jumped into the tunnel and a ladder was lowered. One burly man slung Nigh over his shoulder, then Jace was pushed up the ladder, the last man behind him.

Seconds after they reached the top, what was left of the tunnel collapsed, swallowing the ladder and almost swallowing the last man, but there were others to pull him out.

There was an ambulance waiting and Jace and Nigh were put in it and oxygen masks were placed over their faces. Nigh lay on the bed in the ambulance while Jace sat beside her, holding a mask to his face.

A man in the uniform of an emergency technician looked at both of them. "You all right?" he asked Jace, and he nodded.

Jace removed the mask for a moment. "Who found us?" he gasped out.

"An old man named Hatch. How long were you down there?"

Jace looked outside the ambulance. It was daylight, but he didn't know what time it was.

"Since two a.m.," Jace said.

The technician smiled in a patronizing way. "That's not possible. You couldn't have lived that long," he said as he got out of the ambulance and closed the door. Minutes later, they were on their way to the hospital.

21

Nigh awoke slowly, afraid of what she'd see. The last thing she remembered was being in Jace's arms and knowing that she'd never wake up again. She wondered if she'd open her eyes and see Heaven.

When she did open her eyes, she smiled at her thought. Sitting in a chair, sound asleep, a blanket over him, was Jace. For a moment she watched him, smiling at the sight of him, and slowly she began to remember the rescue. The bucket of a backhoe coming through the wall, then the dazzling sunlight followed by a rush of life-giving air. Men had jumped into the tunnel, ropes about their waists, then someone threw her over a broad shoulder and carried her to the top. She remembered looking back and seeing Jace climb over the ladder onto the grass and into the sunlight. Behind him, with a great roar, what was left of the tunnel collapsed. There was shouting as a man was pulled out of the falling ceiling, then yells of triumph when everyone was safe.

After that, she didn't remember much except lying down with a mask over her face and again breathing.

Jace had opened his eyes and was looking at her. "Hello," he said.

"Hello."

They exchanged smiles, not needing words. Somehow, they had survived the unsurvivable.

She sat up in the bed and Jace got up to help her, moving her pillow about, then handing her water to drink. There was an IV in her arm.

"Tell me everything," she said.

"I can't," he said, kissing her forehead. "I have to go to London."

"London?" She took his arm. "You're going to see Tony Vine, aren't you?"

"Yes. Don't look at me like that. This has become serious. I have to find out who killed Stacy."

Nigh realized that for the first time, he said the name without pathos, without agony, without regret in his voice. She clutched at his arm tighter. "You can't go without me."

"You need to stay here for a day and let the doctors check you out."

"And I guess they didn't tell you the same thing."

Jace gave her a one-sided grin. "Yeah, they told me the same thing, but I have to go. And I have to go alone."

"I'll tell them where you went," she threatened.

He put his hand on her cheek. "Nigh, baby, I can't let you go with me. As soon as we got here last night, I called my uncle and he found out some things. Stacy's roommate Carol was more right than she knew about this guy Vine. He's the head of a minor English organized crime group. No one has been able to prove anything, but he's messed up in some really bad things, like drugs."

"So you're going to go see him and accuse a man like that of killing your fiancée. Do you have a death wish?"

"I'm not going to accuse him of anything. I just want to know what happened."

"Jace," she said, her nails cutting into his arm, "you need to turn this over to the police."

Jace's face turned hard. "You think I wouldn't like to? I've talked to them this morning and I told them about the explosions. But they didn't believe me. They said that what I heard was a three-hundred-year-old tunnel collapsing, and that I should be grateful to be alive."

"Did you tell them about the stereo playing and the doors being open and all the lights on?"

"Of course, but they said it was probably the Priory House ghost, the lady highwayman. They all thought it was a great joke."

"How do you know that this man, Tony Vine, will see you?"

"I had a messenger service in London deliver a note to the address Carol gave us. All I did was give him Stacy's name and he agreed to see me."

Nigh leaned back against the pillow. "You can't go without me. I'm part of this."

"You're going to stay with Hatch and Mick while I go to London."

"Last night I heard someone say that Hatch had been the one who knew where to look for us. How did he know where we were?"

Jace looked away. "You can ask him that when you see him. He should be here in about an hour—if he can get through, that is."

"What does that mean?"

Jace grimaced. "There are about a dozen reporters outside waiting for one of us to appear. Someone in the village told them that Lady Grace's secret tunnel had been found and she'd nearly had her revenge on us by taking it down with you and me inside. The story is making headlines across England."

"And you're planning to leave *me* to deal with them alone."

Jace looked astonished. "You *are* a reporter, did you forget that? You usually have your microphone in someone's face."

"I do not do celebrity interviews and I certainly don't do local ghost stories."

"That's how you met me!" he said, exasperated. "And can you honestly tell me that you haven't followed somebody around with a microphone and demanded that he tell you what was none of your business?"

"No. I mean, not like you're talking about, I haven't. I just reported what people have—" She looked down at her hands.

"Reported what?"

"What people have the right to know," she said. "There! Happy now?"

"No. You've done it to people, so now you can be on the receiving end. I've got to go."

Nigh swiveled and got out of the bed, then was pulled back by the IV in her arm. "If you go to London without me, I'll . . ."

"You'll what?" Jace said, anger rising in him.

"I'll . . ." Her head came up. "After we're married, I'll remind you of this for the rest of our lives together. I'll make you so sorry you didn't take me with you and left me alone to face the reporters that you'll rue the day you did this. I'll—"

"You win," he said, cutting her off. "Where are your clothes?"

"Haven't a clue, but I guess they're in that closet."

As he got her clothes, she took a deep breath, then pulled the IV out of her arm. She started to tell Jace to turn around while she dressed, but then she gave him a little smile and stripped down to her skin in front of him. He was mesmerized, staring at her, taking in every inch of her nude body.

"You approve?" she asked.

"Nigh," he said softly, then crossed the room in one step and pulled her naked body into his arms and kissed her. It was good to know that he desired her, good to know that she hadn't imagined that he'd said he loved her.

"London," she whispered as his hands went down her bare back. "Tony Vine." He didn't stop stroking her skin and she knew that if they didn't want to end up on the hospital bed, she had to make him stop. "Vow of chastity," she said louder. "Remember Lancelot?"

Smiling, Jace moved away from her, then turned his back to her while she dressed. "I want to get this settled quickly," he said.

Nigh laughed. "Me too." It took only minutes to pull her clothes back on. She vowed to burn them as soon as she could because they smelled of the tunnel. They were musty and dirty and the last time she'd worn them, she had been facing death.

"So how do we get out of here without being seen?" Nigh asked.

"Follow me," he said, then took her hand and led her to the door. He checked that the corridor was clear. "Get two bunches of flowers," he said, nodding to the vases in her room.

She hadn't even noticed the flowers. "Ooooh, who sent them?" she asked.

"I don't know," Jace said. "But they'll be our cover. We're looking for sick people to visit."

"As opposed to being sick people," she said. "Right."

Ten minutes later, they were out of the hospital and going toward the parking lot. Jace took his keys out of his pocket and headed for his car.

"How did this get here?"

"Mick."

As she got in, she said, "You still didn't tell me how Hatch knew where we were."

"Danny told him."

"Ah," Nigh said, her eyes opened wide. "Was Ann with him?"

"Do you have a sister?"

"No. Then Ann was with him. Mick said it was a young woman who looked like you."

Nigh kept her eyes on the road. "Did anyone know they were ghosts?"

"Mick doesn't, but I think Hatch did, although I haven't talked to him. Mick said that some man told Hatch where we were and he woke up Mick, then they woke up everybody."

"But Mick saw the man and woman?" Nigh asked.

"Yes. He was matter-of-fact about it. He said Hatch pointed out some guy standing on the sidelines and said he was the one who'd told him we were in the tunnel. I asked Mick who he was so I could thank him, but Mick said he was too shy to come out of the bushes. He wouldn't even let the rescue team thank him."

"I guess you had Mick describe him."

"Oh, yes. Down to the riding boots Danny was wearing."

"And what about Ann?"

"Mick said the man was talking to a woman in a long dress.

Mick thought it was her nightgown except that she had on a belt with it."

"Ah," Nigh said, nodding her head, then she looked at him. "Talking to her? But that means that Ann and Danny are back together. But that's wonderful! He's been haunting Tolben Hall and Ann's been here. So now they can get together forever and live happily ever after. Or go to the 'white light' or whatever."

"That was my first thought too," Jace said.

"But what?"

"I asked Mick some questions about them. I said they were friends of mine from another village and that I'd told them about my explorations of the tunnel and my fear of collapse. I said that they'd had a big fight and I was wondering if they looked like they were back together again."

"So what did Mick say?"

"He said they looked sad, but he figured they were worried that you and I were going to be dead by the time they got to us. It took a while to get a JCB there and it took a while to figure out where to start digging."

"I guess Danny told them. After all, he could move back and forth between the walls and see where we were."

"Mick said that Hatch went into the shrubs and asked the man a couple of times before he let the backhoe operator start digging."

Nigh blinked. "I wonder how ol' Hatch took that? Going to a ghost to ask questions, all done in broad daylight."

"Mick said that during the whole thing, Hatch kept taking deep drinks from a flask he was carrying."

Nigh laughed. "I know how he feels. I've talked to Danny before, but if I had to do it again, I'd want some of Hatch's brew."

"I'd rather face an army of ghosts than ever again have one swallow of Hatch's brew," Jace said, making Nigh laugh again.

He glanced away from the road to her. "It's good to be alive, isn't it?"

"Wonderful," she said. "Truly wonderful. By the way, I need some food and I need some clean clothes. I do not want to meet this gangster wearing dirty jeans and jumper."

"Wives are very expensive, aren't they?" Jace said solemnly.

Nigh took a deep breath. "Yes, and it starts with a ring. Are pink diamonds expensive?"

Jace groaned. "Very."

"Perfect," she said, laughing.

It was late afternoon before they were ready to go to meet Tony Vine. They went to one of the arcades in London's fashionable Mayfair district and bought new clothes. Then they checked into one room at Claridge's and bathed and dressed. They were very polite, respecting each other's privacy, and making no remarks about the one bed. A big, comfortable-looking bed that ate up most of the room.

At 3:30, they were ready to leave.

They were silent as they went down in the elevator, and as they passed the front desk, a man handed Jace a large envelope. He opened it in the taxi, read it, then looked at Nigh. "Tony Vine was in the hospital when Stacy died." He hesitated. "It seems that Tony tried to kill himself on the night Stacy died."

She took the paper from him and read it. It was from his uncle, Frank Montgomery, and it was a photocopy of a report from a hospital near Margate. Nigh looked at Jace in disbelief. "A double suicide? A pact?"

"Aren't those when people kill themselves together?" he asked dryly. "But in this case, Tony lived while Stacy died."

When the cab stopped, Nigh was frowning. None of it made sense. They got out in front of a very modern building, all glass framed in steel, as cold as steel could be.

"Charming," Nigh said, but Jace didn't answer her. His face was set in a rigid mask that she couldn't read.

A man wearing a loose suit—to hide his gun? Nigh wondered—met them in the lobby and took them up in an elevator that had only two buttons on the panel: lobby and penthouse.

They said nothing as they rode up. The apartment was exactly as Nigh would have imagined it: all white marble with a few touches of color obviously put there by some overpriced designer who didn't care about the people living there, just that the place would photograph well.

They passed two more unsmiling men before entering a small, round room that seemed to jut out over London. A table was set for tea. The men left the room and for a moment Nigh and Jace stood in there alone.

"Pretty dishes," Nigh whispered, but Jace didn't speak. His eyes were on the door on the other side of the room. Within a minute, it opened and in walked a man who was only forty, but he looked fifty. His face was haggard, as though everything he'd ever done in his life was etched there. There were huge bags under his eyes. His clothes were as Carol had described them: shiny. They were expensive and made for his heavy-set body, but there was something about them that looked cheap. The man maketh the clothes, Nigh thought.

Graciously, he motioned to the chairs and told them to sit down. His voice was gruff but polite.

"Shall I pour?" Nigh asked. Jace had sat down, but his spine was rigid.

"So you're the bloke Stacy was plannin' to marry," Tony Vine said, looking Jace up and down. "And now you want to talk about her."

"I want to hear what you have to say," Jace said, and there was so much anger and hostility in his voice that Nigh wanted to kick him under the table.

"Tea, Mr. Vine?" she asked loudly.

"Tony, please," he said, smiling as he took the tea, and for a moment she could see the charm that this man had once exuded. He wasn't handsome, but there was something interesting about him. But then, power was an aphrodisiac, wasn't it?

"All right," Tony said, "I'll tell you about that night. I owe that to Stacy. But I'll tell you right away that it wasn't my fault that she killed herself. I had nothing to do with it." He glanced at Jace's expressionless face, then back at Nigh. "The last time I saw her, it was the worst time in my life."

She smiled at him and handed him a plateful of little sandwiches.

Tony looked at Jace. "I know you were engaged to her and you look like the kind of man she should've married, but I can tell you now that I don't have time to sugarcoat the story for you. Can you handle that?"

"I can handle anything you can dish out," Jace said, his eyes flashing.

"How about a cake, Tony?" Nigh said to cover Jace's open hostility.

"You're a real lady, aren't you?"

"Heavens no," Nigh said. "I'm a reporter."

That made Tony laugh so hard he nearly choked. "I like

you," he said. "Would you like to go out with me sometime?"

"Sorry," she said. "I'm taken." She didn't say by whom, but he glanced at Jace, then away again.

"Okay, that's enough chitchat. Let's get on with it. I met Stacy Evans when we were equals. Yeah, I know I was a man and she was a kid in school, but she was a lot older than her years, and, well, I didn't grow up until I had to. Whatever, we were well matched. And, besides, she was rebellin' against her rich father who'd dumped her for his floozy of a wife, and I was crazy with anger against the toffs in the big house."

"Priory House," Jace said.

"Yeah, that's the one. Stace and I met in Margate. She was sneaking into the pub and acting like she was old enough to drink. She fooled the barman, but not me. Let's say that our attraction was instant. She was insatiable!" Tony said, smiling in memory.

Nigh reached across the table and put her hand on Jace's.

"The house was empty then, as it usually was, and we made love in every room."

"And no one knew about this?" Jace said, his tone implying that Tony was a liar.

Tony didn't take offense. "I didn't say that. Nana knew, but then she wanted me to marry Stace."

"Nana?" Nigh asked.

"Everybody knows her as Mrs. Browne, but she'll always be Nana to me."

Nigh could feel some of the tension leave Jace. He was interested in this new twist to the story.

"Your grandmother wanted you to marry Stacy?" Nigh asked.

"She never said so in so many words, but I knew she did. Stacy was a strong-willed girl and her family was rich. I was already involved in a lot of things that Nana didn't like even back then. I think she thought that a good woman could straighten me out."

Tony's features took on a dreamy appearance. "I want to say that Stacy was the love of my life. I've never felt about anybody like I did her. I adored her, the way she looked and smelled. The way she talked. She was everything I'd seen in the rich people that used to live in Priory House, but that I could never have. I never got over that she was in love with me, with common-as-dirt Tony Vine."

"*Was* she in love with you?" Nigh asked.

"Oh yeah. She really was." He looked down at his teacup. "I don't know what would have happened if her dad hadn't come to his senses and let her go home." Tony gave a sigh. "She wanted to stay with me. She wanted to drop out of school and live with me, but I talked her into going back. I said I'd write her, but I never did."

"But why did you send her away?" Nigh couldn't help asking.

"Pride. She didn't think so, but I knew that her rich dad would take one look at me and . . ." Tony shrugged.

"Did you see her again after she left?" Nigh asked softly.

"Not for years. As I said, May of 2002 was a real low point in my life. The lowest. I was in some serious trouble with some goons from Liverpool." He shrugged. "I played the horses and lost everything. They were after me.

"I went to the only place where I knew I'd be safe: Priory House. Nana fed me and mothered me, and I hid in the rooms, sleeping in one bed after another. But I was bored. Bored to being crazy. I had a computer and an Internet hookup and on impulse I typed in Stacy's name. I saw that she was about to marry some rich guy and I wondered what it would be like to see her again.

"The house was for sale and Nana used to make me hide in the old tunnel when the agent brought buyers to look at the place. I used to go up into the tower room and make haunting noises and scare them away.

"Anyway, I cut up a sale brochure and sent her a note."

"Ours again. Together forever. See you there on 11 May 2002," Jace said quietly.

"I see you found the note," Tony said, smiling. "I didn't expect her to show up, but she did." Turning in his chair, he looked out the window at London. "But it wasn't the same. We weren't equals anymore. She was a lady and I was . . ."

"A thug," Jace said.

Tony's eyes flashed anger, then he smiled. "Compared to her, *you* are a thug."

Jace nodded once, as though to say touché.

"She was . . ." Tony paused, as though trying to find the right words. "She was repulsed by me." He grinned. "She tried to hide it, but it was there in that one quick flash across her eyes. I saw it, she knew I saw it, and that was the end of it. All those years I'd thought about what might have been, and I guess she had too because she'd left her wedding plans to come to me."

"What did you do?" Nigh asked.

"We stayed up all night and talked," Tony said, smiling in memory. "We shared a bottle of wine and talked, as friends, not lovers. You know, I think she was relieved that she didn't love me anymore."

"But you weren't relieved, were you?" Nigh asked.

"I was cryin' in me beer, so to speak. I was miserable. She was so beautiful and elegant, while the women I deal with . . ." Tony took a moment to calm himself. "I kept rememberin' that I was the one that broke up with her. She said she'd live over a garage with me because she loved me so much, but I said no."

Tony took a breath. "Like I said, I was too proud to let her stay. I picked a fight with her and told her I wanted nothing to do with her kind. I said all the things I knew she'd hate."

"That's just what she did to me," Jace said.

"Yeah, she told me about that. She felt real bad about what she did and she hoped she could make you forgive her. But she said that she couldn't very well ask her fiancé if he minded if she spent the night with her old boyfriend, now could she?"

"Spend the night," Jace said under his breath.

"Yeah, she spent the night with me, but not like you mean. Nobody took his—or her—clothes off. We drank and we talked. And I thought about what my life would have been if I hadn't been so damned full of pride. Worse, that night, the more I drank, the more I wanted her. I told myself that we were still young. There was still time."

Tony looked at Jace. "But she started talking about you."

"What did she say?" Jace asked and seemed to prepare himself for bad news.

"That she was mad about you, that she wanted to live with you forever and have a hundred children and—"

"What?!" Jace said. "She wanted to have my children?"

"Yeah, sure." Tony looked back out at London. "Remember I told you that when I made her leave Margate I started a fight with her? I told her I didn't want to have kids. That made her cry and . . . and I liked it. I was glad I could make her cry because I was crying on the inside."

"You said you told her you didn't want children and she cried," Jace said. "Then she *did* want children. Are you sure of that?"

"You were planning to marry her but you didn't know that about her?" Tony asked, looking at Jace with a sneer curling his upper lip.

"I thought I knew everything about her until that night when she picked a fight with me. She told me she didn't want kids."

"And you fell for it?"

"Completely. Totally and absolutely," Jace said.

Tony gave a little smile. "She did to you what I did to her, didn't she? That means I taught her something. She carried some of me inside her."

"What else did she tell you about us?" Jace asked. "It's not just prurient interest, it's that I need to know."

Tony played with the heavy gold ring on the little finger of his left hand. "Prurient. I didn't get the education to use words like that. You know what I dreamed of doing? Remember that book where the stable boy runs away and comes back years later a rich gentleman?"

"*Wuthering Heights,*" Nigh said. "Heathcliff."

"Yeah, that's it. I had to read it in school. The girls were all drippy about it, but us boys hated it—or said we did. Anyway, when I told Stacy it was over I had it in mind that someday I'd come back and get her. I'd have made my fortune and would be wearing a tuxedo."

He smiled. "I made a fortune. Actually, I made half a dozen of 'em, but I lost most of 'em. And I've never been in a tuxedo in my life."

"So you two talked all night," Nigh said.

"And drank. Don't forget the drink. I got pretty drunk that night and Stacy was so beautiful. I guess I made a pass at her."

"You tore her dress and scratched her shoulder," Jace said.

"Did I? I don't remember. I know she ran outta the house and got in her car. It's the last I ever saw of her. Later, after I heard what she did, I knew I was a lot to blame. She was pretty drunk that night and I sent her out in a car. I'm glad she stopped in the village and got a room at the pub. If she'd died in a car wreck I never would have forgiven myself."

Jace's face showed his rising anger. "When you heard about her, why didn't you go to the police?"

"It doesn't matter why somebody offs themselves, it just matters that they did it," Tony said, also getting angry.

Jace didn't back down. "Everyone thought *I* was the reason she killed herself."

Tony looked at Jace. "That must've been one hell of a fight you two had. I've never said anything so bad to a woman that she killed herself."

Nigh put her hand back on Jace's arm, trying to keep him calm.

"Maybe she should've stayed with me that night," Tony said, standing up. "Maybe she and I should have—"

"Stop it!" Nigh said, standing up and glaring at the two men. "Stacy doesn't deserve this! Now sit down both of you and act like human beings."

Reluctantly, both men sat down, but they wouldn't look at each other or at Nigh.

"Tony," she said, "we already know that when Stacy died you were in hospital. It seems that you too tried to kill yourself. Would you please tell us the *truth* about what happened?"

Tony looked as though he'd rather do anything than tell them what happened that horrible night.

"For Stacy?" she asked.

Tony took a deep breath. "All right, I did try to kill myself. Is that what you wanted to hear? I said it was the low point of my life. Some goons were after me and I didn't have the money to pay them. But worse, when I saw Stacy that night, I saw what could have been mine. But I threw it away."

He looked across the table at Nigh. "I was drunk, broke, and depressed, so I took a bunch of pills. Washed them down with whiskey."

"Who found you and saved you?" Nigh asked softly.

"Dear ol' Nana," Tony said with a little smile. "She found me and got me to hospital."

"Did you tell her that Stacy turned you down?" Jace asked.

"If I remember correctly, I told her that Stacy was sick at the sight of me."

"What else?"

"What do you want from me?" Tony demanded. "You won her and I lost."

"No," Nigh said. "Everybody lost."

"All right. So I lied. I lied big to my own grandmother. I told her Stacy broke up with me when we were kids and again when we were grown-ups. I told Nana lots of things to make me look good and Stacy look bad, but if you can't lie to your own nana, who can you lie to?"

Nigh looked at Jace and the color had drained from his face. "No one, Mr. Vine. You don't lie to anyone," he said, then he stood up. "We have to go." With that, he turned and left the room.

Nigh made hasty thanks to Tony and scurried after Jace. She caught him at the elevator. "You know, don't you?" she asked.

"Yes," he said. "Do you?"

"Only too well. What do we do now?"

"We go to Scotland Yard."

Nigh breathed a sigh of relief. She had feared that Jace was going to try to handle this by himself.

22

Nigh watched as the police took Mrs. Browne away in handcuffs. When confronted by the police she had easily admitted her guilt. She said that Stacy Evans had deserved to die because she'd broken her grandson Tony's heart not once, but twice.

Before she was taken away, Jace asked if he could talk to her and the police agreed—as long as they could tape record all of it. Jace took her into the main sitting room and treated her as an honored guest, fetching tea for her and even pushing the ottoman toward her so she could rest her feet.

Mrs. Browne had no remorse for what she'd done. She readily admitted that if she had to do it over again, she would. She told Jace that if she'd had any idea he'd come there after her dear Tony, she would have tried to kill him much earlier. "No offense," she said.

"None taken," Jace answered. "You blew up the tunnel, didn't you?"

"Oh, yes. I saw that you had Tony's address in London, so I knew everything and that you had to go. I learned about bombs on the Internet and made some in the kitchen. But the whole tunnel didn't blow. Those old beams were good ones. They used to know how to build."

"Could you tell me about Stacy?"

"Regular little slut, she was. Much like that Nightingale that's always hangin' around you. In my day, women had morals. They had pride. They had—"

"What about the night Stacy died?"

Mrs. Browne's face twisted into a look of hate. "Do you know what she did to my Tony? When I found him, he was half-dead. She'd played with him, like a snake with a mouse. She'd almost killed him with her wicked ways. She came back into his life to tell him she wouldn't have somebody like him. Can you imagine what I went through as I got my Tony to hospital? I had to watch them pump his stomach."

"So you killed Stacy for what she did to your grandson," Jace said calmly.

"That I did. And she well deserved it."

"But how did you do it? Her room at the pub was locked from the inside."

"All of you so smart and you couldn't figure out the simplest of things. I went up the back stairs and knocked on her door. You didn't know there was a back stairs, did you? That uppity Emma Carew don't want people to think she has a back stairs. She wants a new stairs that everybody can see and admire. But I used to clean that pub and I know it well. I went up the back stairs and I knocked on the door of that Stacy."

"And she opened it to you."

"She was drunk. My Tony hadn't had a drink in over a year, but she shows up and he gets drunk again. I said I wanted to talk to her so she let me in. I'd brought a bottle of wine and I knew she had pills with her, so I turned my back to her, opened them, and put them in the wine, then asked her to drink with me."

"And Stacy was always polite so she drank with you."

Mrs. Browne shrugged. "If destroying the life of a decent young man can be called polite, then she was."

"Stacy was alive when you left because she locked the door behind you."

"And put the Do Not Disturb sign on it." Mrs. Browne was smiling. "Did you see my Tony today?"

"Yes, we did," Jace said softly.

"And how is he?"

"Very well and he sends his love," Jace said, then stood up and left the room. He'd heard all he could stand and had been near Mrs. Browne all he could bear.

"She's yours," he said to the inspector, then he went outside to find Nigh. The ordeal of the last three years was over.

23

Nigh would never say so, but she already missed Mrs. Browne's cooking. There was no great roast of beef with four vegetables, but a takeout of curry over rice, a combination of Chinese and Indian cooking.

She and Jace had driven back to Margate after talking to Tony and after Jace had talked to an inspector at Scotland Yard. No one thought that Mrs. Browne was going to escape, so the police had waited until the morning to drive to Margate and arrest her.

Jace couldn't bear to stay in the same house with the woman so they'd camped out at Nigh's little cottage. He hadn't slept much. Three times she'd awakened and seen him standing at the window and looking out at the night. She wanted to go to him and offer him comfort, but she didn't. She guessed that he needed to be alone.

So now they were alone in the big house and it had never felt bigger or more empty. She knew that Jace would put it up for sale soon.

When he came in, he still looked as though he had the weight of the world on his shoulders. "Hatch will fill in the tunnel and plant it full of flowers," Jace said. "Or maybe the next owner will want to rebuild it."

She put a plate down in front of him and handed him a spoon to help himself. Distractedly, he began to fill his plate.

"What about Danny and Ann?" Nigh asked as she sat down across from him.

Jace looked as though he didn't know who she meant.

"Ghosts? Remember? I talked to Danny Longstreet and you had Ann Stuart run through you? Remember them? The two ghosts who saved our lives?"

"Yeah, I remember," he said. "What about them?"

"What's going to happen to them?"

Jace looked at her in consternation. "I don't know. I'm not a clergyman. Maybe you should ask the vicar. Maybe he can—"

"Look," she said, exasperated. "No one does anything without a reason. Those two spirits have had over a century to appear to people but they haven't."

"That's not true. People at Tolben Hall have seen Danny, and lots of people here have seen Ann."

"Mostly kids," Nigh said. "And no one ever saw them together. And I've never heard of their saving any lives before. I'm sure there have been accidents at this house but Ann never intervened. But she did with us."

"Maybe they like us. You are related to Ann, aren't you?"

"Maybe," Nigh said, pushing the food about on her plate. "Maybe. But I keep thinking there's something else. Mick said

the two people in the bushes looked sad. Now that they're together at last, why weren't they jumping all over each other?"

"Maybe they can't," Jace said. "I don't think I've ever heard of
ghosts fornicating."

Nigh looked at him, her mouth open.

"What?" he asked.

"That's it. They can't. And they're not going to leave this
earth until they can."

"Can what?"

Nigh took a big bite of food. "It's okay for a woman to die a
virgin if she gets glorified for it. Think of your state of Virginia.
Named for a virgin queen, right?"

"Right," Jace said hesitantly.

"And all those virgin martyrs. They were known to be virgins.
But it was thought that since Ann Stuart was engaged to a randy
man like Danny Longstreet, then she wasn't a virgin. I made a remark to Danny about Ann having had sex before the marriage
and he nearly took my head off. He was adamant in telling me
that Ann was a virgin."

Jace was still looking at her in puzzlement. "What are you
driving at?"

"I'm not sure, but I think Danny and Ann are waiting for
something."

"And what is that?" Jace asked. "And please don't tell me it's
an exorcism. I do *not* want to go through one of those things."

"I think they want to make love," Nigh said. "Through us."

Jace paused with the fork to his mouth.

"It makes sense," she said. "You've been celibate for three
years and it's been so long since I had sex that I may have become
a virgin again."

Jace reached across the table and took Nigh's hand. "Let's go."

She drew back from him. "When I was sixteen the then-owner of Priory House let me rummage around in the attics so I could write about its history. There's a trunk up there that contains a wedding dress and I think it belonged to Ann."

"I thought her father burned everything."

"He also thought he'd destroyed his daughter. I want to find that dress and—" She looked down at her hands.

Jace went 'round the table to kneel in front of her. "Miss Nightingale Augusta Smythe, will you marry me?" he asked.

Nigh hadn't been expecting his proposal, but she soon recovered her shock. "Yes," she said, then put her arms around his neck, but he pulled back. He handed her a little blue box. She opened it to see the most beautiful emerald-cut pink diamond that she'd ever seen. "Where? How? When?" she asked all at once.

He just smiled at her. "Shall we go to the attic and see if we can find an old wedding dress? We have a duty to perform for some very dear friends."

Epilogue

Nigh cried when Ann and Danny appeared for the last time. There was no more sadness on their faces. They held hands and walked away, through a wall, then to . . . Nigh had no idea where happy spirits went. Heaven, probably.

She and Jace had spent their first night together with their bodies inhabited by others, but they hadn't minded. If it weren't for Ann and Danny, they'd still be in the tunnel. The night hadn't been strange at all, except that Nigh had indeed felt virginal. Had she been fully herself, she would have leaped into bed, but she found herself being shy and waiting with curiosity and a simmering lust that threatened to burn her up.

It had been marvelous to feel sex as though she'd never read a sexy novel, never seen a sexy movie, and certainly never touched a man. Everything was new and wonderful to her.

Nigh had found herself shocked, then delighted at some of the things Jace/Danny had done. There had been tenderness and enthusiasm, gentleness and a laughing roughness. The night had been filled with it all.

But there was also a sadness. She could feel Ann's love for Danny, and his for her, but she could also feel that they knew this was their one and only time to experience physical love. They had waited so very, very long!

That Jace had been a good sport about it all made Nigh love him more. "The next one's for us," he said the following morning, after they'd seen Ann and Danny float away, holding hands and smiling.

Nigh said, "I don't know, Danny Longstreet was pretty good." For a second, a nanosecond, she saw Danny's face behind Jace and he winked at her, then he was gone forever.

"Do you mind if I sell this house right away?" Jace asked. "I really can't take any more of it."

"Gladly," she said. "Where do you want to go?

"Near Cambridge or Oxford for the libraries," he said, getting out of bed. Ann's wedding dress was draped across the foot of the bed. Last night, when he'd seen Nigh in it, he said that if he'd never known that they were related, he would have when he saw her in that dress.

"Cambridge it is, then," she said, looking at her ring. "How long has it been since I told you I love you?"

Jace went dead still. "Actually, you've never told me."

Nigh thought about that. "Maybe I haven't. Why don't you come over here and let me tell you?"

"Why not?" he said, then got back into bed with her.